WHEN IT COMES TO YOU

GENESIS CARTER

This book is a work of fiction. Names, characters, places and incidents are either the product of the author's imagination or are used fictionally. Any resemblance to actual persons, living or dead, or to actual events or locales is entirely coincidental.

This ebook is licensed for your personal enjoyment only. This ebook may not be re-sold or given away to other people. If you like to share this book with another person, please purchase an additional copy for each person you share it with.

Copyright © 2024 Na'Kia Presents. All rights reserved. Including the right to reproduce this book or portions thereof, in any form. No part of this text may be reproduced in any form without the express written permission of the author.

When it Comes to You

By: Genesis Carter

1

JOSIAH MACKENZIE

"Hi My Sonshine." My Mom's raspy voice echoed through the phone the moment I answered it. I was in the middle of grading papers and being that I hadn't spoken to her in a little while, I went ahead and answered.

Before everything happened, you'd never guess that my relationship with my parents would be where it was today. But because of the actions of others, and their condoning the behavior around it; I had no choice but to go low contact with any of my family members. For my own sanity, I had to, there was no way around it.

"Hey Beautiful, what's going on?"

"I just wanted to hear your voice; we hadn't heard from you in a while." The line got quiet as it resonated between us the reason behind all of it. I was justified in my actions and we both knew it.

"How's everything?" I asked trying to maneuver out of the awkward silence we'd found ourselves in.

"It's okay. Hot here in Georgia, as usual. But I'm sure it's just as bad in Dallas already huh?"

"Yes ma'am." I sighed. "But you know, that's the price we pay for living in the south right?"

"Yeah, that's true." She chuckled. "How's everything with you?"

"It's all good this way. Just working; going through tryouts."

"Oh yeah? Anybody good show up?"

"A few good ones came. Most of the team from this year is back, but a few of our seniors are leaving so we need to find a few replacements. A couple of them have been very promising so far."

"That's good." She replied before the line got quiet again.

"Where's the old man?" I asked about my father. Our conversations were fewer between those of me and my mother. He was adamant that I should get over the situation that happened, more on Joshua's side than anything. It strained our relationship tremendously when I just picked up and left.

"Oh, he's out running errands. Should be home in a few though."

"He doing alright?"

"He's fine. You should call him up a time or two and ask after him yourself."

"Ma, he's the parent. He knows my number just like I know his. I'm glad to hear he's doing okay though. It's good to hear your voice."

"Yours too my love. I wanted to call and see if you'd thought about coming home for Thanksgiving this year. Everyone would love to see you."

"Ugh, I don't think so Ma." I shook my head. I knew before I picked up the phone that this was where the conversation was going to end up. It's where it always ended.

"Josiah, don't you think it's time to forgive and forget?" the irritation in my mama's voice rang from the other end of my phone. I bit down on my bottom lip as I had almost forgotten who I was talking to about to cuss her clean the fuck out. There was no forgiving Josh, not for this. "The baby will be here soon, and I just think you'd want to be in your nephew's life."

"Hard pass." I replied. "Aye, Mama, let me get off this phone I gotta get back to work."

"Josiah, Matthew 6:14 says—"

"For if you forgive other people when they sin against you, your heavenly father will also forgive you." I finished the sentence for her. She's been quoting that scripture at me for years since the incident happened. "I'll offer forgiveness on my own time and terms. The Lord doesn't say I need to do it right now."

"It's been four years since I've laid eyes on you in person. You refuse to come home and your father refuses to come to Dallas. You picked up and moved to Dallas just like that. I know you're hurt, but we are your family. I miss you and I honestly think it's time."

"Mama, I gotta go." I repeated. "Tell Pop I said hello. I'll speak with you later."

"Josiah—" I sighed mentally preparing myself for the next words out of her mouth. My brother had broken up our family, yet I was being lectured for the wrong he caused me. "I love you, please be safe."

"Of course. And I love you too Mama."

I disconnected the call before any other words could be said. It seemed like every other conversation Mama was bringing up the past when all I was tryna do was escape it. The betrayal by two people I loved so deeply almost killed me and it absolutely broke me. It was the reason why I had moved almost 800 miles from my hometown in Atlanta to Dallas. I had to get away from the hurt, had to try to start over and this shit has been hard as hell to do.

I thought back three years ago when I first found out that my twin brother Joshua was fucking my fiancé, Angela. I had just come from Dallas, visiting to look at a house Angie and I were supposed to buy. It had been our plan to move from Atlanta to Dallas together. After Rich had moved and we'd spent some time there, we had planned to move as well to be closer to our friends and to start our family. After a grueling trip, I was tired and all I wanted to do was layup with my girl.

I knew something was wrong the moment I walked into our apartment. Nothing was out of place, but everything was just wrong. The TV was blaring in the living room, yet no one was watching it. The smell of Sativa lingered in the air and Angela was nowhere in sight. I dropped my bag at the door and travelled through the apartment, turning off the tv and then opening the patio door to air out the place. I remember calling for Angie and getting no response.

As I made my way back to our bedroom, I heard moaning. I didn't want to believe my ears; my hand was outstretched shakily turning the doorknob. I still remember the way my heart raced as I slowly opened the bedroom door and stood in the doorway shocked seeing my twin brother fucking my fiancé. After that, I sort of just blacked out. The next thing I remember is hearing Angela screaming as my fist pounded into Joshua's face, a mixture of both of our blood on my hands.

It was the first time I ever got arrested. Had my parents not convinced Joshua to drop the charges, I would have served time in jail. Instead, they bailed me out and the first thing I did was call my best friend Rich. I remember him telling me he would be on his way to Georgia to get me. By the end of the week, I had picked up everything and moved to Dallas, leaving Angela behind.

I still remember the screaming she did, trailing me out of

our apartment as I got the last of my things in my car. The begging and pleading, trying to convince me that it was a mistake. But I knew in my heart that it was no mistake. I watched them for a while, watched how intimate they were, and I saw the looks in their eyes as they looked at one another while their bodies were connected. It was obvious that they loved each other.

Previously, Angela had only had that look for me. Hearing my cell phone ring moments later, I quickly picked it up, snapping out of the trance my memories had left me in. Seeing it was Rich, I immediately answered it.

"Richie D, what's up brodie."

"Shit, just checking in on you. What you got going?"

"Nothing much." I sighed and the line got silent. Rich always seemed to call me when I was too far in my head. I don't know how he knew, but he always called. Always!

After three years you would think I was over the situation, but that shit cut me deep. Angela was absolutely the love of my life, or so I thought. We met in college, freshman year and the moment I bumped into her on campus, any chances I had of sowing my oats were out the window. After college, she took a leap and moved to Georgia with me. We planned our entire lives together; never once did I think our lives would end the way they did.

"I'm good Rich." I told my best friend since Kindergarten. "But what's up with you? You good?"

"Ahhh." He sighed heavily and I knew it was about to be some shit.

"Aw shit, what happened?"

"You know Tish had her appointment today?"

"Yeah, how'd it go? Baby all good?"

"Yeah and no." he paused. "They putting her on bedrest until the baby comes. So, I can't come to Puerto Vallarta."

"Damn, is she alright?"

"Yeah, she pissed though. You know she was looking forward to that trip."

"I mean, it's all good. Maybe we can plan something for later. Thanks for letting me know though, I'm sure I can get a – "

"Naw Broski. I don't think you should cancel. I think you should still go. You need a vacation, Mac. You work too hard, and you need a break from those little crumb snatchers."

"Mann, don't be talking about my kids." I laughed thinking about my students. They could be a handful, they could be extra, but I cared for every single last one of them.

When I moved to Dallas, I immediately got a job as a Biology teacher, teaching both basic and advance level classes, with Dallas ISD working for William D. Marshall High School. After the first year, I got the assistant coaching job for the school and then this year when Coach Potter retired, I got his job becoming the head football coach as well as the athletic director.

"Them kids bad as hell bruh. They stay in yo office, I'm surprised one of them ain't in there now." He laughed.

"Don't talk them up." I looked towards my office door, knowing the bell for the last class of the day was going to ring and one of my players would step foot in my office.

"Anyway, don't cancel yo trip Mac. I think this could be good for you. You need to get a break, think about yo life. Tish said you look lonely."

"Tish needs to stop trying to put me in relationships." I laughed. "I'm good. I got my job; I got my students. I did that relationship shit before, it just ain't for me. At this time in my life, all I care about is getting to my money."

"And we both know it ain't shit unless you got somebody to share it with. Let this trip be what you need to get up out of this funk. It's been four years since that shit went down. It's time for you to find somebody to settle down with. Don't let that shit that happened with Angela block you from your blessings. You can't blame every woman for her mistake."

"I ain't blaming every woman." I said defensively.

"You sure? Because you ain't been in a serious relationship since that shit happened. You have these flings where one minute the chick is there, a few weeks later that shit is done. You're a young, financially stable black man, you got what these women are looking for except you don't have an open heart."

"Everybody can't find they happily ever after like you and Tish." I shrugged. "I'm fine with being a bachelor. Relationships ain't for everybody Rich."

"Man, who you think you fooling?" he chuckled. "We been friends since diapers damn near. I know who you are as a man. I know that you crave love, real love. You could have a successful relationship you're just choosing not to because of one bad apple."

"One bad apple that wasted 8 years of my life."

"Don't call that shit a waste, it was just a lesson. Angela is foul as hell for what she did and so might I add is Joshua. But Angela wasn't the end all be all. That girl fucked up right now probably thinking about how she could have had it all being with you and instead she still in Georgia living the same life she was living before only now she got a baby on the way. We both know Josh, he ain't committing to that girl really, even with the baby. Let her rot in her misery, but that don't mean you need to, too."

"I hear you."

"Good." He sighed. "Aye, let me go. I might put some steaks on the grill if you wanna come through later."

"I'll let you know. Bless."

"Bless." He replied before disconnecting the phone.

A part of me knew Rich was right. Deep down inside I had always been a romantic. I loved to cater to my woman, loved to shower them with all of my love; but not anymore. In the four years that have passed since that incident, the most romantic thing I've done for any woman was sent her flowers and fucked her so good she walked funny the next day. That was all I had for women nowadays, dick and honestly, I didn't see that changing no time soon.

Waiting for the last bell to ring, I continued to grade the papers that were sitting in front of me, abandoned during each of my phone calls. I'd given my students a pop quiz in my third and fourth period Advanced Biology classes and so far, from grading the papers, I was convinced we needed to go over some stuff before the final exam a lot more as they had all barely passed. I prided myself on my teaching skills, so I didn't understand why the grades were the way they were. Even some of my brightest students barely got over an 80%.

By the time I got through all of the papers and had them sorted by class, I stacked them up and placed them in my bag just as the final bell rang. I made a mental note to redo my lesson plan when I got home. Gathering my things, I made my way out of my office and turned out the lights. Being that school was almost out for the summer, we had tryouts and I wanted to make sure I was there early as there was a long list of boys who wanted to join the team for next year. After tryouts, I would have a few weeks off before summer practice began and for that few weeks, I still needed to decide if I would be spending them here in Dallas or in Puerto Vallarta.

"Coach Mackenzie." Autumn Murphy, an English teacher smiled in my direction. "A few of us are going out later for happy hour. Did you want to tag along?"

"Nah, I got tryouts then I'm headed home to tighten up my lesson plan."

"Lesson plan? School is out in a week, what more is there to teach?"

"Enough." I shrugged.

"I love how much you care about these kids." She walked up on me, close as hell, almost too close for comfort. Yet my eyes roamed her entire frame, admiring the fabric of the wrap dress she wore as it hugged her hips. I licked my lips, tempted by her scent as she continued to smile in my face.

"Don't you?" I asked. "Besides the fact that it's our job, these are our people. If we don't set high expectations for them now, what are we saying about how much we care about their future. My AP classes barely passed the pop quiz I gave them in preparation for the final exam next week. I can't have that; their success is important to me."

"Well, if you're not going to come to happy hour then how about you invite me to your place, and I can help you with your lesson plan." Her long, clawed fingernail traced my polo shirt. I chuckled taking a step back from her, feeling multiple eyes on us.

"Have a good night Ms. Murphy." I placed the mail from my mailbox in my bag before walking out; feeling her eyes on me as I walked away. Autumn had been flirting with me since I started working here three years ago. But I refused to fuck with co-workers, that shit made for a messy work environment. Besides, the way she was too willing to give it up, I knew she was nothing but trouble.

2

KAHLIA "KALI" MITCHELL

"Hey Kali, the 4pm is here." My assistant Jeremy said buzzing in on the intercom. I was sitting at my desk going over edits.

"Alright, I'll be there in a minute." I said back clicking a few more buttons and pausing my work for now. I grabbed my Canon Rebel T7. It was one of the most expensive pieces of equipment I owned, and it was also my favorite since it was a gift from the most important person in my life, my late husband Jonathan Mitchell.

Jonathan and I had been together since we were 16 years old. We'd been high school sweethearts and when he decided he was going to Hampton, I followed him. I had never known a love like the one Jonathan had showed me and I was convinced I'd never find it again. By the time we graduated from Hampton University at the age of 22, we were happily married starting our lives in our hometown of Chicago. When we were celebrating our 5-year wedding anniversary, Jonathan developed severe headaches; or what we thought were just headaches. Turns out, he'd developed a brain tumor the size of a plum; it was inoperable even with trying to shrink it down with chemo.

We weren't really ready for it, even after getting the diagnosis, it wasn't enough time to prepare. There were so many things for us to consider; so much to plan for. His doctors told us we would only have six months to a year together; Jonathan passed away during month 8. I was devastated and I felt so alone.

That was four years ago, and I still mourned the loss, still missed him like crazy and still remained alone; determined to forever be a widow. Yeah, I'd dated a little here and there, but I never put my feelings into any of it. There was no point; and I was not about to feel the same type of hurt for someone else that I still to this day felt behind Jonathan. Who in their right mind would endure that kind of pain willingly? It wasn't for me, I only had room in my heart for one and his love had consumed me since I was 16.

"Hey Beautiful." I greeted my client, Brianna. She was taking her senior photos and although I didn't really take senior portraits, I owed her grandmother a favor. "You ready?"

"Yes ma'am." She nodded coyly. "I have three outfit changes; I hope that's okay?"

"Yeah, it's fine love." I smiled. "I'm going to go get set up and Jeremy will show you towards the bathroom so you can change. We'll start off in here, I have a few set ups prepared and then we can go outside and take some photos as well. So whichever outfit you want to use for the outside, save that one for last, okay?"

"Yes ma'am." She nodded. "Thank you again for doing this. My Nana showed me some of your work and I fell in love with it. I know you don't usually do pictures like this."

"It's no problem." I smiled. "I appreciate a person who knows good work when they see it. Go change and meet me back out here when you're done." She nodded then followed Jeremy towards the back.

I went over to where I had a green screen backdrop getting the area set up to capture her photo. This would be a quick $500 in my pocket just to do what I loved to do most. Plus, when Ms. Winona told me how much of a fan Brianna was, it was a no brainer for me to get it done.

I placed my Canon on the tripod and focused my lenses, peering into them every so often before going to adjust something in the setup I was working on. It wasn't long before Brianna came out wearing a two piece pants suit. She was a work of art herself, a beautiful black queen in her own right and I felt privileged to be capturing her beauty for her senior pictures.

After a few poses, she went to change her outfit. The second outfit was a pink and green ensemble and while talking to her, she let me know that her grandmother and her mother were both AKAs and it was her dream to pledge as well when she went off to college this fall. As a member of the Divine Nine myself, I took pleasure in capturing those photos, even if the sorority she intended on pledging wasn't my own. The last outfit was a flowy yellow dress that was giving very much summertime vibes and it was in that dress that we took the session outside, in the small garden off my office building taking pictures of her with the beautiful flowers that were growing there.

It took a few hours to complete, but at the end of it, I promised her I would have them edited and sent to her by the end of the week. It was the deadline I'd given to myself especially knowing that the day after, I'd be on a plane to Mexico.

"Hey, I'm about to take off." Jeremy said not long after Brianna left. I was cleaning up my space and getting ready to leave myself. "You need anything before I go?"

"No, thanks Jeremy." I smiled. "I appreciate you as always. I'll see you tomorrow and lock up on your way out."

"See you tomorrow." He gave me a quick hug and exited the building. Jeremy had been working for me for three years. He started off as an intern and when his internship was over, I realized how valuable he'd been to me, so I hired him on. He was finishing up his junior year in college and even with a lot on his plate, he'd been by my side faithfully.

I finished cleaning then made my way to my office to drop off my equipment, removing the memory card from the camera then packing it away. The memory card went into my desktop until tomorrow when I would tackle the task of editing the photos. My day was far from over as I made my way out of my office and towards my dark room. I had been working on other photos I'd taken with my Nikon Z for a project I had. It was pictures of different people, places, and things around the city that I loved. A lot of it would go on display in my home, or here in the office, but some of it, I hoped to display in an art gallery soon.

Flipping the switch, the red light illuminated the dark room. I pulled my hair up into a high bun on top of my head, then placed my Air pods in my ear getting in the mood to lose myself in my work. Grabbing my phone, I went into my Apple Music and found Lucky Daye's *Painted* Album which had been on repeat for weeks. My best friend Jamie had put me on to his music and he'd had me in a chokehold since the first song played.

I couldn't tell you how much time had passed since I'd been in my dark room, surrounded by my work, hanging photos to develop. The only thing that broke my concentration and brought my attention to the time was the phone call that suddenly blared through my Air pods. Looking at my phone, I saw it was my sister Parris calling me, then I glanced at the time in the corner of the phone seeing it was nearly 9pm.

"Shit." I said to myself before declining the call instead going into our text thread.

> Hey Boo, I'm in the darkroom, finishing up. I'll call you back in five minutes.

> Parris: Don't forget Kali.

Shaking my head, I slid my phone into my back pocket then cleaned up the mess I had made in my dark room. Once all my materials were put away, I looked at the film I'd been developing and smiled seeing the photos I'd taken. I was proud of myself. I slowly took them down and laid them across the long island countertop I worked on, figuring I'd finish up tomorrow.

On my way out of the darkroom, I flipped the light off then hurried to my office to grab my stuff so I could head out, making sure I had the memory card from the pictures I'd taken earlier. I locked up my building and ran over to my 2023 Lexus RX 500h. It had been my dream car and I'd finally taken the plunge and purchased it for myself a few months ago. It had an all black exterior and interior, a panorama sunroof, memory seats, a heads up display and pretty much any other bells and whistles you could imagine.

It was the first bit of money I'd spent from my husband's insurance policy money. Jonathan knew I wanted this car and after a few years, I felt like it was time to treat myself. It had been the first bit of true happiness I'd experienced in a while. Plugging my phone in so the Apple Car play could connect, I asked Siri to call Parris and waited patiently for the phone to ring as I buckled up and pulled off.

"That was more than five minutes Kali." Parris immediately fussed at me. I rolled my eyes as I focused on the road.

My big sister was eight years older than me, and she'd been bossing me around since before I could walk. But she was all the family I had left so I rarely complained.

"Hi Parris, how are you?" I attempted to correct her bad manners.

"Girl, go to hell." She snipped causing a chuckle to escape my lips. "It's late, you're just now leaving your office?"

"Yes." I sighed. "I lost track of time. You know that happens whenever I'm in that darkroom. But I accomplished a lot today, so I'm not complaining. What's up? How's my nephew?"

"Mason is fine Kali, he asked about you today."

"I'll call him tomorrow. You know he be answering his phone during class."

"Yeah, I do know. I keep having to pay money to get it back after he gets in confiscated." She sighed and I laughed.

My nephew was 14 going on 30. He had just entered high school and from the conversations I'd had with him, he already had a bunch of little girls on his line. I wasn't surprised, he was handsome and as the fun rich auntie I kept him in all the best gear. He was spoiled and my sister hated it. Since he was already down one parent through no fault of his own, I tried to make up for it in whatever way I could.

"Has he spoken to Lamar?" I inquired silently wishing his deadbeat had offered some form of communication. I hated Lamar with a passion. When Mason was born and Parris caught him cheating, she immediately filed for divorce from him. When Parris refused to get back with him, he wanted nothing to do with Mason. It was a shit show to witness.

"Girl no." she sighed. "At this point, Mason is old enough to see what it is and I'm not going to attempt to broker a relationship with them anymore. Evelyn called him though, and he's been in regular communication with her these past few months."

"That's something." I offered.

"Yeah." She replied. "Anyway, what's up with you? You ready for your trip?"

"Um, just about." I replied biting my bottom lip nervously thinking about my upcoming vacation.

"Are you going to do it this time?"

"I'm going to try." I shrugged as if she could see me. "I just—I know once I do it, it will make it final, you know?"

"I know Babe, but it's what he wanted, and it's been four years. You got your necklace made, you gave some of the ashes to his mom and Jamie; now it's time to get the rest of it done."

"It's easier said than done Parris. But I'm going to do it."

"You gotta move on and until you do this final step, you won't get anywhere near moving on."

"I've moved on." I said defensively, my hand going to the heart shaped pendant on my neck that contained a bit of Jonathan's ashes.

"Yeah? How many dates have you been on? And no, those couple of one night stands do not count." Again, I bit down on my bottom lip. I didn't want to admit to Parris that she was right, so I said the first thing to come to mind.

"Two."

"Girl, stop lying." She replied. "Jonathan wouldn't have wanted you to be lonely like this. You're still young. I get it, the thought of dating anybody is scary, but it's a part of life Babe."

"I miss him every single day Parris. I'm just not ready to let him go. Believe me, I know I do, but I just can't. And I most certainly don't want to love anybody else; that shit hurt too much when you lose it."

"It's not love if it's not a little painful. But the pain, is what lets you know that it's real. And besides, didn't you make him a promise? You know he's up in heaven shaking his head at you like only he could do." That made me laugh.

"Yeah, I know."

"So, get it done and then think about finally moving to Dallas. You need to be around family, and I would love seeing your face every day. My house is big enough, or I can look for a place near mine for you." Again, I rolled my eyes. Parris had been trying to convince me to move to Dallas since the day after Jonathan's funeral. But I loved Chicago. It was the place I felt closest to Jonathan.

"I'm not moving to Dallas, Parris."

"I don't know why not."

"My business is here."

"Your business can be anywhere. What is here in Dallas are your sister and nephew who both need you. What's here is a fresh start and opportunity. Besides what you're paying in rent there, you could own and pay less in mortgage here. There's a three-bedroom 2 bath ranch down the street from me for 250k which is a steal. I went to the open house they had the other day; you know I like to be nosey, and they completely renovated everything. The master is huge and the master ensuite is gorgeous. That gives you space for your art room, and you could have a dark room too if you want to. Think about it Kali, I think it could work."

"How are you planning my life in Dallas before I could even think about it?" I chuckled. "Be for real Parris."

"I am being for real. I know I keep asking and you keep saying no, but I really think it would be a good move for you."

"I'll think about it." I sighed, knowing I would consider it for a few seconds before giving up on the idea like I always did. "Let me go, I need to grab something to eat before I get home. I love you Parris, kiss Mason for me."

"Love you too Kali."

I disconnected our call and immediately the Lucky Daye album I'd been playing earlier began to boom from the speakers. No matter how loud the music played though, nothing could drown my thoughts. Any time Parris called me, she got me to thinking about shit and I hated it. I knew she only wanted what was best for me, but I didn't understand why she didn't trust that I knew what was best for myself.

I missed Jonathan and I know he wanted me to have a fulfilling life, but a huge part of me knew I wasn't ready for it. Still, she was right; I'd made a promise to him, and I had been procrastinating on spreading his ashes in Mexico as he'd requested. Mexico was where we'd honeymooned and every year, we revisited the same hotel and resort.

We had planned to go one last time, but he transitioned weeks before the trip. He wanted me to still go and spread his ashes, but after losing him, I was stuck in bed. The dates for the trip came and went and I had broken my promise. Since then, I had told myself and others that I was going to get it done, then always found an excuse on why I couldn't. I felt it in my heart that it was time; so, three weeks ago, I booked my flight and hotel determined to get it done and fulfill his wishes; I owed him that much.

3

JOSIAH

The flight to Puerto Vallarta was short and comfortable since I'd splurged on myself and opted for first class. The extra legroom was well worth the extra $250 I'd spent on the ticket to upgrade. Standing at 6'1 200lbs, my body appreciated the extra space and the comfort that only first class could offer.

I had slept most of the way to Mexico opting out of my meal service just wanting to get there already. The last week had been trying. I'd gotten another call from my Mom and this time she had me speak to Pops as well. Needless to say, that conversation went exactly how I thought it would and not at all how she expected as it ended with shouting on both our ends. Them constantly trying to convince me to forgive my brother was getting more and more annoying with each call. As if he deserved it.

It wasn't like Josh had fucked Angela once which was a horrible thought on its own, but they remained in a relationship after as if I didn't matter. Somehow their betrayal turned into me being the one who was being stubborn. And yeah, it had been four years, and I probably should have been over it, but I wasn't. I loved Angela more than I loved any other girl in this world and she and my brother; the man I'd literally come into the world with, gutted me like I was nothing. So needless to say, this vacation was very well needed; so, I was packed and ready to go two days ago.

After getting the announcement that we'd arrived and to fasten our seatbelts to get ready for landing, I suddenly became excited for what was to come for me. I'd been to Mexico a time or two, but Puerto Vallarta was a new destination and the hotel I'd chosen, Secrets Resorts was an adult only all-inclusive resort. Anytime I travelled out of the country, I always booked with Secrets. I'd researched this location in particular and looked forward to the amenities that would be offered to me once I arrived. But first, after landing, I needed to take the nearly 45 minute journey from the airport to the hotel.

After landing, I gathered my backpack which I'd carried on then made my way off the plane up the runaway and followed the line of people to customs with my passport in hand ready to collect my stamp. It took another forty minutes to get through customs and collect my luggage. I stopped at the exchange center and got a few pesos to use throughout my trip. I made my way through the airport, avoiding the time share offerings and found the transfer company I'd booked.

"Welcome to Puerto Vallarta." A short Hispanic man smiled when I reached a sign with my name on it. "My name is Pedro; I will be driving you to your hotel. I understand you were originally a part of a group, but it is now just yourself, is that correct?"

"Yeah." I nodded. "Just me."

"In that case, if you do not mind, instead of the bus, we have a sedan that will be taking you to your hotel." He pointed towards a small Toyota before grabbing my luggage and wheeling it to the car. He opened the door for me then placed my suitcase in the trunk. I made myself comfortable preparing for the ride there. When he got in, he buckled up then offered me a beer from the cooler in the front seat which I declined. "The ride will be about 45 minutes, may be a little longer depending on traffic. But I promise to get you there safely."

"Thank you."

Nestling against the window, I figured I'd get another nap in, and I hoped and prayed that the driver wasn't talkative so I could have peace. He was friendly, but I wasn't a conversationalist, at least not when I was jet lagged.

Thankfully the journey passed without much talking. When we pulled up to the large gate for the hotel, the driver gave my name, and they allowed us in. I went through the check in process which took another twenty minutes and finally I was escorted to my room on the first level.

Once inside of my room, I admired the furnishings, cloaked in all white with a dabble of green. There was a large king sized bed in the middle of the room, an ensuite near the room door and a large patio door which led out onto a long walk out patio that housed a set of chairs as well as a hot tub.

Looking around the space, I made a mental note to try to enjoy myself and my peace. Rich was right, I deserved this break, and I deserved this vacation. Ever since I'd gotten to Dallas, I had poured myself into my work, barely taking vacations only being out when I was absolutely too sick to come in. Even during the summer, I taught summer school as well as being involved in sponsoring after school activities to keep myself busy.

I think my hard work and throwing myself into work was a symptom of my trauma and of the pain I'd endured in the betrayal I experienced. Some days I felt good, other days I missed both Angela and Joshua so much it was disgusting. I don't know why but a small part of me wasn't that surprised that Angela had done what she did. I was more surprised by Josh than anything. As my brother, my closest confidant it didn't seem possible that he could hurt me in the way he did; especially since I would have never dreamed of doing the same to him.

Still, I pushed them out of my mind and went over to my luggage so I could unpack and get settled. The next four days would be spent enjoying myself, dismissing the conversations I'd had with my parents and not allowing negative thoughts to consume me. This time was about me and only me. I just wanted peace and as I put my phone on do not disturb, I was resolved to have it.

∼

I SLEPT LONGER than I intended to. What was meant to be only a 15 minute nap to rest my eyes turned into three hours of deep sleep I didn't even realize I was in until I woke up. When I first got to Mexico, the sun was shining brightly, beaming down on me. My room was on the same level as the hotel lobby, and there was a small bar in front of the lobby that seemed to now have live music.

I had left my patio door open a little to allow the fresh breeze to come into my room and now I could hear the music. Stretching and rubbing the sleep from my eyes, I sighed before getting out of the bed and going over to the patio door, opening it enough for me to be able to step out of it and walk towards the end of the patio near the banister enclosing it. Only, it wasn't fully enclosed as it was open enough where if I wanted, I could lift my leg, step over the hedges, and access my neighbor's patio if I wanted to.

I looked down over the banister observing the people in the resort moving about from location to location. I could see from my patio the open lobby area, the vibration from the live music seemed to radiate through me the longer I sat and watched them. It was a Mexican band, singing American music, old hits like Dionne Warwick, Stephanie Mills, The Temptations. The female lead singer was doing a great job and her partner, the male, was keeping up with her to the best of his abilities. It was a nice little vibe, but I thanked God the patio door was soundproof so I wouldn't hear it if I hadn't had the door cracked a little.

Turning to my right, I looked down at the main pool area, which was surrounded by shops and restaurants. Smiling faces were maneuvering in and out of those spots; couples with their hands connected, girlfriends laughing boisterously. The view of the beautiful women was very much appreciated and suddenly Rich's suggestion to find something nice to get into didn't seem so bad; so I made a mental note to stop at the little gift shop I saw on my way up to the lobby to see if they had condoms as I didn't bring my own. I hadn't planned on sliding into anything until the sea of beautiful faces were paraded in front of me.

Suddenly, I saw something move to my right, out of the corner of my eye. Turning slightly, my eyes seemed to automatically zoom over to one of the most beautiful rich chocolate women I'd probably ever seen in my life. She was on her patio as well maybe three rooms down, only she didn't seem to be out to enjoy the music. In fact, her face seemed to be concentrating, not on anything in particular, but more on her thoughts. There was a sadness in her eyes as she wrapped her arms around her slim thick frame.

She was wearing a yellow and orange haltered maxi dress. While her breasts were average size, a B cup at most, her waist was slim, and her ass seemed to poke out in the way that maxi dresses seemed to make them do. Her hair was pinned up in a braided bun with two loosely curled braids left out in the front framing her face. She had gold bracelets on both arms, with big hoop earrings in her ears. I couldn't see from this far, but I wouldn't be surprised if she didn't have one in her nose too, she seemed like the type, the free spirit, art loving type.

I didn't mean to stare, but I couldn't tear my eyes away from the beauty. The longer she looked out over the resort, the more pain I seemed to see in her eyes. I wondered what her pain was about. Maybe she was like me and had experienced hurt because of somebody she loved. I half expected someone to walk out of the patio to go after her; surely a man who had a woman like that wouldn't leave her sad and would do what they had to do to make her happy.

As if on cue, her eyes seemed to find mine and when they did, she nervously twirled her finger around one of her left out braids. I lifted my hand to greet her with a quick wave and a smile. I had been caught staring at her and since I was only a few doors down, I didn't want her thinking I was a creep. I didn't know how long she'd been on the trip, but it would certainly make for an awkward run in, which I was sure we'd end up doing since the resort wasn't that large. I watched as the beauty lifted her hand up in a wave, politely smiling back. Before I could yell across the way, she turned and walked into her room disappearing behind the patio door.

The moment she was gone I seemed to gain my breath back. I hadn't even realized I had stopped breathing until she was gone. Besides Angela, no other woman had ever taken my breath away, until now. I placed my hand over my beating heart and willed it to calm itself. I was trippin'. I didn't even know her name, yet my sweaty palms and rapidly beating heart didn't seem to care. I wanted her, there were no ifs, ands or buts about it.

Grabbing my room key, I figured now was as good a time

as any to go explore the resort. I'd read up on it before I got here, so I had an idea which restaurants I wanted to hit up, but I saw some brochures by the front desk with the different excursions they offered, and I figured I'd grab some of those to look over. Four days was a long time to be here to not get into some kind of fun.

When I was out of my room, I turned to my left and looked down the hall where I knew the nameless beauty's room was. My mind was rampant with thoughts of her chocolate skin. I wondered if she smelled as good as she looked, and I wondered if she tasted as good as she looked. These thoughts were crazy, so I chuckled, shook my head, and went on about my way.

I stopped by the lobby, grabbed some flyers for snorkeling, scuba diving, ATVs and for a tour of the city. I walked past the live band and saw they had a small crowd, some people were dancing along to the music, others were enjoying drinks at the bar. I made my way down to the lower level, making my way to the gift shop I'd passed earlier. Once inside, I immediately went to grab a few things I figured I would need. When I got to the personal hygiene area, the selection of condoms stared me in the face. I grabbed two boxes of the 3 pack of Magnums, just in case. The silent judgement from the cashier as she rang up my items was funny, but there was also a sparkle in her eye that most women got when they fully looked into my face. I knew it was my eyes, they were hazel in color, something Joshua and I had inherited from our Pops.

Once I was done in the gift shop, I walked around making note of where certain restaurants were. Since I was a Preferred rewards member, I had access to the Preferred lounge and *The Premier*, the restaurant exclusive for Preferred members. Finally, I made my way to the beach and after snatching off my shoes and finding a beach chair, I sat and listened to the waves crashing against the bright sands. The sun was almost fully set now, the hues of blue and orange spread across the ocean. Pulling out my cell phone, I snapped a picture of its beauty, grateful to God that he allowed me to see it.

∼

"Good evening, what can I get for you?" The bartender asked as soon as I sat down. It was a small bar outside of an Italian restaurant I had wanted to eat at but didn't feel like eating alone. Since I didn't have a choice, I figured I would just eat at the bar instead, after a few drinks.

"Coke and Hennessey." I replied.

"Of course." She smiled before busying herself to make my drink. I turned my eyes towards a small tv mounted on a wall just behind her head. They were replaying a Lakers vs. Phoenix game on ESPN.

Although my phone was on DND, I saw a new message come through from Rich. Shaking my head, I could imagine him clicking the 'notify anyway' button.

> Rich: How's Mexico? Slide into anything yet?

Rich was always living vicariously through me. He married Tish straight out of college, and she was the reason he moved to Dallas to begin with. For nine years she had been the only woman he'd been with. I respected him because he stayed faithful no matter what. I was happy for him, happy that he found his happiness so early on. I truly believed I had that with Angie, how fucking stupid I was.

> Not yet. Just enjoying the views.

I added the picture I took earlier at the beach. A picture I stared at for just a short while longer before being presented with my drink. I thanked the bartender with a smile and a nod before grabbing the glass and taking a sip of it.

> Rich: Don't think about it, just do it. You ain't never going to see them again. Strap up so you don't leave with something you can't get rid of.

I laughed at my friend and the bartender looked my way.

"Can I help you with anything else?" she asked licking her lips. Her accent was heavy, but I could understand her broken English perfectly.

"Not right now sweetheart." I replied. "Thank you though."

"Well, my name is Maggie, if you need anything else." I nodded in acknowledgement of her statement, before looking towards the restaurant. I had a small snack earlier, but I knew I should be eating more in order to soak up some of the liquor I planned on consuming. It didn't take me long to finish my first drink and then I was on to the next, continuing to watch the game.

"Is anyone sitting here?" A soft melodic voice from my right asked. There was a sweet scent that came with the voice, the smell of strawberries and vanilla. I slowly turned in the direction of the voice, stealing my attention from the screen, focusing instead on who was speaking. To my surprise, the beauty from earlier was standing in front of me with a coy smile on her face.

As my eyes met hers, my heart again began to accelerate the way it had done earlier. Her chocolate skin seemed to glow even more in front of me now than it had done before. Her hair was out of the bun, instead her braids hung loose framing her face. As if nervous, she raked some of her braids out of her face pulling them to the back.

"Huh?" I finally managed to say, and she chuckled.

"This seat, is it taken?" I looked around and noticed that a few other seats at the bar had been filled, the seat in question was to my right.

"No." I shook my head. She smiled before taking the seat next to me. I turned my body towards her, giving her my full attention. "You want a drink?"

"I need one." She replied and I gestured for the bartender to come over.

"Hey handsome, what can I get for you?"

"Another coke and Hennessey." I told her. "And for my friend…" I looked towards the beauty, and she twisted her lips in thought.

"I think I want a red wine; do you have anything sweet?"

"We have a 2018 Chateau Montelena or the 2019 Cabernet Sauvignon. Both are very good, but I do prefer the Montelena myself.'

"Then I'll take a glass of that." Nodding the bartender again left us to make the drinks. "So, do you have a name?" she looked at me batting her long eyelashes.

"J-Mac." I replied and she chuckled sweetly, the sound of her giggles sending tingles through my body that I didn't know could even be possible.

"That is not what your mama named you."

"Josiah." I extended my hand to her.

"Hi Josiah, I'm Kahlia, but you can call me Kali." She accepted my hand, giving it a gentle shake.

"Are you here alone Kali?"

"I am, you?" she accepted the drink the bartender gave her and placed it to her lips covered in bright red lipstick. My eyes roamed her body, admiring the material from her mini dress that clung to her chocolate skin. She was taller than I thought, but it could have just been the gold heels she wore on her feet. Without them, she had to be no more than 5'4.

"I am." I nodded. "It was supposed to be a group trip for me, but everybody else bailed on me. I didn't want to waste the trip or my money, so here I am alone sitting at a bar, contemplating on going into that restaurant to get a table for one or going back to my room and ordering room service."

"You sound like me." She chuckled. "I didn't want to go through the embarrassment of asking for a table for one." Her shoulders shrugged.

"Why are you alone in Mexico? Most women, black women at that, have a fear of traveling alone."

"I had to." She replied taking another sip of her drink.

"Please explain."

"I probably shouldn't, you'll think I'm crazy."

"Are you on the run?" I laughed taking a sip of my own drink.

"No." she shook her head before biting down on her bottom lip. I noticed the sadness I saw earlier flash in her eyes, then her hand went towards the heart shaped pendant on her necklace, twisting it in her fingers.

"I'm not trying to pry." I assured her, absentmindedly placing my hand over hers. The moment our skin touched; an electric shock ran through me. We looked at each other and there was no doubt in my mind that she had felt it too. "Sorry."

"You're good." She slowly snatched her hand away. "I'm here to honor a promise I made to someone special to me. It has taken me several years to get it done, but I'm here to do it."

"Do what?"

"Spread my husband's ashes." She guzzled the rest of her drink and that's when I noticed the tan lines on her left hand's ring finger. "Can I get another?" she asked the bartender who immediately came and poured her another glass of wine.

"I'm sorry for your loss."

"Me too." She finally looked over at me, her eyes swelling with tears, yet she seemed to be able to keep them from falling. "Anyway, I'm a mess and I didn't want to be alone so thank you for letting me sit here with you. Have a good night." She started to get up from her seat and I stood up as well.

"Wait…" I said grabbing her arm and preventing her from walking off. "Have dinner with me."

"No, you don't have—"

"Neither of us wants to be a table for one, so how about we be a table for two." She again bit down on her bottom lip, her plump red lips sexily tucked between her teeth. She probably didn't even know how sexy that gesture was for me. A woman biting her bottom lip would always be chef's kiss, but this woman doing it, seemed to send me into overdrive.

"I just unloaded a shit load of info on you in less than ten minutes. You sure you wanna have dinner with me?"

"Seems like we could both use the company." I shrugged holding out my hand. "Let's go eat." I waited patiently for her to take hold of my hand and when she slid her soft hand into mine, I prayed my palms weren't too sweaty. She made me nervous.

Smiling, I escorted us towards the Italian restaurant and when we got to the hostess, we were immediately seated. I pulled her seat out for her before taking the seat opposite to her. We remained quiet as we browsed the menu, only speaking to let the waitress know which drinks we wanted.

"So, I told you something personal." She sighed breaking the silence that surrounded us. "Now it's your turn." I looked up at her from my menu contemplating on if I wanted to be as sharing as she was with my business. I didn't know shit about her, but also, I figured this could be good therapy considering the fact that after these four days I would never see her again so I could care less about any judgements.

"What you wanna know?"

"Are you married? You said you were here alone but for all I know you're on a business trip and your wife and kids are home waiting for you."

"Not married." I chuckled showing her my left hand for good measure. "Why do you ask?"

"Just wanted to make sure I'm not having dinner with somebody's husband." She shrugged. "So, no marriage; but do you have a girlfriend, kids?"

"No and no. I haven't been in a relationship in a little while."

"What's a little while?" she inquired.

"No judgement?" I asked, eyebrow stretched high.

"No judgement, scout's honor." She smirked.

"It's been about four years." I sat my menu down and stared across at her, waiting for something in her eyes to change. When women found out I hadn't been in a serious relationship in so long, they tended to judge me.

"Can I ask why?"

I looked around the restaurant before answering. I didn't want to be vulnerable; it wasn't who I was. But this woman seemed to make me feel so at ease, so comfortable and we'd only been interacting for all of twenty minutes. Rubbing my hand down my waves, I sat up straight preparing to give her an answer.

"Last person I was in a relationship with did some shady shit." I said and her eyes seemed to urge me to continue. "I was engaged to my college girlfriend; had just proposed maybe three months before I came home and found her fucking my twin brother."

"Whoa." Her eyes widened. "I wasn't expecting that. I'm sorry that happened to you."

"Yeah, me too." I repeated the same words she'd told me earlier. "But it's all good. You live and you learn."

"Fucking your brother is wild. Do you still talk to them?"

"Nah." I shook my head. "Haven't said a word to either of them since it happened. Found out from my Mama that they got a baby on the way though, she keep tryna get me to forgive and forget."

"No offense to your mom, but fuck that." She scoffed. "You better than me. If my sister did some shit like that to me, I'd beat her ass every day until I felt vindicated. And the fact that they are still together is crazy, that's really fucked up."

"Yeah well, I'm grateful at the end of the day. God just showed me that I didn't need either of them in my life no more. I did fuck his ass up though before I left." We both laughed at that, and it felt good to joke about the situation.

"Good, because if you said you didn't at least get a couple licks in I would have been disappointed." Finally, the waitress returned with our drinks; another coke and Hennessey for me and another glass of wine for her. We ordered food and when she left to put in our orders, I turned back to Kali.

"So, how long were you married?"

"I was married for almost six years, but we were high school sweethearts and had started dating at 16."

"Sheesh, that's young. You knew that soon that he was the one for you?"

"I knew he was going to be important to my life. Sometimes, you get those feelings from people you know?"

I did know. I had felt it with Angela and now... with her. Yet, I didn't let on to that as I just nodded my head slightly sipping from my own glass.

"How long has it been since you lost your husband?"

again her hand went towards her necklace, fidgeting with it. This was the second time she'd done it. "You don't have to say, if you don't want to. I was just curious."

"Four years." She admitted. "Four very long years and here I am still pinning over him. It's pathetic right?"

"You loved him, why is that pathetic? It takes however long it takes to grieve. What made you finally decide to come here and do it?"

"I don't know." She shrugged. "Something just told me it was time. I had been scheduling this trip and cancelling it so much it was ridiculous."

"Why here?"

"We honeymooned here, and this was one of our favorite places to vacation because of it. We were among the first guests at this hotel when they built it years ago."

"I saw you earlier and you looked sad. Is it because you'd already done it? You spread the ashes?" she nodded her head.

"Yeah, it was the first thing I did when I arrived earlier this morning. I had to do it then, because if I waited, I wouldn't have gone through with it."

"That had to be hard, I'm sorry." I reached across the table, placing my hand in hers to comfort her.

"Thanks." I didn't pull my hand back for a minute, instead choosing to keep our hands connected while staring at her. She was the first to break the embrace again and I understood why. The connection, the feeling, the emotion going through me from just being in her presence was overwhelming. She was overwhelming.

We continued to talk and converse throughout the rest of the dinner. We laughed, talked, ate, and drank good. I enjoyed her company, enjoyed being around her. When the restaurant was closing, we found our way to the bar in the lobby. We had another drink or two and I was starting to feel good. By 1AM, we were headed away from the bar and towards the rooms. We passed my door and went towards the end of the hallway stopping at room number 1107.

"This is me." She nodded towards the door. "Thank you for keeping me company, it's been a rough first day."

"You got plans for tomorrow?"

"Now that I've gotten today over with. I was going to head up to the Preferred Lounge and relax, get drunk. I don't want to waste my all-inclusive alcohol. You?"

"Same plan." I chuckled. "But I'mma wake up and have breakfast first, coat my stomach so I don't get too fucked up."

"Oh, that's a must. Which room are you in? I'll stop by in the morning to see if you're up."

"1104." I nodded down the hall towards my room. "I'm an early bird, so just stop by."

"Okay." There was the lip biting again. Feeling compelled to do so, I leaned towards her placing a kiss on the side of her mouth.

"Have a good night, Kali." I turned to leave, knowing that if I didn't, I would have invited myself into her space. She didn't need that from me, not after what she had to go through today. But tomorrow was another story.

4

KAHLIA

The temptation to visit Josiah in his room last night was real. From the moment our eyes met earlier in the day, I felt this intense pull towards him, and I couldn't explain it. He was handsome, of course he was. He had to be at least 6 feet tall with an athletic build, muscles protruding from his shirt with ease. And his eyes were sexy as hell, entrancing and pulling me in. When he looked at me, I immediately felt a puddle develop in the seat of my panties.

Nasty thoughts consumed me throughout dinner. Any time he would lick his thick pink lips, anytime he smiled, anytime his eyes pierced into mine all I could do was imagine his beard soaked in my juices. I was horny and I needed some dick. But that was the last thing I should have been thinking about after the day I'd had.

I wasn't kidding when I told him that the first thing I did when I arrived at the resort was spread the ashes. Not even five minutes after checking in and unpacking my bag, I was back out the door, the remainder of Jonathan's ashes in tow on my way to the beach. I'd had to give myself several pep talks in order to even get on the plane, another set on the drive to the hotel and finally after checking in, I gave myself one last pep talk to just get it done. The moment I saw the clear blue water, I almost chickened out. But then I felt Jonathan pushing me forward, heard his voice telling me it was time.

I cried for hours when I got back to my room. I cried for so long and so hard that I fell asleep. When I woke up, the sun was setting, and I felt Jonathan's spirit compelling me to go onto the patio to watch it falling. Imagine my surprise, moments after walking outside to see Josiah staring at me intensely. It was the first time I'd felt the pull to him and when our eyes connected, this feeling washed over me, an overwhelming feeling that the life I had with Jonathan was finally over and it was time for me to move on.

That only saddened me more.

It took a while for me to leave the room after that. I needed a drink, needed to drown in my sorrows but I also didn't want to be alone. I got dressed, intending to go inside of the Italian restaurant I had passed on my way to the beach earlier. As I neared the restaurant however, I realized how pathetic I would look asking for a table for one. I started to turn back until who do I see just outside the restaurant at a small bar but the mystery man from earlier. My legs had a mind of their own as I walked in his direction, compelled to say something. After learning his name, I knew the universe, God or Jonathan were fucking with me; hell, probably all three of them were.

Josiah… it was the name Jonathan had been adamant he wanted to name our child should I ever had gotten pregnant. He'd loved the name since we were teenagers. Jonathan's family were religious and well into the church. He told me all about the King who ruled Judah with love and devotion. He'd mentioned it several times and I would laugh him off each time; knowing we were too young to even be having the kids conversation.

It was hard to believe, but I would swear that the pull, this meeting, it was all a sign from Jonathan. It was why I had been feeling so adamant about coming here to finally spread the ashes. He had to have been bringing me here for this reason.

"Don't be fucking stupid." I thought out loud sighing as I laid in bed. I looked to my left at the patio, the blackout shades were slightly open showing me the sky. I looked towards the alarm clock on the nightstand seeing that it was a little after six in the morning; the sun was rising, and I was sure it was going to be beautiful.

Slowly, I got out of bed and walked over to the bathroom needing to relieve my bladder. I had a slight headache from drinking so much wine last night but other than that, I was fine. After relieving my bladder, I went over to my carryall and pulled out my camera before walking the short distance towards the patio.

Stepping out of the door, the crisp early morning air hit my face. Still, I led my bare feet towards the banister so I could take pictures of the beautiful sunrise. The sky was blue, a bright blue, with big white clouds. The sun in all its glory, in all its beauty shined in hues of orange and yellow. It's reflection against the waters and sands of the beach just as beautiful.

Immediately my hands and camera worked together to start snapping pictures, attempting to capture the beauty I saw in person through my lens. It was magnificent to witness in person. The view was always one to remember. After snapping the last of my pictures, I found my way back inside so I could get ready for my day.

An hour later, my hygiene was taken care of, and I was dressed in a pair of biker shorts and a cropped t-shirt along with a pair of Crocs. My stomach was empty, and I needed to fill my stomach. I grabbed my room key as well as my cell phone before making my way out of the room. As I walked past room 1104, I hesitated, wondering if he was up. He'd offered to have breakfast with me, but I knew I was an early bird and the last thing most people wanted to do while on vacation was wake up early. Still, I knocked quickly and waited, shifting from leg to leg, my nerves beating through my body, wondering if he would answer.

When more than a minute passed, I started to walk away. I was only a few steps away when I heard the click of the lock and the door creak open causing me to turn around to face him.

"Good morning." I smiled bashfully, feeling like a damn teenager in the presence of her crush. Even as he rubbed the sleep out of them, his light bright eyes seemed to mesmerize me. "I was about to head to breakfast; I didn't know if you wanted to join me or not."

"What time is it?" he asked flicking his left wrist up but soon realized he didn't have a watch on. "Aw shit."

"It's almost 8." I told him. "I'm sorry I woke you. Get some rest, I'll see you later." I turned to walk away again but he quickly grabbed my hand stopping me.

"You are good. Let me just get myself together and we can go. You can wait in here or you can head up and I'll meet you."

"I guess I can wait if you don't mind." He smiled before stepping aside to let me in. His room was the same as mine. Same king bed, same tv, same bathroom, same layout; yet I looked around as if I was seeing something new, my head on a swivel.

He went over to his suitcase and grabbed some stuff before making his way into the bathroom. Not a single word was exchanged between us as I sat at the small two seater round table near the patio door. He seemed to be focused on getting himself together, so I remained quiet; not wanting to interrupt his stride with my words.

I continued to look around the room taking note of his open suitcase. Some things were inside neatly folded, and nothing seemed out of place anywhere in the room. He was a neat freak which was a little funny considering I was a bit messy myself.

Not wanting to wait in silence, I turned the tv on seeing that it was already on ESPN. They were reporting about the upcoming Olympics. The show temporarily distracted me as I waited patiently for him to finish. I was nervous but I was also very hungry.

Nearly thirty minutes later, he was dressed, and we were heading out of the room. There was a buffet for breakfast that included different food stations. When we made it, we gave them our room numbers and were escorted to a two seater table on the balcony overlooking the property. We were served drinks by the waiter then we made our way around the buffet picking up our food selections. Once I had everything I needed,fruit salad, 2 pancakes, 2 sausage, 3 strips of bacon and scrambled eggs, I went back to our table holding two different plates as well as a bowl for my fruit. It wasn't long before he made his way back and he gawked at the plates of food surrounding me.

"Don't judge; I'mma eat every last bit of it too." I said buttering my pancakes then pouring syrup all over my plate saturating the pancakes and meat.

"I ain't judging you." He held his hands up on mock surrender. "I saw how you got down yesterday. You ate your food and mine. I had to order room service when I got back to my room, I was still hungry and fucked up."

"Sorry." I giggled finally cutting a piece of pancake then placing it in my mouth. I silently moaned at the perfection of the fluffy batter and the crisp sides. They were buttery and sweet, just like I liked them.

"Good?" he asked, his eyes seemingly roaming my face, always falling to my lips. Instinctively I licked the corner of my lip, savoring the syrup residue that was left over. "You have beautiful lips." I stared into his eyes as he stared back at mine. I didn't know what to say, nobody ever complimented my lips before.

"Thank you." I mumbled focusing again on my food.

We ate in silence for the most part, each exchanging glances and quickly looking away when the other had caught on to it. I studied his face during my glances. I found myself admiring the blemish free caramel skin covering his body. His hair was in deep waves with tapered sides. His nose was big but didn't distract from the rest of his face. He had beautiful lips of his own, they were big, thick, and perfectly pink. Then there were his eyes, his beautiful hazel eyes that sparkled in the light of the sun.

When we finished breakfast, we took a walk around the resort eventually ending up on the beach where we walked barefoot down the shore. There were people starting to gather, couples enjoying the peace of the waves, venturing off into the water, cuddled up underneath the cabanas that had been made available by the resort. We walked and talked about ourselves.

He shared with me that he was from Georgia and coincidentally had moved to Dallas. He told me he was a teacher and football coach. He told me that he moved to Dallas to be closer to his best friend Richard. He was excited about being an uncle to Richard's child and the excitement in his eyes at the mention of small kid made my uterus swell.

I shared with him how I was from Chicago and still lived there. I told him about my photography and artwork, and I told him my sister had been trying to get me to move to

Dallas for years, but Chicago was home, and I wasn't ready to leave yet. After telling him Parris had been trying to get me to come to Dallas, he attempted his own convincing but even his beautiful smile couldn't persuade me. I wasn't ready for that move yet.

We talked about our hobbies, outside of my art, I loved to cook and bake. He agreed that he loved to cook as well but he hadn't been much of a baker. He told me he played football up until college and that was why he had taken on the role of coach when it came open. He talked about being a gym rat as well, often going to work out six days a week. While I wasn't much of a workout buff myself, I did enjoy a good workout which is how we'd agreed to wake up early tomorrow to get a workout in.

Without warning we seemed to have planned our entire days together. He was to leave in two days while I had an extra day ahead of me. As we made our way back from the beach, up through the resort and towards our rooms, we meet up again in the Preferred Lounge where we'd have access to a private pool for only Preferred members.

Once I made it back to my room, I quickly freshened up before slipping into my yellow two piece. I grabbed a pair of Chanel sunglasses I purchased right before the trip and filled my beach bag with candy, my room key, my cellphone, and some sunscreen. I placed on a black cover all before pulling my hair into a tight high bun on top of my head. Not long after, there was a knock on my door and I was out of it, falling in step with Josiah.

When we made it to the pool, we grabbed beach chairs near the pool and took turns rubbing sunscreen on one another before entering the pool. With my sunglasses over my face, I enjoyed watching him swim. His body was even nicer outside of his normal clothes. He had an athletic build, his muscles on a constant flex. On his chest was a football

GENESIS CARTER

inspired tattoo of a skull with a football in its mouth. The vivid colors in the tattoo had my eyes yearning to study every part of it.

"Can you swim?" he asked coming up out of the water towards me where I sat on the ledge of the pool, my feet kicking in the water. He took my left foot into his hand, the water still cascading down his body, yet his hands did the lord's work as they rubbed my feet.

"Yes." I responded, trying hard not to moan at the feel of his hands massaging my feet.

"Why aren't you swimming with me?"

"Because my braids are cute, and I don't want to mess them up." I replied honestly with a chuckle. "You know how black women are about their hair."

"Oh, I know." He chuckled, continuing to dig into my tissue. I tried to squirm out of his reach, yet his hold remained. "So, you're not going to get in at all?"

"I am, but I won't be underwater." I shrugged. "And I have to ease myself in. Just from it being on my feet, I know it's cold as hell. Only a psycho would just walk all the way, in with no cares." That caused a hearty laugh to escape his lips. "Fair enough." He continued to dig even deeper, and the moan threatened to escape my lips. "I love the white polish on toes. It's sexy." I gave him a coy smile before playfully rolling my eyes.

"How often does that line work?"

"What line? I do love white polish especially against chocolate skin."

"Can we be real for a minute?" I asked thrilled and nervous to venture into the conversation I had planned on having with him. As a 31 year old woman, I had no time to play around. I knew what I wanted from him, and I was sure it was the same for him with me.

"Haven't we been being real this entire time? Or you been

playing me?" The sexy smirk forming on his face sent chills down my spine.

"I want to have sex with you." I told him cocking my head to the side matter of factly. "And I think you want the same from me?"

"I do." He responded after a moment of silence. "So, what that mean?"

"Can we agree that this will be just for this weekend? No feelings, no promises of reconnecting in the real world, just us in our little Mexican bubble."

"I'm not looking for nothing besides this weekend." He assured me and I felt a slight sense of relief. "I am not a relationship type of man anymore. I can give you a companion for the next few days. I can romance you if you'd like or I could just fuck you. Either way, I'm leaving here alone."

"Let's toast on it." I said nodding towards a waitress who had been walking near us. Before we got in, I had stopped at the bar and ordered a bottle of tequila with limes and two shot glasses. Once she was gone, I poured two shots, handing one of them over to Josiah. "To good sex and no feelings."

"To good sex and no feelings." He repeated before we both chugged our shots.

After a bit of time and a few more shots, I found myself inside of the pool engulfed in Josiah's arms. My legs wrapped around his waist as his hand cupped my ass. With all the uneasiness behind us and the truth out in front, it was easier to be in his presence without the expectation of anything more. Our eyes connected, flirtatiously consuming the both of us. I had agreed to be his and he agreed to be mine for the rest of our time here.

Wrapping my arms tightly around his neck, I lowered his head down so that I could feel the softness of his lips. I stuck my tongue out before tracing his lips then placing a peck on them. Soon our lips were smashing against one another, swipe for swipe of our tongues causing silent moans to escape both of our lips.

We didn't care that we were surrounded by a small group of people who had also ventured to the Preferred Lounge. Nobody else mattered except for me and him. Had I not already been in water, I knew my bikini would have been soaked. My pebbled nipples would never be able to hide my arousal. Sitting at his waist, I could feel what he was working with, and it was growing steadily, the longer our lips remained connected. From underneath me, I felt his hand go towards the seat of my bikini before swiping it to the side then placing one of his fingers inside of me.

The loud gasp escaped my lips and was only muffled by the fact that our lips were still connected. His lone finger moved in and out of me and when he entered a second it became increasingly hard to fight the moan.

"Unless you're trying to get fucked in the middle of this pool; I suggest you stop kissing me like that." He whispered. "But if you are tryna get fucked in the middle of this pool, just let me know and I'll make it happen. I can be discreet, can you?" he finally removed his lips from mine before looking at me. His fingers never stopped moving inside of me and I tried so hard to keep my face neutral, yet he was slowly breaking my resolve. "Should I stop." I wanted to tell him no, but I knew damn well that if he didn't everyone in our vicinity would know what we were up to. I was adventurous but public sex was never on my bucket list.

"Please." I groaned and with a sly smirk, he removed his fingers from inside of me before placing a quick peck on my lips then backed away from me. Staring in his direction, I slowly made my way towards where I'd left the bottle of tequila, pouring myself two more shots, and then grabbing a towel walking off towards the bathroom so I could get myself together.

If I wasn't careful, he had the capability of making me completely undone.

∼

WE SPENT NEARLY three hours at the pool, finishing off the bottle of tequila and ordering lunch. Needless to say, neither of us were sober when we took the elevator down to our room level. The elevator ride was silent, though I knew we both had the same thing on our minds. I wanted him to finish off what he'd started in the pool, I wanted to feel him inside of me and I prayed to God that he didn't disappoint when it came down to it. I'd learned the hard way that just because a nigga had a big dick didn't mean he was able to put in work with it. I wondered, as the numbers descended from the 20th floor to the 11th, if he would be able to satisfy me the way I liked.

We exited the elevator as soon as the doors opened on the 11th floor. We reached my door first and as I fished my keycard out of my bag, I could feel his eyes on me. I looked up at him once I'd retrieved it.

"I'm not going to offer to come in." he assured me with a smirk. "Now isn't the time. But I happen to know that most single women travel with vibrators on vacation; if you got a vibrator, I'll give you permission to use it this once for the rest of the weekend."

"Permission?" I asked confused and intrigued.

"Yeah." He walked up on me, my back against the door leading to my room. "Permission. You told me your body would be mine for the weekend."

"I didn't—"

"Oh, but you did." He chuckled sexily causing a shiver to run down my spine. "So, since your body belongs to me,

I'mma give you permission to let anything other than my tongue and dick please you."

"You talk a big game, Josiah." I licked my lips, squirming under the intense gaze of his beautiful hazel orbs. "I sure hope you can back it up. I'd hate to be disappointed."

"I love having the opportunity to prove you wrong." He took the keycard out of my hand, placing it against the lock. When we heard the click, he turned the knob and pushed open the door. "Dinner is at 7:30, I'll meet you here around that time." Placing a final kiss on my forehead, he walked away from me leaving me stuck temporarily until I came to my senses and made my way into the room.

I stumbled over to the bed, kicking off my sandals and throwing my bag on the bed. With no shame in my game, I grabbed the vibrator I'd purchased from Amazon. It was made by some company called Tracy's Dog. It had been a big deal, months ago since someone left an Amazon review for it, and it went viral. As one could imagine, my sex life was not consistent. I never kept anyone around enough to have sex on a regular basis, so toys became my go to. At the price they were offering for this one in particular, and since the review intrigued me, I purchased it on a whim. So far, it had lived up to its reputation and I needed that, in this moment, because of that man.

So, I eased out of my bikini top and bottom, tracing my skin; the chills of the fan hitting the droplets of water that still remained on my body. I moved my hand over my left nipple, biting down on my bottom lip I traveled further down, across my belly then between my leg. I rubbed my clit smearing the juices that already leaked from me over my clit to get it lubricated.

The first level of the vibrator was strong, intense, but I needed more power to get rid of the electricity building up in my body. I imagined his voice in my ear telling me to rub my pussy and me being willing to oblige. I clicked the button on the vibrator to bring it to the next level, my heart skipping in anticipation of what I knew the third level would bring me. Still, I placed the suctioning cup with the mini tongue over my clit the other side curving fitting snuggly inside of my walls. I moaned biting down on my lips feeling the euphoria covering my body. Finally, I clicked the button a third time and my entire body seemed to shake as an intense orgasm built up inside of me, slowly, methodically.

I felt his fingers inside of my pussy again, stroking in and out of me. His lips against mine, his body pressed against mine. I imagined his tongue which I had tasted with my own tongue, tasting my other set of lips. The faster the vibrator worked, the more intense the buildup stayed until finally, I could no longer hold it in, and I exploded, juices flying every which way like a faucet.

Slowly, I began to come down off that high, breathing hard, my heart pounding in my chest. I felt weak as I attempted to get up so I could get under the blanket. That had taken a lot out of me and after the dizziness from my impending hangover had passed, my eyes seemed to close on their own and soon snores were the only sound coming from room 1107.

The sound of my phone blaring woke me up what felt like only an hour later. However, after I stumbled around blindly for my phone, I finally found it buried deep inside of my beach bag pulling it out and observing the time displayed on the screen; 6:35pm. I had slept for three hours, and it didn't feel like it. The brightness from the phone displaying my sister's name almost blinded me.

"Hello." I answered the phone groggily seconds later.

"Eww, wake up you sound a mess." Parris laughed into the phone, and I sat up realizing I was naked finding my vibrator next to me. "Why are you sleep on vacation?"

"Had a long day." I said rubbing slob from the corner of my mouth. "What's up?"

"Nothing, just calling to check on you. How's the trip?"

"It's good." I sighed. "Today has been a good day."

"Did you, do it?" she asked, and I paused before answering her.

"Yeah, as soon as I got here I did it. I had to, so I just got it over with."

"You, okay? Why didn't you call me after?"

"I needed some time." I replied honestly. "I felt like shit afterwards even though I know that's what he wanted."

"Understood. Besides that, everything else is good? Are you enjoying yourself?"

"I am." I told her. "I met a friend."

"A friend? Like a male friend?"

"Yeah." I replied picking lint and looking out towards the open space of my blinds. The sun was going down and although I wanted to get my camera to take pictures, I knew I wasn't sober enough to get a good one.

"What's his name?"

"That doesn't matter."

"Is he fine? What does he look like?"

"He's gorgeous." I admitted. "And for the weekend he's mine."

"Yours? Kali, be careful."

"I have been being careful, since Jonathan died, I've been being careful." I told her. "This weekend, I decided to be reckless."

"You fucked him?"

"Not yet, but I plan to. I haven't been fucked in almost a year Parris. If you saw him, you would understand why the first person I want to touch my body in almost a year needs to be him."

"All I'm saying is stranger danger. Make him show you his

clean bill of health, even if ya'll are using condoms which I hope to God you are—"

"We will be." I assured her.

"Even if ya'll do use them, please be smart and ask for that full panel screening. I'm all for you getting your groove back Stella, but make sure he's clean. He is still a stranger."

"I already know that. We're having dinner in an hour, and I was planning on getting through those specifics. I'm not stupid Parris."

"No, you're very smart. But you're also reckless." Her words soaked into my brain. She knew what spreading those ashes would do to me, what frame of mind they would have me in. I was absolutely being reckless, but I didn't care. This was the only feeling I wanted to have, it was the only way to mask the pain that I had been burying deep inside of me.

"I gotta go Parris." I finally spoke after a few moments of silence.

"If I don't get regular check ins from you, I'm going to call the Mexican police and tell them someone kidnapped my sister. What's his room number, I know you know it."

"1104." I laughed. "And no, I'm not giving you, his name. You are just going to have to trust that your baby sister knows what she's doing. But I will make sure to check in; at least by text."

"How am I going to know it's you giving me the updates and he didn't kidnap you and is using your phone."

"We can use a code word. How about we use Mason's birthday 0626."

"After your text use that number and I'll know you're fine."

"I love you Parris." I shook my head, before disconnecting our call. With another deep sigh, I removed the blanket from my naked body before standing up and slowly making my way towards the bathroom. I cut on the shower then came back out and grabbed a bottle of water and found my bottle of Excedrin which I knew I was going to need.

I made my way towards my suitcase, grabbing a panty and bra set as well as my shower bag. I stepped into the hot water, cleaning the day off of me. After a quick shower, I got out wrapping a towel around my body then walking into the room looking in my bag for something to wear for the evening, settling on a two piece pink skirt and matching cropped tank. I grabbed my white Jimmy Choo Sadea pumps; the ankle wrap made of rhinestones that resembled an anklet.

After massaging lotion all over my body, I got dressed then I sprayed my Gucci Guilty perfume all over my body. I took my braids out of the bun, letting them hang down my back instead. I found my white clutch placing my phone and some pesos as well as my ID inside.

By the time the clock struck 7:25, I was ready to go just as a knock sounded against my door. I braced myself before opening, trying to calm my pounding heart. I was ready for him, ready for whatever happened tonight.

"You're prompt. I like that." I smiled up at Josiah, leaning slightly against the door frame. He was dressed in a white polo with blue khaki shorts. He had white vans on his feet.

"You're beautiful." He stepped closer to me and wrapped his arms around me, placing a soft kiss on my forehead.

"Thanks. Should we head out?"

Nodding, he took my hand escorting me towards the stairs. We seemed to walk past all the restaurants, and I became confused as we made our way instead towards the beach. Once we made it to the beach, we went a short distance away coming up on a table set for two surrounded by a tent and lights.

"When did you set this up? No way you were sober enough to do it after the pool."

"After the first drink, when I went to the bathroom; I stopped by the bar on my way and had them set it up for me. I told you; I was going to romance you. After dinner, there's a club I want to take you to, don't worry it's a speakeasy here on the property and after that, I'm going to take you back to your room and fuck you so you can forget about using that vibrator ever again while you are mine." A chill went down my spine as he kissed the back of my neck near my left shoulder, then he pulled out my seat. After he was seated, we ordered drinks and appetizers before being left alone to talk.

"So, if we're going to do this, I figured we should set some ground rules."

"I thought the only rule was that this doesn't go beyond this weekend."

"I want to make sure we're being safe. Are you able and willing to show me your most recent test results?"

"I can and will." He pulled his phone out of his pocket and started scrolling. Assuming he was pulling up his results, I pulled my own phone out of my clutch and began doing the same. I got to the portal for my doctor's office and went to my most recent panel screening which was only last month. I slid my phone over to him and I accepted his, picking it up and reviewing his result. He had been cleared and his tests were from the past three weeks.

"How long has it been in between these results and today since you were with anyone?" I asked.

"I haven't been with anybody since those results. I usually get tested after dealing with anybody, just to be on the safe side. What about you?"

"I haven't been with anybody in over a year." I decided to be honest. "But I'm a health nut so I keep my results as up to date as humanly possible; just to be on the safe side."

"A year? Damn. As beautiful as you are, I can't believe it's been that long."

"I'm picky about who I give my body to, Josiah. Besides my husband there have only been three other men who can say they've had me; well, you will make number three. Like I said earlier, I hope I won't be disappointed."

"I guarantee you won't be."

5

JOSIAH

I couldn't help but stare at her as we ate our food. She was beautiful and embodied the word sexy. The richness of her chocolate skin glistened against the fabric of her clothes. Her braids framed her face, and the gold necklace reached the groove of her breasts, laying perfecting between them; those chocolate mounds threatening to escape her top. I yearned to have them in my mouth, yearned to suck her nipples while my fingers explored her tight pussy. By the end of the night, I looked forward to fucking her and conquering her sexy body.

"You, okay?" Kali asked waving her hand in front of my face. I snapped out of it with a smile, placing my fork in my mouth to buy some time. "What were you thinking about?"

"The real?" I asked, eyebrows raised, wanting to see how far I could go, trying to gage what would be too much for her.

"The real."

"I'm thinking about tasting your skin. I want to run my tongue over your entire body and make you cum. I want to know which positions you like the best, which ones will get the best orgasm out of you. I want to know what your pussy tastes like and I want to know what kind of faces you're going to make while I'm buried deep inside of you."

"So, let's go make all of that a reality." She replied cupping her head in her hand as she leaned it on the table.

"Can't." I said sipping my drink. "You're not ready for me yet."

"Who says I'm not ready?"

"I say." I replied crossing my hands on the table. "Did you use that vibrator when you got to your room?"

"I did."

"What did you think about when you were playing with your pussy?"

"You. How I wanted you to be the one to please my body and how good it's going to feel to have you inside of me."

"Come here." I commanded, flicking my finger towards her. She smirked before getting up from her seat and walking over to me. I pulled my chair out and grabbed her hand sitting her on my lap. I rubbed my hands up and down her thick thighs and grabbed her chin placing her lips on top of mine. We sat there; our bodies intertwined for what felt like hours before the loud sound of a throat clearing interrupted us.

"Sorry to interrupt sir." The waitress smiled coyly at the both of us. "Were you ready for dessert?"

"Beyond ready." I replied looking into Kali's eyes. I was almost desperate to taste her, knowing she tasted as good as she looked. How she had me feeling like this? I didn't know. Maybe she was some kind of voodoo witch using a love spell on me, my infatuation was unreal.

"I think she means actual dessert." Kali smiled placing a peck on my lips before turning to face the waitress. "Can we take it to go please?" nodding, the waitress walked off. "I want you in my bed as soon as possible." Another peck of my lips caused a deeper kiss, a deeper connection to form. This girl was going to drive me crazy, I knew it, I felt it in my spirit and in my soul. Built in the perfect package, she was a trap, and I was foolishly falling for it.

Once our dessert was packed up and in hand, I signed the slip for the service to be charged to my room number before grabbing Kali's hand and escorting her back up the beach, through the resort, finding an elevator so we could get to our floor faster.

Between the two of us, I couldn't tell who was more anxious. There were people on the elevator with us so I couldn't do much besides wrap my arms around Kali and hold her close enough for her to feel the erection growing in my pants. I wanted her in the worst way and any disappointment she planned on having would be forgotten. We were amongst the first to leave the elevator when it hit our floor. We were going to reach Kali's room first and that was the bed we were going to end up in.

I stood behind her still as we both stood in front of her room door. She was fidgeting with her bag, trying to come up with the key. It was reminiscent of earlier in the day. Only this time, it wouldn't end with her using a toy to satisfy her needs; but with me, balls deep inside of her. When she managed to get the door open, and we had crossed the threshold of the door; she jumped into my arms wrapping her legs and arms around my body.

The room was pitch black but still I walked her over to the bed; having a similar floorplan had its benefit. I laid her down on the bed gently her body fitting perfectly under my own. Her lips had been enjoyable since the first kiss we shared earlier in the day. My hands rubbed all over her body, sliding ever so softly across her pebbled nipples.

"Remind me again of the agreement." I whispered breaking the connection between our lips and instead kissing a trail along her neck while at the same time lifting the small shirt she'd worn tonight over her head. She wasn't wearing a bra which gave for easier access to lick her nipples alternating between thumbing the opposite of the one I suckled on. Her skin was just as sweet as I imagined it would be. Hershey's kiss had always been my favorite candy.

"No strings, no attachments. After we leave Mexico, we won't look back. For the weekend you are mine and I am yours."

"No strings, no attachments." I affirmed, my hands now on either side of her skirt, shifting my body further down the bed. I kissed her belly, licking every inch of skin that appeared as I pulled her skirt all the way down to her feet. Her pussy was clean shaven, pretty, pink and had to be every bit as juicy as it looked to be. I could smell her orgasm and it made my dick harder than what I knew it had the capacity to be, the fabric from my shorts the only barrier holding it back but just barely.

"Promise?" she asked, and I looked up at her. The look in her eye almost pleadingly asking me to uphold my end of the bargain; while I was hoping that she would uphold hers. Two broken people didn't make for a happily ever after; and we were absolutely both broken individuals.

I couldn't keep that same promise, knowing the things I already felt, I would never be able to make that promise feeling like this already. So, instead of making it, I spread her legs swiping my tongue between her folds and from the first drip of her nectar on my tongue, I groaned hungrily getting my fill of her. I licked and sucked her pussy devouring every bit of her. Her legs seemed to tense up around my head and I used my hand to pry them back open.

Looking up at her, her face contorted in the sexiest ways, biting her lips while loud pleasure inducing moans escaped her lips. I used my left middle and pointer fingers to dip inside of her pussy. I could feel how wet her pussy was, but also how tight. I wanted her more and more the longer I tasted her. When I felt her walls tighten around my fingers, I knew she was going to cum for me. Without warning, her hands found the top of my head, pushing me away from her. Confused, I looked up at her as I sucked her clit.

"Stop, please." She begged while at the same time the position she had on my head seemed to no longer be as strong as it was only seconds ago. She started fucking my face and with one last tight squeeze, her sweet nectar shot across my face taking me by surprise, a good fucking surprise. "I'm so sorry, I—"

"You are so fucking sexy Baby." I groaned wrapping my lips around her pussy, catching the remnant of it that was dripping between the both of us. My beard was saturated, I'm sure my lips certainly were, and I licked up as much excess that I could.

Placing one last kiss on her sweet pussy, I stood up and pulled my shirt over my head. I stepped out of my shoes then pulled my shorts down but not before grabbing one of the gold wrappers I'd placed inside them earlier. Peeling off the wrapper with my teeth, I grabbed the condom, rolling it onto my hardened dick.

"Be gentle."

"I make no promises." I replied rolling the tip of my dick between her folds, using her own nectar as a lubricant. "I'mma show you how to handle it, if you're scared."

"You've been talking a good game all day she said grabbing hold of chain around my neck and pulling me down so I could kiss her. She stuck out her tongue and swiped it around my lips, tasting her own juices on my lips and moaning. "You better fuck the shit out of me."

"Is that a challenge?" I asked and before she could respond, I watched as the words got caught in her throat the moment I entered her. If it wasn't so sexy, it would have been comical to see how she'd quickly decided to take her words back. Her hand made its way on my chest trying to push me back. "Just relax." I coached her, placing soft kisses along her face and lips. "Breathe, I got you."

"I asked you to be gentle." She groaned, her lips baring between her lips.

"You also told me to fuck the shit out of you. So, which one do you really want?" I asked inching more of my dick inside of her; again, her hand found its way between us, attempting to back me up. "Kali, you gotta breathe."

"Both." She finally said ignoring my previous words, but hers caused my eyes to pop directly onto her. "I want you to do both." She exhaled and soon her breathing seemed to slow the longer she looked into my eyes. "I want you to be gentle and fuck the shit out of me." Her hand that was previously against my chest eased down before wrapping around my dick. My eyes widened as she guided it further in. "Mostly though, I want you to fuck the shit out of me."

I lifted her legs over my shoulders before stroking in and out of her. Her moans were no longer silent as she talked shit to me. My right hand wrapped around her neck, while the left thumbed her nipples. Her pussy was wet and tight, drowning my dick inside of its juices.

"Fuck, yes, please don't stop." Kali begged. Her walls sucked me in with each stroke I delivered between them. My dick was in love with her pussy, and I clearly saw Shawty for the trap that she was. As I looked into her eyes, I leaned down and placed a sloppy kiss on her lips, and I knew without a shadow of a doubt that regardless of what I thought this was; it was quickly turning into something completely different.

6

KAHLIA

As I woke up out of my sleep, my body felt tired. Thinking back on the night, I smiled before finally opening my eyes immediately being disappointed not to see his face lying next to me. That's when I thought about it; this was just for fun, no strings attached which meant no staying over. He had his own room, I half expected him to still use it regardless of our little arrangement.

Josiah worked my body over last night and any disappointment I may have imagined having was completely thrown out the window with the first swipe of his tongue between my folds. I moaned out loud just thinking about it and butterflies appeared in my stomach at the very moment the image popped in my head. The sex was everything I needed it to be, but after being celibate for a year, my body obviously needed time to adjust.

Slowly sitting up in bed, I looked again to my right this time catching a glimpse of a folded up piece of paper left on the pillow. Picking it up, my hands started to shake nervously; I didn't know why I was nervous, but all I could do was pray that he wasn't writing a Dear John letter thinking sex with me was trash. My eyes scanned the letter and with each word I read, the anxiety calmed.

> *Kali,*
> *Thank you for last night.*
> *I hope we're still on for exploring town. You promised me you'd show me your favorite spots. I look forward to seeing you.*
> *Josiah.*

I smiled after reading the note for the third time before getting out of bed on shaky legs. After the shaking subsided, I made my way to the bathroom to get myself together. After relieving my bladder and showering, I stared at myself in the wide mirror, the memories from last night flooding through my brain. I felt alive, I felt free, and it was all because I had decided to be reckless with a man, I barely knew anything about.

After washing my face and brushing my teeth, I made my way out of the bathroom and went to pick out something comfortable to wear for the day. The sun was shining but I could see some clouds looming in the distance. Still, I decided upon a pair of biker shorts, a graphic tank, and my Nike walking shoes. I grabbed my small backpack, tossing in my essentials, wristlet, a couple of bottles of water, sunglasses, my Sony camera, and a fresh memory card.

The day I got here, I had arranged a trip to town with the company that shuttled me from the airport to the resort. They had separate tours and transportation packages available where the driver would take me all around town to visit some of the most popular spots in Puerto Vallarta. After the walk I had with Josiah yesterday discussing all of our plans, I called them to let them know another person would be coming with me. I paid the extra $50.00 and from that moment on it was a reservation for two.

Checking the time on my Apple Watch, I saw that it was just after 8:00 am so I exited my room and made my way down to 1104. I knocked a couple of times then waited on bated breath for the door to be opened. The moment I heard the lock click and saw the doorknob move, I looked up to see those beautiful hazel eyes staring back at me.

"Good morning."

"Good morning beautiful." He smiled in my direction leaning against the door frame. He was dressed in a pair of basketball shorts, a white t-shirt and had a basketball cap going to the back of his head. He had apparently decided on comfort just like I did; I peeped the Yeezy 350s on his feet.

"Um, I got a text from the shuttle service they should be here in about thirty minutes. I was thinking we could grab a quick bite from the café downstairs while we wait."

"Sounds like a plan." He agreed. "Let me grab my stuff right quick. He went into his room, and I stepped in the door frame waiting for him to come back out which didn't take long. "Ready?" he asked moments later, and I nodded. As we walked back out of the room, his hand found mine, lacing our fingers together. I looked down at our connected hands and immediately felt at peace.

We got to the café in no time, ordering breakfast sandwiches and two bottles of orange juice. As we sat and waited for the car to arrive, we ate in silence watching as people were emerging from their rooms and starting their day.

"News said it was going to rain later this afternoon." Josiah finally broke our silence.

"A little rain never hurt nobody." I shrugged. "But we can head back whenever we want. There's just a couple of things I have to get pictures of, and I'll be good."

"What kind of camera do you use primarily?"

"Mostly Nikon, but I have my Sony with me because it's the best at capturing natural sunlight."

"I tried to look you up this morning." He said and my eyes shot over to his. "I know it's against the rules, but I had to." He shrugged. He was right, last night we'd set more rules for this. We knew first names only no social media info would be given. The good thing for me was that I didn't have much of a social media presence. I had my business page for IG and Facebook, and I had a personal Snapchat that I only used for the silly filters. I did also have a Tik Tok that I sometimes posted glimpses of my artwork on.

"What did you find?"

"I found a Tik Tok when one of your videos popped on my FYP. I was just scrolling after I'd given up on my search when it randomly came on my phone. I'm beginning to believe that the feds are watching us for real, there was no way it should have happened. Then I started to think maybe the universe wanted me to find you and this was its way of helping a brutha out. That Tik Tok led me to your IG page, which led me to your Facebook. I swear I'm not a creep, but I wanted to be honest."

"We agreed though Josiah." I mumbled and he nodded.

"Yeah, we did agree."

The stare down between us was just as intense as it always was. Those beautiful eyes bore into mine, daring me to act out of character for what this was. But I couldn't let up. This was nothing more than what it needed to be. I could not get caught up with a man who was probably only meant to be in my life for this one season.

"You can't." I sighed helplessly. I knew deep down it was inevitable. These feelings were unreal, I was almost ashamed of them considering the fact that this was a place that was dear to my husband and I, now here I am falling hopelessly for another man. It was happening too fast; I was not prepared for it.

"I know." He replied reaching across the table and grabbing my hand. "But if we did; how bad could it really be?"

"Two broken pieces don't make a whole." I told him. "If you think you can't get through this I will understand."

"No." he replied letting go of my hand and sliding back in his seat. "We're good."

I could see a glimmer of hurt flash across his face. I hated it, hated that it had to be this way; but there was nothing I could do about it. I was doing my part to keep from falling, I just needed Josiah to do his part as well. The silence was quickly filled as my phone rang. Recognizing the number for the car service company, I answered.

"Hola! Yes, this is Kali. Hey Pedro." I stood up and walked towards the pickup area. I immediately recognized Pedro as he was the person who dropped me off when I arrived a few days ago. "We'll be right over." I hung up the phone and headed in that direction, Josiah maintaining a step behind me.

The drive into town was silent but tolerable only to the fact that when I went to snake my fingers between his, he allowed it; like it was the most natural thing to do.

"Our first stop is to Church of Our Lady of Guadalupe." I said leaning into his body. He unattached our hands momentarily to fling his arm around my waist only to reconnect our hands. "It's a beautiful church both inside and out; it has some magnificent lines. I just need to get a few pictures inside of it and then we can go do touristy stuff."

"I'm with you." He replied looking down into my eyes.

"Good." I leaned up so our lips connected.

We made it to the church thirty minutes into the city limits. Our driver dropped us off in front of the church and then went to find parking. The moment I stepped into the building, as always, my breath was taken away. Immediately I pulled my camera out of my bag and started snapping photos.

I found myself inside of my head, in my element as I moved with fluidity throughout the building. My faith had been put to the test so many times over the past four years since I lost it. I had been slowly trying to rebuild my relationship with God, but so far it had been a trying journey. Needing to memorialize this feeling, I turned just in time to view Pedro walking into the church. I beckoned him to me, and I handed him the camera once he arrived.

"Can you get this picture of us?" I asked and he nodded. "All you have to do is press this button twice." He gave me a thumbs up letting me know he got it, and I grabbed Josiah's hand pointing to the camera so we could get a shot of us.

After we left the church, we went to the pier, visited some souvenir shops, and grabbed lunch before we both recognized that it was probably the best idea to head back to the resort. Dark clouds were starting to form in the distance and neither of us was interested in getting caught in a storm.

"I had a good time." Josiah said pulling my back against his chest. "I was thinking, since it's going to rain and we'll be stuck indoors, how about you pack a few things and spend the evening with me in my room. I have plans for you."

"What kind of plans?"

"I been thinking about being inside of you all day. I want to taste your pussy again and I'm tryna feed you, my dick. Those are the kinds of plans I have for you." I snapped my neck in his direction, admiring his boldness and getting wrapped up into his toxicity.

"Pedro, how much longer?" I asked causing a hearty laugh to escape Josiah's lips.

"Not long ma'am." He replied from the front seat. "Fifteen minutes."

As promised, he got us to our destination in fifteen minutes. Before I could do so, Josiah pulled a few bills from his pocket to tip him. As he was driving off and we were walking onto the property, the first rain droplet fell.

Once on our floor, we parted ways agreeing that I would meet him in his room after I packed a few things. I went into my room, undressed, and got in to take a quick shower. I pinned my braids up then dressed in a swimsuit before putting on a t-shirt along with distressed jean shorts over it. I slid into my Croc slides before packing a change of underwear, my toothbrush, and my phone charger.

When I was ready, I made my way down the hall, knocking on his room door and waited patiently for him to answer. It wasn't long before I heard the lock click and the door opened with Josiah standing in front of me in bright red swim trunks with no shirt on.

"I got the hot tub heating; you need to change into your swimsuit or something?"

"No." I replied walking into the room and setting my bag down on one of the sitting chairs. I pulled my shirt over my head and stepped out of my shorts revealing my red ensemble. Of course, this was completely unplanned, but it garnered a chuckle from each of us. Because of the turn in weather, none of the pools on the resort were open so instead we found ourselves in the hot tub, taking full advantage of the amenity offered to multiple Preferred level rooms.

Walking onto the patio, Josiah placed two towels on a chair before climbing the small set of stairs and getting into the hot tub. He held his hand out to me, and I accepted it. My body relaxed as I slid into the heated water.

"Is it always that intense when you're in your creative vibe?" Josiah asked sitting opposite me with my foot in his hand, rubbing it. He didn't know how much I needed it; my feet were killing me with how much walking we'd done.

"What do you mean?" I asked enjoying the feel of his hands digging into the curve of my foot.

"I don't know how to describe it. Once you started with the first picture, you're hand just went crazy and the camera was just snapping. It felt, oddly satisfying to experience you in that way. The shots you captured; they were amazingly beautiful."

"Thank you." I smiled. "I just kind of go with the flow when it comes to my art. Whatever inspires me, I try to capture it in a way that other people will appreciate it's beauty as much as I do."

"Were you always into art and photography? Like, when you were younger did you know that's what you wanted to do with your life?"

"No." I replied shaking my head. "I wanted to be a lawyer believe it or not."

"Why didn't you continue to pursue that dream?"

"Because I realized when I get mad the first word that pops out of my mouth is usually the word bitch before fists are thrown." I laughed. "Imagine me in a courtroom and the other attorney or judge says one wrong thing, now I'm in jail being held in contempt of court." His laughter carried, disturbing the water as he continued to hold my foot in his hand. "No but seriously, I was always good at art, and I took a few art classes. I didn't get into photography until high school, maybe junior year. I needed an elective and that was the most interesting thing to do. My sister had to scrape to buy me the camera needed."

"Your sister? What about your parents?"

"My parents passed when I was young, car accident."

"I'm sorry—"

"Thanks." I shrugged. "After they passed my sister and I

both got sent to live with our grandmother. When I was fifteen and my sister was 21, our grandmother passed as well. My sister stepped up in a big way, so I wasn't put in foster care. I thank God for her every single day because she could have let me go in the system and lived her life, but she didn't. My sister is such a good person."

"She sounds like it."

"What about you, did you always know you wanted to be a teacher?"

"Uh no." he shook his head laughing. "I thought I was going to be in the NFL, but I had to lower my expectations a little when I wasn't getting that much playing time. I figured, if I had a scholarship, I was going to make the most of it, so I got my degree in Education. I like kids so it was almost like a natural thing to get into. The coaching gig sort of fell in my lap. The school I was at when I first started teaching, they needed a coach, so I stepped up and got the job. We were pretty good too. After everything blew up and shit went down with my brother and me ending up getting arrested, I thought I was going to lose my ability to teach and coach for good. I'm lucky that charges were not pressed against me, so nothing went on my record, and I was able to get a new job when I moved to Dallas.

"How was that transition for you moving to a new place? Besides college, I don't have much experience living somewhere other than Chicago."

"It was hard at first considering the circumstances but eventually I figured it out and was able to navigate through my new normal. Why, you thinking about taking your sister up on her offer to move there?"

"No." I lied. "I was just curious."

"Probably for the best that you don't move there. Wouldn't want to run into each other after this."

"I've been to Dallas to visit quite a few times, it's a pretty big city. I doubt we'd run into each other."

"Maybe, or maybe not. The only thing I'm focused on is here and now." Josiah grabbed my hand and pulled me into his lap so that I was straddling him. "But if I do see you in Dallas on one of your little visits, best believe I'm going to be all over you." He put his face in my neck placing soft kisses against it.

"Yeah right." I licked my lips enjoying the feel of his lips on my skin. "You probably won't even remember me after this is all said and done. I'll just be another face you pass by."

"You think so?" he asked, and I nodded. "I don't. I think there's a reason we met on this trip. I doubt I'll ever forget you or this entire trip. I'm getting to experience a lot of new things and it's because of you."

Dark clouds seemed to surround us as the rain started to drizzle down. The hot tub was in a covered area, but still open enough for a passerby to catch a glimpse of the things Josiah and I were up to. Cupping my chin, Josiah pulled me towards his lips, filling my mouth with his tongue. Soft moans filled the air between us as I grinded on his dick feeling it come to life below me.

"You ever had sex in public?" Josiah asked, his lips trailing my lips onto my neck. I tilted my head back to give him better access to the sweet spot on my neck that gave me chills.

"No."

"You want to?" My eyes shot open into his direction. His hands found the clasp on my bikini top, unhooking it effortlessly. Josiah slowly pulled both sides of the straps down until the bra hung just below my breast, urging me to assist with removing it the rest of the way. "Hhmm?"

"Josiah we— "his fingers moved my bikini bottoms to the side before slightly lifting me up. I never noticed he'd freed himself from the confines of his shorts, just felt the brush of his mushroom head over my pussy lips before he eased me down on top of him. A loud hiss erupted from my mouth the lower I slid down his dick.

"I know we agreed— "

"Don't say it." I begged continuing to slowly bounce up and down on him, the water splashing violently around us. He was going to say out loud the thing I had been avoiding and saying in my mind from the moment the day started. If we weren't careful, this was going to be more than either of us bargained for.

"But— "again I interrupted him placing my lips against his. I bounced steadily harder feeling my orgasm rising inside of me.

I couldn't stop the cry that escaped me, couldn't stop how good he made me feel. Two days was all it took for me to be nearly undone by him. I hated it; hated this feeling of longing, the feeling of need of him.

"Fuuuck." I groaned as he crashed me down on top of him one last time before a throaty groan escaped his lips. I felt him pulsating inside of me, releasing his seeds inside my walls.

The reality of what he did set in all over his face. Josiah was just as reckless as I was; taking his chances to go in raw with a woman he barely even knew. His face was comical as I slowly came down from my euphoric high with a chuckle.

"I'm on birth control." I assured him taking his hand and rubbing it on the side of my right arm. I had gotten the Nexplanon three years ago when I decided I was not consistent enough for the pill. I would need to get it replaced soon, but for now it was in place and working effectively.

"How well does it work?"

"Pretty darn well considering I haven't had any issues since I got it put in three years ago."

"Good." He kissed my pebbled nipples. "Your pussy feels even better without the rubber. Though, I don't think it was a good idea for me to slide in you without it. I want you even more now than I did before." His lips traced kisses over my skin. "How am I supposed to let you go after this?"

His dick sprang back to life and without warning he lifted me off his lap and instead planted me, so my knees were on the small seat in the hot tub. My back was to his chest, my arms resting on the ledge of the tub. A loud gasp escaped me when he entered me from behind. Holding my neck, he squeezed if gently as he slammed into me. My moans were loud, he felt so good. Surely, we would have an audience soon. I bit down on my arm to keep from screaming.

"Josiah, please." My words were barely audible over the yearning inside of me.

"Please what?"

"Don't stop."

After another earth-shattering orgasm, my body relaxed against the ledge of the hot tub. The rain was steadily falling around us, and the ripple of the water around us sloshed around us. I felt Josiah pull out of me before placing soft kisses on my back. The sound of the movement from the water slapped me out of my trance.

"Let's go in." Josiah said adjusting himself in his swim trunks. I fixed my bikini bottoms as best as I could, losing all hope for my top which was completely off. Josiah used a towel to dry off before extending the towel in my direction, wrapping it around my body and then lifting me out of the tub like a father would do for their child. He held me bridal style, close to his chest as we moved inside. I was exhausted and it showed in the way I snuggled into his body.

Josiah pulled back the covers on the right side of the bed then he laid me down. My eyelids were heavy as I tried to focus on his face but the euphoric high from the bliss, he had me in weakened my resolve and I lost the battle; my eyes closing all together falling into a sleepy stupor.

∽

I WOKE UP AN HOUR LATER. The TV was on and when I rolled over, he was sleeping next to me. I moved to lay my head on his chest, looking up at him as he snored lightly in my ear. I was happy, so very happy considering what I had come on this trip for. I wasn't expecting to find him, damn sure wasn't expecting to have this intense feeling of joy and passion, but I did. The semblance of happiness washed over my entire body, and it felt so right. What if he was who I had been looking for? What if he was the one meant to fill my life with happiness and joy? I started to question how he could possibly be the one when I didn't feel worthy of it, and it felt too easy.

Getting out of bed, I walked over to the bag I dropped earlier, digging inside for my cell phone before heading to the bathroom closing the door behind me. As I used the bathroom, I scrolled on social media noticing I had a notification on Tik Tok that someone had viewed my profile. Clicking on it, I saw the username JMac_89. Clicking on the profile, I laughed at the few videos I saw of him and his students doing Tik Tok dances together. He had videos of himself playing football in college and I found myself going down the rabbit hole of his videos. Before long, I clicked on the Instagram icon from his Tik Tok page which took me down another rabbit hole of viewing his pictures and video.

I had been sitting for so long looking at pictures and video from his page that my ass had gon numb. Realizing the amount of time that passed, I got up, washed my hands then made my way back out to the bed where Josiah was still laying peacefully. I took a picture of him in his peace and smiled seeing how intent he looked.

I let him sleep longer before finally waking him up so we could figure out dinner. A part of me wanted to go out to one of the restaurants on the property but the other half wanted to stay in so we could remain in our little bubble.

"Josiah." I nudged him awake and his eyes glanced in my direction. He reached over, grabbing my waist then proceeded to pull my body into his, burying his face in my neck. "Wake up." I chuckled moving out of his reach. "I'm hungry. Are we staying in for dinner or going out?"

He yawned and stretched a little before replying groggily.

"If we stay in, I can keep you naked. But on the flip side, we can go out and I can see you in another one of your tight outfits." I playfully rolled my eyes. "You know what you was doing when you packed that shit, fabric be hugging the fuck out of your chocolate skin and I'm thoroughly enjoying the view. Still, the thought of keeping you naked is more tempting so let's order in; grab a bottle of tequila then fuck all night."

"I'll order the food. The sooner it gets here the sooner I can have you back inside of me." I grabbed the tablet that would allow me to access the room service menu. I ordered both of us a meal from the menu along with a bottle of Luna Azul tequila. Josiah got out of bed heading towards the bathroom.

While I was waiting on him, I looked again at his profile contemplating if I was going to send a friend request. Despite what I had told him earlier, maybe it wouldn't be so bad to keep in touch at least via social media. Before I could send the request, I clicked off his social media.

"Did it say how long it was going to be? Didn't realize how hungry I was."

"It said 35 minutes." I snuggled into him again. We were

quiet as we watched the tv. I wasn't really paying attention to what was playing, instead I was thinking about how complicated I was making my life while trying to deal with different feelings of lust, happiness and even guilt for liking someone besides Jonathan as much as I liked Josiah.

"What you thinking about?" He asked gently rubbing my skin with his fingertips.

"Nothing." I decided against sharing. "Just thought about having to text my sister to let her know I'm still alive. She told me stranger danger and look at me, in a stranger's bed being reckless."

"You think this is reckless?"

"No." I said honestly. "Those were her words when I told her what I was up to. She's always been thinking I was reckless. But I think that's the big sister in her. She thinks everything I do is reckless because it's not something she herself would do."

"I don't think it's reckless either. Well, maybe a little. It's a dangerous game that we're playing."

"I agree." I sighed. "I was hoping it wouldn't be as complicated as this has been. But I realized I'm not that kind of girl and you don't seem like that kind of guy. I like you as a person."

"Same."

Those words magnified in my head through the silence in the room. I could feel his heart beating through his chest, it had a steady beat like a drum. It was in complete and total contrast to the beat of my own which was beating rapidly. I wanted more from him then what either of us saw coming. This should have been a simple feat, almost transactional. The issue is that we got to know each other in between the sex, and I saw how dope of a person he was. I needed that good energy in my life, but I refused to allow it in. I couldn't.

GENESIS CARTER

Being hurt again from losing someone I had love for was unfathomable for me.

When the food came, we wrapped up in robes sitting at the table eating and making small talk. There were a lot of things not being said between the two of us. Words that should have been spoken and words that shouldn't be because of the level of complications it posed to our situation.

After dinner we found ourselves back in bed, taking shots of tequila and joking, talking with one another. I smiled so much, laughed so much, more than I had in years. I felt comfort when I was with him. Too comfortable almost.

I found myself staring up at him as he laid between my legs later on in the night. My legs had been opening, willingly to him; our essences blending, connecting our souls and our spirits together. Josiah was sent to me in my time of need, during a trip that had the potential to break me. He pulled me out of the darkness before I could get too far into it.

As I came down from my high, his dick still pulsing inside of me, his eyes connected with mine. I started to see and imagine things, things that could mess with my trajectory in life. After Jonathan passed, I was resolved to be the fun aunt for Mason, forever the widow as I couldn't see myself being with anyone else. But as Josiah's bright hazel eyes stared down at me, I started to imagine a future with us. I imagined what it would look like to fall in love with him, to move in together, to meet each other's families. I saw our engagement, the wedding, my pregnancy announcement. I saw our lives in his eyes…

And I fucking…panicked.

"Stay with me." He begged, almost as if he could see the moment it happened. "Stay in this moment with me baby." He placed a soft kiss on my lips, locking me in for such a passionate kiss. I could feel the emotions he conveyed to me, and my own emotions pounded through my heart; begging to be set free. Images of Jonathan was the only thing that kept me from what could be my new reality. I simply couldn't do it.

So, I returned his kiss. I wrapped my arms and legs around him, pulling him closer into my body, if we could be any closer. I didn't want to break his spirit, I didn't want to hurt him, but I also knew I couldn't stand to be hurt again either.

7

JOSIAH

When I opened my eyes, I looked to my left feeling for Kali, yet my hand encountered a cold void. I knew I hadn't been dreaming, I could smell Shea butter and vanilla on my sheets and the pillows. Figuring she just dipped off to her room, I got out of bed stumbling towards the bathroom so I could take a piss, shower, and brush my teeth.

I was ready for the day, already having it in my mind to go speak to the front desk to make my plans for the day. The sun was out and since it was my last night here, I wanted to spend it going on adventures with Kali.

The need to be in her presence was overwhelming me. Rich had fucking jinxed me and after showering, brushing my teeth and getting dressed, I grabbed my cell phone and called my friend. It was after 9am here, so I knew he was up.

"What up brodie." Rich asked coming into view on the Facetime request.

"Man, you out here jinxing niggas." I chuckled and he looked at me confused. "Ole girl I told you about."

"The cutie from the Chi?"

"Yeah man." I sighed rubbing my hand down the back of my head. "She got me in my feelings a lil' bit. I'm thinking about how we can make this shit work long distance."

"After two days?"

"After two days." I replied shaking my head at my own foolishness. "This shit kind of scary Rich."

"I bet; but we both know the kind of man you are. Tell her that shit and work something out. You said she got family in Dallas, right?"

"Yeah. She told me her sister lived there. Am I trippin?" I asked my friend needing and wanting his complete honesty. I felt like I was, but also, I felt like I wasn't. Whatever it was that pulled me to her from the moment I first saw her was rooted deep inside of me. It was terrifying, but it was real.

"I think it's fast, yeah." He sighed. "But I think when you're as old as we are; when you know you know. Niggas ain't got time to be wasting no more; we ain't just giving feelings to any ole person. If you feel like that's yo girl, then that's your girl."

"Bet." I smiled appreciative of his thoughts. "Let me get myself together. It's my last day so I'm about to make the most of it, got some plans to make."

"Be safe, I'll see you tomorrow afternoon." I gave a brief nod before disconnecting the call.

Standing up from my seat, I sprayed some cologne over my black t-shirt and tan cargo shorts, grabbed my black fitted cap, placing it over my head to the back then slid into my black slides. I made my way out of my room looking towards my left. The cleaning lady's cart was near her room door, and I knew I wouldn't be able to get around it, so I went to the right instead so I could make my way to the lobby.

It didn't take me long, just the short 2-3 minute walk for

me to reach the front desk. With a smile on my face, I approached the attendant behind the desk.

"Good morning, Senor." She smiled in my direction. "What can I do for you?"

"Uh yeah, I wanted to see about setting up a few things for today."

"Of course." She replied typing away at her computer. "What is your room number?"

"1104." I told her digging into my pocket and taking out my wallet so I could get my ID in case she asked for it. "Josiah Mackenzie."

"Ah Mr. Mackenzie, yes." She bent down and grabbed what I saw was a small envelope. "The guest in room 1107 asked me to give this to you." I accepted the envelope and hurriedly ripped it open. Seeing the beautiful cursive writing on the page, I began to read it.

Josiah,

I'm sorry I couldn't stay. Things between us were getting heavy and honestly, I got scared. I didn't think I would come here to feel like this. I came here to spread my husband's ashes. Never in a million years did I imagine I'd find you here too. From the moment I laid eyes on you, I felt this magnetic pull and it hasn't gone away. You have been the most kind, most generous and so very special to me. I wished it didn't have to be like this, wish that I wasn't so scared to feel anything for you. But the moment I stared into your eyes last night, I knew that if I stayed, I was going to be done for and I just can't put myself through

that again. We've both been hurt and the thought of loving you then losing you is something I couldn't even begin to bare. Please don't try to find me. I wish things were different. I really, truly do.
Kahlia.

WITH EACH WORD I read my heart seemed to break a little bit more. I wasn't expecting it, wasn't expecting to feel like this so soon for someone I barely even knew. This shit hurt and it was tough because I had gotten attached too soon and there was nothing, I could do about it.

"Mr. Mackenzie, is everything alright?"

"When did she give you this?" I asked holding up the paper and envelope.

"This morning, when she checked out."

"She told me she wasn't leaving until tomorrow."

"Yes sir, that was her original reservation. However, she advised she needed to check out early. I'm sorry sir, there's a line developing; were you still needing to set up those activities?"

"No." I replied folding the paper and putting it back in the envelope. "Thank you." I balled the envelope in my hand making my way back to my room.

I was at a loss for words, confused pulling my phone out to look up her social media. I'd found it before, added her as a friend. Yet as I typed her name to search, nothing popped up. She had blocked me on all social medias.

I felt dazed and confused at this turn in events. I wasn't expecting this when I woke up this morning. I was expecting to spend our last day together. I wasn't expecting that last night would be the last time I laid eyes on her. Instead, she had run away from her developing feelings scared of what they could be.

A part of me couldn't blame her; this shit between us was scary as hell especially when you considered that we'd only known each other for three days. But at the same time, it was exciting and exhilarating and I thought that maybe, just maybe we could figure out a way to make things work.

Damn, was I wrong.

⁓

When I made it back to Dallas the next evening, I collected my bags then met Rich outside as he'd come to pick me up from the airport. I spent my last day in Puerto Vallarta occupying the same seat at a bar in the resort. I kept going over the last few days. All the emotions I had gone through in such a short amount of time.

I thought about my first time seeing the beautiful woman I now knew was named Kahlia Mitchell thanks to her social media. I remembered our first conversation; even remember the first real smile I was able to pull out of her during dinner. I thought about her sweet tooth and how she always had to have dessert with her dinner. I knew she was sexy as hell in a bikini and even sexier naked. I knew most importantly that, that woman had me hooked on her mind, body and pussy and there was nothing I could do about it.

When I woke up this morning, I packed everything I'd come with and was calling my shuttle service to get me to the airport early. I was thankful that the airline was able to get me on an earlier flight. I wasn't in the mood to sit around waiting on the scheduled flight. I wanted to leave Mexico and everything from the past four days behind me.

"How was the flight?" Rich asked pulling away from the

toll booth at DFW airport then heading south towards Arlington where he lived. I had parked my car in front of his home, so I needed to grab it before I made my way home to Dallas.

"It was alright." I shrugged. "Slept the entire way there, still nursing this damn hangover."

"We ain't as young as we used to be." Rich laughed. "We gotta watch how much we drink now."

"Yeah." I agreed leaning my seat all the way back. "I just need my own bed and some rest; jet lag ain't shit."

"So, you gon' tell me what happened?" I was quiet, contemplating if I wanted to go into detail with my best friend how I had fallen in love with a woman who wanted nothing to do with me. I didn't want to explain to him that I had contemplated making a fake social media account just to stalk hers. I was fucking sprung off a cute smile and some good pussy."

"Nothing, just got caught slippin'." I admitted. "Momentary lapse in judgment judgement, it won't happen again."

"There's a reason you feel the way you told me you felt about her. You can't just give up on those feelings all together. Hell, I'm just glad to see that you're still capable of it."

"Come on Rich, I ain't heartless."

"Nah but you ain't exactly been yourself either, my nigga. You let that shit with Angie break you and for so long I watched you pass over good women. You fucked them then ducked them without so much as a goodbye. That ain't you Josiah, that ain't the man I been friends with all my life."

"Maybe this is my karma then."

"Maybe." He replied patting my shoulder. "It's not too late to change."

Rich's married ass got on my damn nerves sometimes. I couldn't stand how right he was about women as if he was some expert. Back in the day you couldn't keep Rich from fucking different bitches until Tish waltzed her ass into his life and hooked his ass. I was glad for it too, back then Rich was on some bullshit; got caught up a few times and had to be at the clinic taking antibiotics. He tried for a little while to still do what he wanted when he first got with Tish, but she nipped that shit in the bud. She gave him an ultimatum either he straightened up or he would lose her forever. It was the first time I was ever jealous of a nigga getting an ultimatum.

I wished I had that, wish I had it with anybody. I clung to that notion that if I had a woman I would give up my life for or risk losing; a woman that wanted to see me grow and change for the better, then my life would be better for it. I wanted that kind of love, and I wanted it so bad I looked for it in Angela only to realize that she was far from it.

Deep down inside I still hadn't given up on that dream. I wanted to give up on it, had thought about giving up on it, but I never did. I just figured now; it was going to take me a hell of a lot longer to achieve it then it would have before. It was a battle; one that I was willing to fight.

8

KAHLIA

3 MONTHS LATER

"Sissy, I can't believe I have finally convinced you to move to Dallas with me and Mason. I swear, you're going to love it." Parris smiled excitedly as we finished packing the last box of my things. The majority of it would be going to storage until I found a permanent spot in Dallas. For now, I would be staying with Parris and Mason. Her house was nice, and I always had my own space whenever I visited her; but I couldn't help but to think of the things I would be giving up when I left Chicago.

I hadn't come to the decision lightly. I no longer had any ties to the city, hadn't had a tie to it in years. When Jonathan died, the only reason I stayed was because of his sister who happened to be my best friend, Jamie. Jamie moved to Baltimore last year so really, I was there alone, and I couldn't stand to be alone anymore.

The four days I spent with Josiah left a deep imprint on my mind, body, and soul. Some days, a lot of them actually, I thought about him and wondered what he was doing. I had kept the promise I made to myself and didn't unblock him but that didn't stop me from still viewing his social media posts. I missed talking to him, missed laughing with him. I missed having someone to talk to who listened without judgment. I missed him and how he made me feel like the sexiest woman in the world.

I hated how I left, hated that I wrote that Dear John letter; but I was terrified of who I would become with him. I had made many efforts to move on, to figure out my new normal; but deep down it was my comfort zone, and I wasn't ready to change.

Then I came home from Mexico to my lonely two bedroom apartment and realized being lonely wasn't something I cared to do anymore; especially when I had a taste of happiness. I knew what it felt like to be in a man's company. I knew again what it felt like to be safe in a man's arms.

"I'm excited." I told her. "I'll only need to stay with you for a little while; just until I can find a place."

"You can stay with us for as long as you need to."

"And thanks for getting me that job at the school." I told her using a Sharpie to write the word Kitchen on the box I was working on.

I had decided to take a step back from my photography and would focus solely on my art. Parris was Assistant Principal at a high school in Dallas. The school happened to need a new art teacher and after telling Parris I would move to Dallas with her, she offered me the position without hesitation.

"Girl, thank you." She waved me off. "Principal Woods had been stressing over finding a good candidate. I told him my little sister is the best artist I know. The good thing about it is its only during the school year, you get summers off and during that time you can pursue other stuff."

"What other stuff Parris?" I glanced over in her direction.

"I don't know Kali, maybe date, find you a man and make me an auntie."

"Parris, stop." I rolled my eyes before grabbing the box and pulling it closer to the front door; the movers would be here in a few to pick up my things and take them to my storage unit. My clothes and essentials were packed away in suitcases and a few boxes already in my car. The drive from Chicago to Dallas was 14 hours long and it was a drive I wasn't looking forward to.

"Just saying Kali." She shrugged. I ignored her and instead, I began looking around my apartment. It was the first place I moved once I sold the house that Jonathan and I had bought. It was supposed to be our forever home; yet not even a year into owning it, my husband was dead, and I couldn't stand the sight of it.

I was going to miss this apartment, this city but I knew it was time for me to move on. Parris was right, I needed my family and she and Mason were my family. Moving to Dallas meant a new start for me, a new chance to explore love and to be loved. Not to mention the fact that there was nothing in Dallas that reminded me of Jonathan.

We waited for the movers to come and supervised while they placed everything in the truck. After everything was out, I quickly took pictures showing how the apartment looked on move out and then I made my way to my car getting in the driver's seat to head to the storage.

The last of my boxes was placed in the storage over an hour later and finally I was able to get some rest before the long drive. It was nearly 7pm and we'd been packing and moving things all day. I was exhausted and I just wanted to get some food in my system, take a long shower and lay in bed for a little while.

"What do you want to eat?" Parris asked as if she was reading my mind.

"We can stop by Greek Corner and get a gyro plate. It's

the only thing I'm going to miss when I get to the land of overcooked barbeque."

"Don't be like that." She laughed. "The brisket is usually good."

"What time are we getting Mason?" I asked looking at the time on my dashboard. He was spending time with his paternal side of the family while we handled business.

"We can actually head that way after we get food." She replied typing on her phone. "I just told him to be ready. That way neither of us has to come back out tonight and we can get some rest before this long drive. I still don't understand why you wouldn't take me up on my offer to have it shipped down here. It was only going to be like five hundred dollars, and I could have gotten us flights home with my miles."

"It was seven hundred dollars." I corrected her pulling into in open parking space right in front of Greek Corner. I felt lucky, seeing as parking in this area was always terrible. "And shipping it meant I would be without my car for a week."

"Oh, wow a whole week." She mocked me. "I have two cars; it wouldn't have mattered. I swear Kali you be making life so much harder than it needs to be. In case you've forgotten your sister has a little bit of money." She whispered it, in the neighborhood we were in, you didn't exactly announce how much you were worth.

"I know that would have been easier, a lot quicker for sure." I said turning off the car. "But I just wanted to drive myself. I don't know why and even if I did, I'm sure I couldn't even explain it. I just know that I needed to drive myself."

We went inside of the restaurant ordering our food and grabbing something for Mason as well. After leaving there, we made our way to pick him up. I didn't want to go inside but Parris didn't want to go in by herself and they wanted to speak to her before we left.

I sat with Mason in the living room, speaking to some of his relatives I had known since I was 15 and Mason was just being born. Lamar's people weren't good people; I knew that even at a young age. Lamar was an ain't shit nigga and that was because he was birthed by an ain't shit bitch who guzzled the sperm of another ain't shit nigga. I hated that Parris was so nice, hated that she fell prey to him and his family. But, on the flip side, if she hadn't; we wouldn't have Mason who was worth every single piece of bullshit we encountered along the way.

By the time we left, it was nearly 9pm. We made our way back to the hotel they booked and once I had my overnight bag in hand, we made our way to the 4th floor of the Hyatt Regency. We ate, I showered and was in bed within two hours of arriving.

We woke up early and were checked out and gone on the road by 6am. I had the first 7 hour drive which wasn't so bad with my playlists updated and ready. For the most part I thought about what my new life would look like when I got to Dallas. I wondered if this was a good move for me to be making and I wondered if it was a bad move. Then, I wondered if by some type of divine intervention, I ran into the one man who was constantly on my mind since the day I left him sleeping in his hotel bed. He lived in Dallas and yes Dallas was a big city; maybe we would never meet again. But… if we did, what would it mean?

We made it to Dallas in a little under 13 hours; I was glad to see Parris' two story home when we pulled into the driveway. I loved this house from the moment my sister told me she was buying it. Whenever I did visit Dallas, it was my home away from home.

It was a 5 bedroom 3.5 bathroom home in Lancaster, a

city bordering Dallas separated by a major freeway. The house was massive, way more space than Parris and Mason needed, yet it was exactly the kind of house I expected my sister to have.

She hadn't been here long, had moved in about three years ago and paid for it in cash. A lot of people didn't know but around that time, Parris had hit the local lottery, winning a prize total of 5 million dollars after taxes. She had money to burn, and she set that shit ablaze. The home had two living spaces one upstairs and one down. There were four bedrooms upstairs, two on each side of the second living space; each bedroom separated by a bathroom.

The room I had opted to sleep in was on the opposite side of the house as my nephew's bedroom on the second level. When I finally accepted moving here; Parris gave me both bedrooms; a space for me to sleep and the second being my art room; it was the only real ask I had in all of this, I needed space to create.

All three of us walked into the house carrying suitcases and boxes having to make multiple trips in order to get everything inside and once it was inside; they helped me take it all upstairs to my space putting the bulk of it into the second bedroom.

"Home sweet home." Parris cheesed in my direction before wrapping her arm around my waist. "I know I keep saying this Kali but I'm so glad you're here with us. I know how much losing Jonathan broke you, but I'm hoping being here with family will help you on your journey to pick up the pieces."

"I appreciate everything you've done for me and will do." I told her. "Being here just felt like the right move."

"Well, I'll give you some space to get situated. If you need anything let me know." I gave her another hug before she exited my bedroom closing the door behind her. I flopped down on my bed looking around the room I'd spent quite a bit of time in realizing it was going to be my safe haven for the next few months until I was able to get my life together.

∼

"How many people are we meeting up with?" I asked Parris as I sat in the passenger seat of her candy red Tesla Model Y. I was dressed in a yellow cropped hoodie, dark high waisted blue jeans, and yellow Christian Soriano pumps. My hair was in its natural curly state, pinned up in a bun on the top of my head. I wore diamond hooped earrings with a few diamond bracelets around my wrist.

Parris had convinced me to come out with her to meet a few of her co-workers. Mason had left us opting to spend what remained of his summer with his best friend Patrick and his family going to Galveston.

I had been in Dallas for over two weeks, and this was the first time I was really getting out. Next week we'd all be starting the school year together with a weeklong teacher's orientation. Parris thought I should meet some people before then as she wouldn't have time to make introductions during the orientation. As the assistant principal her schedule was even busier than the rest of ours.

"Um, not many just like five or six people. You're going to like this lounge, we come here during happy hour sometimes." She had taken her hands off the steering wheel and every time she did that it freaked me out. I felt like Will Smith in iRobot; AI was not natural and self driving cars did not excite me.

"Can you keep your hands on the wheel please?" I rolled my eyes. When I glanced in her direction, she laughed.

"You're such a scary cat." She shook her head. "It's safe."

"Tell that to all of them lawsuits Elon Musk has." I stuck my nose up at her.

"Anyway." She rolled her eyes. "Are you excited about the orientation? We'll probably need to drive ourselves and not carpool; our schedules will be different."

"It's fine." I replied waving her off. "My GPS will tell me where to go until I get the hang of it myself. I can't wait to see the layout of the classroom, so I'll know how to decorate it. I'm nervous to be teaching."

"Why? You've taught private art lessons before."

"Yeah, but I ain't never taught a classroom full of teenagers. I have never had to just deal with a lot of teens before in general."

"They are nasty little creatures, but they can also be very sweet and caring. They are all funny and they stay tryna get you to do a Tik Tok with them. They are going to have their attitudes but as adults it will be our jobs to guide them. That's why I got into this work, because of schools like ours in an underprivileged area, serving underprivileged kids who are our future. And these kids are so smart Kali, they are all beautiful kids in their own ways."

"You sound like you memorized the school pamphlet." I laughed and she flipped me off.

"I helped write it; fuck you very much."

Not long after we were pulling up to a parking lot in Deep Ellum. We parked then exited the car walking towards Grafton House. When we walked up to the door, there was a few people ahead of us; yet when we got there, seemed like the bouncer's attention was in our direction.

"Miss. Parris." He smiled once the others had their IDs' checked and were entering the building. "Ain't seen you in a little while, how you been doing?"

"I'm good Fabian." Parris smiled and I stood back, watching her flirt with him and I could see why. Fabian reminded me of those wrestlers the Uso Brothers. He had four braids pulled into a low man bun with the sides tapered. He was big, at least 6'4 and he was solid; like he could bench press the fuck out of any bitch on the planet; yet I knew my sister had to wish she was the happy contestant. "How you doing?"

"Better now that I'm seeing you back here." He smiled. "When you gon' stop playing with me and give me your number?"

"Who said I was playing?" she asked. "You are not ready for me; I keep telling you that."

"Let me decide what I'm ready for." He bent down to meet her 5'4 frame whispering something in her ear that caused her to giggle like a schoolgirl. He was whispering for so long I was starting to think they forgot I was here, so I cleared my throat to get their attention.

"Oh God, sorry Kali." Parris mumbled taking a step back from him. "Fabian this is my little sister Kali, Kali this is Fabian."

"So, I heard." I smirked. "Very handsome and I agree Sissy, you need to stop playing games and give this man your number."

"I like sis." Fabian pointed in my direction while looking at Parris. "Come on now, let me take you out and we can go kick it."

"Fine." Parris playfully rolled her eyes before handing her phone to Fabian. "Call yourself, then we can lock each other in."

"Me and you locked in, ooh wee I like the sound of that." Fabian continued to flirt, and Parris' simple ass continued to cheese in his direction. Shaking my head, I waited a little longer for their exchange to be done. Finally, he opened the door for us. "Enjoy your night ladies, Parris; I'mma hit you up."

"You better." She replied and I grabbed her hand, pulling her inside.

"Girl, what?" I asked over the loud music. "He is cute Parris."

"I know right? He been flirting with me since we first started coming here. His family owns the place." She looked around the lounge and my eyes followed hers admiring the laid back ambiance; hues of dark blue, purple, and red surrounded us. The DJ was raised on a stage towards the back of the place, there was a long bar covering the left wall with seating throughout the building. There was a dance floor in the middle of the room.

"Well, you need to stop playing and make sure you answer his phone calls. He's a good look for you."

"You think?" she asked, and I nodded. "I do like him. He's a gentle giant, as sweet as can be. He's exactly what I need in my life."

"Anyway, where are your friends?" I asked looking around the place wondering which table her people sat at. Whenever I came to visit, I had only met one person which was a lady named Autumn. She and Parris had worked together for years. She would often go out with us whenever I visited, and she seemed like an okay person; except I noticed she was a bit possessive of Parris at times as if she was scared, I was going to come steal her away.

We found her friends a short while later joining them at the small section they had. There were bottles of alcohol already lining the table in front of them. When we approached, I saw that there were 3 women and 2 men in the group; all of which hugged Parris individually.

"Everybody this is my little sister Kahlia; she's going to be starting at William T. as one of the art teachers."

"Hey everyone." I smiled with a wave.

"Kali, you know Autumn already." I nodded glancing at

Autumn who gave me a condescending smirk. "This is Jocelyn Spears, she teaches Chemistry, Michelle Little she teaches English, Pedro Lopez teaches Spanish and Oliver Wilson who teaches Geometry."

"It's good to meet you, Kahlia." The woman introduced as Michelle said. "Your sister tells us you're a very talented artist. Do you have a social media account where we can check out your work?"

"Yeah." I went into my purse grabbing a couple of business cards. "All my info is on here. I also do photography if you know anybody needing to get some pictures taken."

"I love the networking." Autumn said. "Gotta hustle so you can get outta your sister's house as fast as possible huh?" I didn't respond to her, just looked over at Parris who shook her head, pleading with her eyes for me not to say anything. She knew me well enough to know I hated backhanded compliments.

"Uh, Coach Mackenzie said he was coming out tonight." Oliver interrupted the awkward silence. I couldn't tell you why a shiver ran down my spine at the mention of that name, but I ignored it.

"How did y'all convince him to get out the house?" Parris asked, her eyes wide in shock. "He never comes to anything we invite him to."

"I don't know what changed but I asked if he wanted to come then he said he was coming. We had a long practice today so he might need the drink." Oliver shrugged.

"Practice?" I asked attempting to follow the conversation.

"Oliver is an assistant football coach at the school." Parris said. "You want a drink?" She pointed to the alcohol on the table, and I nodded. I watched as Pedro poured the entire table shots of Tequila. The bottle of Luna Azul struck a nerve as I remembered it from Mexico. I loved it so much when I had it there that I had been only drinking this brand of tequila since I'd been home.

As we took shots and sipped drinks, dancing became a necessity. Parris and I along with Michelle and Autumn were on the dance floor. It felt good to be out. I hadn't had fun like this in a long time. Despite the icy start, Autumn was starting to grow on me and Michelle, who looked to be about my age was a cool person as well.

"I gotta pee." I suddenly heard Parris scream over the music. I nodded and took her hand as she pulled me along. We were both a little tipsy and we never went to the bathroom alone when we were out in a club like setting. When we made it to the bathroom, we grabbed the first two empty stalls. After relieving my own bladder, I adjusted my clothes and then left the stall to wash my hands.

"I like them, they seem like cool people." I told her. "But I'm telling you now if Autumn keep up with that slick shit talking I'mma knock her ass into next week."

"I know." She chuckled. "I get it, she be doing the most but she's a good person. I'mma talk to her about that. She know I don't play when it comes to you, so I don't know why she tried it."

"She better not try it again, I'mma show her ass how I get down."

"I'll talk to her." She repeated. "Come on, let's get back to the table, I need another drink." She grabbed my hand again escorting me out of the bathroom and we made our way back towards the table.

As we neared the table, I noticed that someone had joined the group and figured it must have been the man they mentioned earlier. The closer we got, butterflies began to fill my stomach and my heart started beating faster than normal.

"What the hell?" I mumbled and Parris looked at me concerned.

"What's wrong?"

"Nothing, it's fine."

"Coach Mackenzie, you made it." Parris smiled and when he turned in her direction I stopped in my tracks. He gave her one short glance before his eyes immediately hit mine; those beautiful hazel eyes staring into my own with the same intensity, the same veracity as he had in Mexico.

What were the fucking odds?

9

JOSIAH

The room seemed to spin slightly as my eyes landed on hers. Everything went quiet despite the table my colleagues sitting at being closer to the DJ booth. Nothing in this world mattered to me as I stared at the woman I'd been thinking about every single day for the past three months. It was surreal to be standing in front of her even though I thought I'd never see her again.

"Josiah?" My name rolled off her tongue and the sound of her voice snapped me out of my own thoughts. I stood up from my seat and closed the distance between us. "How are —" she couldn't finish her statement before my lips found hers.

I didn't give a damn what her situation was, if she had a man, if she was promised to somebody, none of that mattered as I pulled her body into mine enjoying the softness of the skin on her back. She wrapped her arms around me and kissed me back. She felt and smelled just as I had remembered, just as I had imagined whenever I thought about her. This moment was unexpected, but it was everything.

Our bodies stayed connected in the middle of the dance floor and I didn't have a care in the world for who was watching. I had missed her, and I craved her. The impossible was happening right now, so impossible that I never thought I'd see this woman again only for her to be here. I never fucking agreed to come out with my colleagues preferring to keep my home and work life separate. But today, after practice, I needed a drink or two. I was starting to realize though, that what I really needed, was her.

"Uh, hey, we're all still here." Parris said appearing next to us. "Unhand my little sister." Confused I looked from Parris to Kahlia. I could see how they could be related, but only because they had the same lips and nose, everything else was different. I backed up but only slightly then grabbed Kali's hand. Having her next to me wasn't enough, I needed to feel her.

"She's your sister?"

"I just said that Mr. Mackenzie." Parris replied before turning to her sister. "Explain please."

"He's the man from Mexico that I was telling you about." She smiled up at me coyly.

"Mexico, Mexico?"

"Yes Parris." She chuckled.

Parris turned to me her eyes roaming my body and I wondered what the hell Kahlia had told her. It was already awkward enough that she was my boss, but knowing I'd imagined bending her over her desk once or twice didn't make it no better.

Parris Nettles was a beautiful woman there was no doubt about it. Her skin was a shade or two lighter than her sister's and she had big doe eyes. She was short as hell, I'm talking 5'3 tops but what she lacked in height she made up for in body. Basically, she was a baddie, and she knew it. Seems their family kept a baddie in it.

"Can we go somewhere and talk?" I asked looking in Kahlia's direction.

"You just got here." Autumn said and I finally realized we had other eyes and ears on us.

"And now we're leaving." Kali replied reaching over the seat and grabbing a white clutch. She turned to her sister and gave her a quick hug. "I'll call you later."

"Be safe." Parris replied before looking up at me. "I have access to all your information; think about that before you try anything stupid." I chuckled, shaking my head. It was like she hadn't known me for four years.

"Ya'll have a good night." I yelled over my shoulder before escorting Kahlia towards the same direction I'd only arrived from just five minutes prior. Neither of us spoke as I escorted her out the door, towards the parking lot where my car was parked. When we made it to my car, I opened the door then jogged around to get in myself.

"Where are you taking me?" Kali asked the moment I pulled out of the parking lot not long after.

"I don't know." I said honestly. "I just want to be with you for a little while before—"

"Where do you live?" she asked. "It's okay if you want to take me to your place."

"You sure?"

I didn't want her to assume that I was assuming anything about her. I didn't want her to think that this was about sex for me. It may have started that way between the both of us, but it wasn't what I was on now.

"I'm sure." She replied grabbing my hand interlocking our fingers. I pulled her hand to my lips placing a kiss on the back of it. "It's good to see you. How have you been?"

"I've been good." I smiled. "You?"

"I moved to the place I said I was never moving to." She chuckled. "How do you think I'm doing?"

"You wanna talk about it?" I rubbed her hand with my thumb, glancing over in her direction anticipating her response.

"Not yet." She sighed leaning back in her seat a little.

Our hands remained connected in the thirty-five minutes it took for me to get back to my house in Desoto. I had purchased this space a month after I got to Dallas, purchased it during the pandemic so I got it for a steal. 4 bedrooms and 2.5 bath, 1500 sqft ranch style home. I was proud of myself when I bought it, had told myself that I wanted to be a home-owner for my 30th birthday so that's what I did. I pulled into the 2 car garage then cut the car off looking over at Kali.

"You good?" she had been staring blankly out the window, not speaking much as we traveled to this destination.

"What were the odds?" she mumbled still staring out the window, with her elbow against the door frame, subtly rubbing her lips as if she was in heavy thought.

"What odds?"

"What are the odds that you knew my sister and we never made that connection."

"You never mentioned her name and I never talked about what school I worked for; it was a part of the rules remember; nothing too personal, no identifying information."

"It's weird though right?" she asked. "How the hell did we end up at the same resort at the same time?"

"Maybe it was kismet." I shrugged and finally her eyes connected with mine.

I had been thinking about that same thing as we drove. The commonalities, the things that seemed to be pushing us together, things that were outside of our control. We were meant to just be temporary lovers. But after spending time together, getting to know one another, it grew into something more so fast and with such intensity that I doubt either of us could have stopped it even if we wanted to.

"God is a mysterious being." She chuckled shaking her head. "I asked him for this, I think. Well, I asked him to give me strength, to help me heal, to give me peace. I asked him for those three things for an entire year and everything I went through, everything I dealt with or didn't deal with, it all was preparing me."

"Preparing you for what?" I asked hanging on to every single word she was saying.

"For my happiness, for my strength and for my peace. When I got the strength to let go of my husband, he sent me to the place I had promised I would make his final resting place. A place I had been avoiding for years since he died. And when I got back there, I finally fulfilled my promise to Jonathan. A few hours later, I saw you standing on your patio, and I felt—" her pause intrigued me. I squeezed her hand urging her to go on. I had a feeling I knew exactly what she was going to say, because I had felt it too the moment, I looked at her. "I felt like everything was going to be okay. I felt like you were there to make it okay. Then with the time we spent, the conversations we had, the chemistry was—"

"Amazing! I ain't never felt nothing like it before. I had never wanted anybody more. I too had asked for strength, for happiness and to be healed. After all that shit went down with my ex and my brother, I said I was never going to trust another woman. I was out here reckless, making bad decisions and treating some women like they were the ones that hurt me, projecting my past bullshit on them. I had intended on doing the same thing in Mexico, I was there alone and there were some beautiful women. When I laid eyes on you, I remember thinking how sad you looked and how I hated that shit. I didn't know nothing about you, but I hated the fact that you were sad, and I wanted to make it better. I knew I was fucked up the morning after I first had you." My head fell back against the head rest remembering the first time I entered her walls. "I wasn't really tryna leave that room after, but I knew what we said at the pool, and I knew what it was; so, I got my bitch ass up and left to my room. You consumed me, consumed my mind and my soul. I couldn't wait to see you and I fucked up, looking you up on social media, saying fuck the rules. When you shut me down before we went to visit town, I was salty as fuck."

"You were distant at the church."

"Yeah, I was." I confirmed. "But then we kept kicking it all day and I watched you in your element and I was enthralled again, on accident. I couldn't wait to get you back to that hotel, I planned on showing you for the rest of the night that I was worth the risk. I was willing to figure it out with you, regardless of the distance. But then you fucking left me and that crushed me."

"I'm sorry—"

"Nah, I get it." I stopped her. "I really do. I read that note you left me so many fucking times; read in between the lines, read the words you couldn't say and the words you did say, and I pieced it all together. There was no doubt in my mind that there was something there and that if it was meant to be it would be. Kali, I never fucking accept the invitation to go out with my colleagues. They cool people, but I fuck with my guy Rich and that's about it. Tonight, for whatever reason when Oliver asked me, I just said why the fuck not. After practice, I came here, got dressed, procrastinated a bit, but I got my ass out the house, in the car and started driving. I had no fucking idea that you would be in there; but I'm fucking glad you were."

"I hoped I'd find you here in Dallas. I knew it was a longshot, knew that there was no way I would run into you this soon. What were the fucking odds?" a light chuckle broke out between the both of us before the car got quiet and we just stared at one another.

"You wanna come in? Or I can take you home."

"I don't want to be apart, not when I just found you again." She whispered and I sighed with relief. "I'll stay, if that's okay." Nodding, I got out of the car, walking over to the passenger side and helping her out as well. Our hands remained connected as we entered my home through the kitchen. It was dark, the only light I had was the light on my ring doorbell plug in.

"You want a drink or something?" I started towards the fridge, but she stopped me, pulling me back to her. She stood on the tips of her toes and placed her soft lips on top of mine.

"I want you to make love to me." She kissed me again, grabbing the t-shirt I was wearing, beginning to lift it over my head.

Once I was out of my shirt, I helped her out of hers, throwing both to the ground. I lifted her in my arms, and she wrapped her arms and legs around my body. I carried her to my bedroom, kicking the door open and walking her over to the bed then sat her down on her feet.

"You're so fucking beautiful." I admired her chocolate skin, rubbing my hand down the side of her face. Her big doe eyes stared up into mine. She stepped back from me then unclipped her bra strap letting the bra fall to the ground. I started towards her, wanting to get to her chocolate mounds but she moved away from me again. She unbuttoned her jeans then slid them down. When she went towards her panties, I stopped her.

"I planned on getting those off with my teeth. Don't take that away from me." I walked up on her, backing her up against the bed before gently pushing her back.

I ran my finger along the seat of her panties, feeling the moist center. I got on my knees then placed my lips on her stomach, trailing kisses down towards the lining of her panties. Using my teeth as promised, I pulled them down.

Kissing back up her left leg and thigh, I finally kissed her lower lips. I felt her tremble the moment I swiped my tongue against her bud.

I buried my face in between her legs, licking and sucking her pussy while listening to the loud moans escaping her lips. Spreading her legs a little further, I stuck my tongue between her walls, while simultaneously sucking her bud.

"Oh God." She screamed, pulling my face deeper between her legs. Her back slightly lifted off the bed and I knew I had her where I wanted her. I stuck two fingers inside of her wet walls still licking and sucking her bud. I finger fucked her and each time my fingers entered her juicy pussy, her walls tightened around them until juices squirted all over my fingers.

"Fuck." I groaned feeling how hard my erection was, the fabric from my jeans constricting its release.

I stood up and unbuckled my belt before taking off my jeans and boxer briefs. I went over to my nightstand, grabbing a couple of condoms. Before I could open one of them, Kahlia was off the bed and on her knees in front of me. She licked the precum that was leaking from my mushroom head before opening her mouth as I fed her my dick.

"Mmhhm." she hummed causing my head to fall back. When I lowered my head to look back down at her, her swollen lips were wrapped around me bobbing up and down my shaft, milking me for everything I had in me.

I grabbed the back of her head feeding my dick further down her mouth, making her gag. Her eyes watered each time she gagged and when she didn't stop, I didn't try to stop her. Her left hand was stroking me while she sucked my mushroom head, her right hand was between her legs rubbing her own pussy. When I couldn't take it anymore, I felt my seeds coat her tongue. Her two fingers on her right hand were coated in her sweet juices. I placed those fingers in my mouth, licking her essence from them.

This time around, Kali pushed me onto the bed before climbing on top of me. As she slid down on my dick, my hands immediately went to her breasts, squeezing them and then leaning up licking her gumdrop nipples. Feeling her walls tighten around my dick, I bounced her up and down aggressively, pulling her juices from her, her body shuddered in my arms. I had missed being inside of her, didn't know how much until I was. She'd clearly made a big impression on me and on my dick; just being inside of her felt like a dream.

Our hearts beat fast; they were almost in sync. Suddenly, I felt a shudder as sniffles soon followed it. Sorrow consumed me as I held on to Kahlia. I didn't know what to say, didn't know if I should say anything. So, I sat there with her; our bodies connected, her arms around my neck while mine wrapped around her waist. I rubbed her head, comforting her as best as I could.

"Tell me what's wrong." I whispered as her sobs slowed and her shudders almost fully stopped.

"Don't fucking hurt me." She cried before another rumble of sobs started. I continued to rub her back, hoping my touch would calm her.

"I can't promise you that and that's just me being real. I won't do anything to intentionally hurt you; but I ain't a perfect man nor do I think you're perfect so I wouldn't expect perfection of you."

"Promise me anyway." I pulled back from our embrace looking into her wet eyes, pools of tears flowing down her face. "Please."

"I promise." I finally gave in, knowing I was making a promise no man or woman could ever keep. Still, I told myself that I would do all I could to keep the promise regardless of how impossible it seemed.

∼

"Good morning." I spoke to Kahlia as she trailed out of my room, wearing one of my t-shirts that looked way too big for her. I was in the kitchen fixing her an omelet the same way I noticed she had them when went to breakfast while in Mexico.

I had woken up earlier than normal and for the first five minutes, I stared at Kali wanting to pinch myself to make sure this was real. I had been completely sober last night; I had only gotten there in time to take a few sips of the drink I ordered before she showed up. Still, I couldn't believe this was real; she was in my bed, and I had gotten to wake up next to her.

"Good morning." She replied walking over to me and wrapping her arms around my waist while I flipped the omelet. She laid her head on my back, and I basked in her warmth. When she backed out of the embrace, I turned around and placed a quick kiss on her lips. "Smells good."

"Sit, it's almost done." I nodded towards the chair that was pulled up to my island countertop. I grabbed a plate before placing the omelet on top of it. I gave her a few pieces of bacon as well as some toast then I slid the plate towards her, and she looked at it.

"I'm not going to eat this entire omelet, cut it in half and split it with me?"

"I was going to make my own."

"Seriously Josiah, I'm not going to be able to finish this."

"Okay." I nodded going to grab another plate and a knife.

I cut the omelet in half placing half of it on my plate then grabbing bacon and toast for myself. I put the plate at a seat next to her then went to the fridge grabbing the orange juice as well as a bottle of Moet I had, pouring both into two glasses. After that, I grabbed silverware then sat down next to her handing her, her items. We ate in silence, the only sound coming from the occasional scrape of our forks on the plates.

Once we were done eating, I cleared the plates setting them in the sink. Turning to look at Kali, I leaned back against the kitchen sink and folded my arms across my chest. There was a lot to discuss and the silence that resounded around us proved that to me. We were both in our heads, saying things in our brains that we were scared to say out loud. Even with our conversation in the car, not enough was said, not enough was out in the open.

"You, okay?" she asked, and I nodded. "You wanna talk?"

"I do but, I don't."

"What does that mean Josiah?"

"It's weird that you're here in my house." I shrugged. "I like it, but it's weird. I didn't think I'd ever see you again. You blocked me on social media and honestly, I started to make a fake page to contact you. Can you believe that? I was mad when I got that letter Kali, I was pissed. I went downstairs, about to plan a bomb ass final day and before I could, I got that fucking letter."

"Josiah—"

"I know I said I understood why you just left, and I do; but I'm still salty as hell at it. Would it have been so bad if what we had lasted beyond that weekend?"

"I wasn't ready for you." She whispered. "I knew I wasn't ready, and I was also terrified on what would happen if I stayed longer. I was falling for you, and I had never fallen for anybody other than my husband. We were together since we were 16 years old, so for me to have this intense connection with somebody else; I felt like I was betraying him, and I was scared that I would hurt you which is something I didn't want to do."

"But you did though." I shrugged. "You really fucking did."

"And I'm so sorry about that." She replied getting up from her seat and moving into my space. "It's been three months and in these three months I have discovered so much more about myself and it's all because of you. I realized I was holding on to a life that was steadily passing me by. Every single day all I could think about was you. I would be lying if I said I came here for something other than you, but I didn't. I planned on finding you eventually and I hoped that when I did find you again that you would be open to me. Did I think within weeks of me being here that, that was going to happen? Hell no. But I swear to God, Josiah, God had other plans for us and I'm here now because I'm giving up control and giving it to him. If we weren't supposed to be together then, how did we end up here? How am I in your home? How am I standing in front of you now?"

"You sure this what you wanna do?" I asked needing to make sure this wasn't just another thing we were doing. "I'm almost 35, I got plans and I'm not tryna just fuck around and play games. I am looking for somebody to share my life with, to have a family with. If you're looking for something else, or if you're not ready for that, then let me know now." She stepped closer to me before wrapping her arms around my waist.

"I'm yours." My heart inflated as I wrapped my arms around her before leaning down to place a kiss on her lips. Without warning, I lifted her off her feet and she screamed, laughing as I placed kisses all over her face while walking her to the living room and sitting down on the couch.

"I can't believe you're here." I said holding her face in my hands. "I don't want to let you go."

"Then don't." she started to take the oversized shirt off,

GENESIS CARTER

but the ringing of my doorbell stopped her in her tracks. I looked towards the door, then looked at the bright white numbers on the cable box. Seeing it was almost 9AM, I cursed silently knowing exactly who was at the door. I lifted her off my lap before walking over to the door and opened it slightly.

"Fuck you doing?" Rich asked as I blocked him from coming in.

"I forgot about us hitting the gym." I sighed. "I need to do a raincheck."

"Nigga what?" he chuckled. "Hell naw, I'm already here. Get dressed and let's go, nobody told yo ass to go out last night knowing we had an early morning workout."

"Rich, I can't right now." He looked at me confused before pushing his way into the door anyway, walking past me and stopping in his tracks seeing Kahlia sitting on the couch, her feet beneath her.

"Aw shit." Rich said looking from Kahlia to me, then back to her. "Who this?"

"Nigga, get the fuck out." I shook my head walking towards Kali.

"How you doing Miss Lady? I'm Rich, Mac's best friend." He said moving around me and approaching Kali with his hand out.

"Hi Rich, I'm Kali." She replied accepting his handshake. As soon as she said her name, he looked at me shocked then smirked in her direction.

"Mexico Kali?" his question was directed towards me, yet his eyes never left her, nor did his hand.

"Alright that's enough." I removed their hand from one another and possessively stood in front of Kahlia.

"Damn nigga, ain't nobody tryna steal yo girl." Rich laughed. "It's nice to finally put a face to a name. You got my boy sprung or something, nigga ain't shut up about you in months." I wanted to punch his ass but hearing the sweet laugh come from Kali's lips stopped me.

"It's nice meeting you Rich." She finally stood from the couch, and I saw Rich's eyes roam her body, if he was anybody else, I would have checked his ass. But I knew the nigga wasn't stupid and he wasn't tryna lose me as a best friend or his wife and child. "I'll let ya'll talk. I should probably go call Parris before she sends out a search party." She placed a quick kiss on my lips before walking off. I watched her as she did, biting my lip seeing the cusp of her ass peeking out from under the shirt. Only when she closed the door behind her did I turn to look at Rich.

"What the fuck? How that happen?" Rich asked and I walked towards the kitchen to clean up the mess I'd made. There was still leftover bacon which I offered to Rich, and he accepted sitting down at the island countertop.

"Man, I'm still figuring it out myself." I replied rinsing the dishes from the sink and then putting them in the dishwasher. "When I went out last night, she was just there. Her sister is Parris Nettles, the Assistant Principal at the school."

"Nigga what? And neither of ya'll had any idea?"

"No." I shook my head. "I was shocked as hell to see her there. When I saw her, all I could do was..." I paused thinking about last night, thinking about how I felt in that moment. "All I could do was kiss her. I wasn't even in that joint for five minutes after seeing her and having her close, I wasn't tryna stay either. I just wanted to be with her, so I left with her, and we been here since."

"You hit?"

"What you think?" I smirked. "I been dreaming about that shit since I had it last, and she definitely didn't disappoint." My smile got wider, brighter. There was no doubt in my mind that Kahlia Mitchell was inside of me and that she had me gone.

"My boi." He laughed and we dapped up with our signature handshake. "So, what's next? Ya'll about to be on some long distance shit?"

"Don't got to. She moved to Dallas a few weeks ago." I replied. "And she's about to work at the school."

"Wait, hold up? This seems like some stalker shit." He lowered his voice. "You sure she didn't plan this?"

"No nigga." I laughed. "She was just as surprised to see me as I was to see her. I never told her what school I worked for and neither of us had any idea we had a connection via her sister. This took us completely by surprise."

"Man, this is wild." He placed his last piece of bacon in his mouth. "So, it's up from here huh?"

"Hopefully." I shrugged. "I'm literally in shock still, I don't think this shit has hit me yet. I never thought I'd see her again and now she's just here. I'mma marry that girl, Rich. Ain't no doubt about it."

"Look man, I'mma support you in everything you do; you already know that. But I wouldn't be a good friend if I didn't tell you to take it slow, make sure this is what you want with who you want to do it with. That girl is beautiful, but from what you told me ya'll both got some shit ya'll need to get over. I just want to make sure ya'll both deal with it before ya'll get too deep."

"I'm not dealing with shit; I'm over that bullshit."

"Just like that, Bro?" he asked skeptically. "You think just because this girl walked back into your life that all is well? Yo ass ain't over shit man and we both know it."

"Man, I ain't thinking about that shit from Atlanta. All I care about is my future."

"Yeah Mac? Then how come you still refusing to go see Miss. Claudette for Thanksgiving then? You all healed and over it, but you refuse to confront the issue head on."

I busied myself with cleaning the counter and sink area

then started the dishwasher. A part of me knew he was right, but the other part refused to admit it because if I wasn't healed, why was I ready to be with Kahlia? Serious relationships weren't even on my mind until I met her and all I could do was think about what a future between us could look like. I was ready for her.

"Rich man, I don't know how to describe it. I ain't saying I'm 100% healed but I'm ready for her. I been ready for her, been waiting for her. I'm not tryna rush into nothing but I got her here with me and I would be a dumb ass nigga not to go after what I want. We tryna be together and all I can do is see where it goes."

"Alright man." He sighed. "But aye look, we hitting this gym or what? I only got a limited amount of time before Tish come calling me."

"Let me go get dressed." I replied before walking out of the kitchen, going towards my bedroom. Once inside, I observed Kali sitting on the bed talking on the phone. When I shut the door, she ended her conversation.

"Parris is on the way to come pick me up."

"You ain't gotta leave." I assured her. "I told Rich I would go workout with him, but it shouldn't take long."

"It's okay." She smiled as I sat next to her on the bed. "I need to get back home."

"I want to take you out later." I swiped a few of her curls back from her face. "Be ready by 6." I grabbed her phone from where she'd dropped it after ending her phone call. I dialed my number and let it ring a few times before hanging up. I clicked on the number and added my name then handed it back to her.

"Let me get dressed, it won't take her long to get here."

We both got dressed; me in workout gear; and her in the clothes she'd worn last night. She was right, it hadn't taken Parris long to get to my house, she was pulling up as we were exiting. I was riding with Rich, so I locked up and walked Kali to her sister's car.

"Good morning Ms. Parris."

"Coach Mackenzie." She shot in my direction. "I see she's in one piece; I appreciate it."

"She's safe with me." I replied before turning my attention to Kali. I wrapped my arms around her pulling her into my body then connecting our lips. "Text me the address and I'll see you at 6."

"Bye Josiah." She smiled when I finally let her go. I opened the car door for her then closed it once she was inside. I backed away so they could drive off, not moving from my spot until they were clear down the street.

"Come on sprung ass nigga." Rich shook his head walking over to his car and I followed, getting into the passenger seat. When we were buckled up, he pulled off. "You about to go into this shit foot first; I can see it already. I just want you to be careful Mac."

"You know careful is my middle name." I smirked in his direction. "But man, for that one, I think I'mma decide to be reckless."

10

KAHLIA

When I got back home, I showered then got dressed in a pair of black leggings, my blue Hampton University sweatshirt with matching blue thick socks. I wrapped my hair in a white scarf then I made my way downstairs. I needed to find an art store. Inspiration had struck me and all I could think about was creating.

"So, you just gon walk around here and not give me information?" Parris asked, she was sitting in the living room on the couch waiting for me so we could go shopping. "And it's hot as hell, where the fuck you think you going in that?"

"It's going to be cold in the stores." I shrugged underestimating the Texas heat. "Come on, we can talk in the car."

We made our way back out of the house and hopped in the Model Y; until I learned my way around, I had Parris drive everywhere. I settled into my seat, letting the sound of Coco Jones fill the car. I didn't say anything right away, didn't know how to put into words what I was feeling.

"Talk Kali."

"He's Mexico." I shrugged, that's all there really was to say.

I had confided in her what I had experienced while in Mexico. Had shared how in such a short amount of time I slowly started to fall for a man after I told him I only wanted sex out of him. I told her about the conversations we had, the moments we shared. She knew what that meant to me and she also knew how guilty I felt about it afterwards.

"How crazy is it that I know him? I mean, I've worked with Josiah for four years since he first came to Dallas. I know he's a good dude, but also, I know he sleeps around."

"I know that too." I told her. "We were honest with each other. Hell, we didn't think we'd ever see each other again, we told each other things we wouldn't tell anyone else. I was that comfortable with him. He knows my secrets, he knows me, the me I don't show other people."

"And you trusted him to know that part of you?"

"I did and I still do." I told her. "Because I think he was sent to me, and I was sent to him. How did two people like us just come together? How were the feelings we developed over three or four days that fucking intense, that deep? Parris, that man is inside of me. I tried to get over him, but who gets over those kinds of feelings that developed in less than a week? Who could ignore that? How dumb would I be to fumble this because by society's standards I shouldn't be feeling like this? I know it's crazy, but it's real Parris."

"If he hurts you Kahlia, I swear to fucking God." She sighed shaking her head.

"I'm just hoping I don't hurt him." I bit down on my bottom lip as memories of Jonathan, and I flashed through my head. I missed him still, but not as much as I had previous to Mexico. I felt bad about that, but it also made me feel hopeful for my future.

"After all of that, that you just told me about that man knowing you; neither one of ya'll better hurt each other." She huffed before focusing back on the road.

I smiled, happy that she was content enough not to give me a hard time about it. Hell, I couldn't explain to you even if I wanted to, what these feelings were. It felt unreal to know he was back in my life so soon. The amount of shock, anxiety, extreme joy, and happiness I felt when I was back in his presence was unreal. He was inside of my soul, and I needed this kind of positivity in my life.

Feeling my phone vibrate, I looked down to my lap to see that I had a text notification. I grabbed my phone, opening the text thread smiling as soon as I saw his name.

> Josiah: I can't wait to see you again. Is it crazy that I miss you already?
>
> I miss you too. You have inspired me, on my way to the art store.
>
> Josiah: Oooh, ya boi get art?
>
> We'll see. Enjoy your day Josiah 😊

I placed my phone back in my lap while biting on my nails and smiling.

"You in deep Babe." Parris said shaking her head. "Please don't make me have to kill that man."

Our first stop was to a small art store called Pandemic. I had visited here a couple of times during past visits to Dallas and I loved their offerings which were high quality made without the price tag. I'd even had Parris come in to get some things and send them to me in Chicago, brands I'd gotten used to and loved that weren't available in my city.

I grabbed so many things while I was there. While the majority of it would be going in my art room, quite a few pieces would be going with me to work next week as I designed my classroom décor. By the time I left, I had spent nearly $500. Parris thought I was crazy, but I wasn't when it came to my art supplies and the quality.

Our next stop was to the Parks Mall in Arlington. We stopped by several stores, looking at clothes, shoes and I was able to find some cute items for next week as well as a pretty red dress for my date tonight along a pair of gold strappy heels.

After the mall, we went to get a bite to eat before heading back to the house. I put away all of my things in my bedroom, hanging up the new items I got in the closet then I went to my art room and started putting my art supplies up. With the things that I had brought with me from Chicago, I had semi set up the space over the time I'd been here; I just filled in the empty spaces I had saved for my new supplies. All of my cameras were on a small desk in the corner facing the window. I had a mounted 42 inch tv courtesy of Parris, my easel set up just to the right of it. I placed my first canvas on the easel then grabbed a pencil to start outlining the image I had in my head all day.

I spent nearly three hours in my art room, listening to music and painting before the alarm I'd set for myself blared through the speakers interrupting my Lucky Daye album from playing. Sighing, I took a step back looking at my art feeling butterflies form in my stomach. I almost didn't want to stop, but I also didn't want to miss a chance to be near Josiah. So, reluctantly, I set my paint brush down and removed my apron before leaving out of the room, shutting the door behind me.

I stopped by the bathroom to run a shower and clean the day off me, relaxing as the hot water hit my body. Then, I went into my bedroom and grabbed my underwear, excluding the bra since the spaghetti strapped dress I'd picked up would look ridiculous with one on. I made my way back into the bathroom, took a quick shower, moisturized my curls restyling them in the high bun leaving a few tendrils out to frame my face. I gave myself a very light beat, the boldest thing being my full lips with shiny gloss on them.

I went back into my room slipped into my dress and heels then paired it with a gold bracelet, gold hoop earrings and a few gold rings on my right hand. I found a gold clutch stuffing my things inside then I made my way downstairs.

"You cute." Parris said sitting on the couch curled under a blanket with a bowl of popcorn in her lap.

"Thank you." I smiled going into the kitchen and grabbing a bottle of water from the fridge. "You staying in tonight?"

"Yeah, I didn't really feel like going out." She shrugged as I sat down on the loveseat to the right of her.

"You should call the guy from the lounge." I told her taking a sip of the water. "He was cute Parris, and you being here alone on a Saturday night does not sit well with me. Next week is back to work for the both of us. I have to get used to having a 9-5 again."

"I'm sure it will be fine." She sighed. "And as for Fabian, I am not about to call him. Those Samoans be playing games with people."

"How you know? You dated one before?"

"I heard things." She scoffed popping a few pieces of popcorn in her mouth. "And the people I heard it from, be knowing."

"Girl shut up." I laughed. "Get that phone and call that man."

"He's probably working."

"You won't know until you call him. It's 2023, women are asking men out on dates all the time. Go after what you want."

"Now you all in love, you wanna start passing out advice huh?" she shook her head.

GENESIS CARTER

"First off, I'm not in love. I care about Josiah a lot, but love is a huge stretch." I rolled my eyes. "Secondly, I was telling you to call him before I even knew Josiah would be back in the picture. I want you to be happy, it's been longer than me since you had a serious relationship."

"I don't have time for one." She mumbled. "I'm a boss in my own right and I have a teenage son who—"

"Is living his own life which is why he left both our old asses in this house as soon as he possibly could. Mason is not thinking about you, he probably got some little girl in his face."

"He's not in no little girl face, shut up."

"Yeah okay." I chuckled. "Whatever helps you sleep at night. It's probably time to give him the talk Parris, get his ass some condoms before you be a 36 year old grandma."

"Fuck you Kali, don't wish that shit on me."

"I'm just saying." I shrugged. "If you want me to be there with you, when you discuss it, I will be. I'm here to be helpful wherever I can." Before she could reply, the doorbell rang, and I got excited quickly standing up from my seat then straightening my dress and fluffing my hair. "How do I look?"

"I already said you were cute bitch, just answer the door." I smacked my teeth walking towards the door, willing my emotions to calm themselves, exhaling before opening the door.

"Damn." Josiah's eyes roamed my body. A smile crept on his face, and I blushed under his intense stare. "You look good baby." He moved in and wrapped his arms around my waist placing a kiss on my forehead. "You ready to go?"

"Yeah." I replied walking back towards the living room to say bye to Parris. "Hey, I'm about to head out. I'll see you later. Call that guy and get out of the house, please."

"Have fun you two." She dismissed me. Slightly offended,

I shook my head and rolled my eyes. Knowing Parris, she wasn't going to leave that position on the couch.

"Where your bag?" Josiah asked when we went back towards the front door.

"What bag?" I asked confused.

"You're staying with me." He replied. "And we're chilling tomorrow."

"I didn't pack anything." I told him. "Come up with me right quick and I will." Instead of going out the door, we shuffled up the stairs and I led him to my bedroom. I grabbed a small duffle bag from the closet then packed a few things. When I was done, Josiah grabbed the bag from me and we went back downstairs, said bye to Parris again before heading out.

We took a short drive north of where we were towards downtown. The ride was quiet, but I enjoyed just being with Josiah. Our hands were connected the entire time. My entire body tingled with giddiness at being here. I felt like a little girl with a childhood crush who had just paid her some attention. It was bad, the way I was feeling about this man.

When we pulled up to the restaurant, I observed the name Dakota's in a neat script at the top of the building. Josiah gave his key to valet and then came around to my side of the car, grabbing hold of my hand and walking us inside. As soon as we approached the hostess stand, he told them his name and not long after we were shown to our seats. Once seated, we immediately ordered drinks and then the waiter quickly left to fill in the order, telling us he'd come back and give us more time for our food orders.

"So, tell me what you've been up to since Mexico." Josiah said taking a sip of the water that was at the table while we waited on our drinks to arrive.

"Nothing much, just semi closed my business and let my sister convince me to move to a new city." I smiled.

"Semi closed? What that mean?"

"The photography studio is closed, but I am still selling my art on my website and via social media. I have an intern who is helping me still. Anytime a new piece gets sold, he ships it out for me."

"You think about opening a studio here in Dallas?"

"I thought about it." I shrugged before resting my elbow on the table and placing my chin in the palm of my hand. "I'm just going with the flow and letting God guide me."

"Understood. I saw some of your pieces on Instagram before and from what I saw you're very talented."

"Thank you." I smiled bashfully. "I appreciate that. It's been a while since I have been inspired to create anything. Today when I went to the art store, I was like a kid in a candy store. I wanted everything, touched everything, tried everything. Then I got home and set up my art room, put on some Lucky Daye and was in a zone for hours, creating."

"You like Lucky Daye? My homie Rich's wife been tryna put me on to it. I heard a couple of songs, he's pretty dope."

"His voice is amazing; I can listen to my playlist for him all day."

"What's your favorite song from him?"

"Ugh, I don't know if I want to pick." I told him. "I love all of it, but I will say the one I have been listening to the most lately is *That's You* or *Maybe Misunderstood*. There's too many to choose from."

"Is that your vibe with music?"

"Honestly, I like all kinds of music. I don't discriminate. Whatever resonates with me and inspires me, I love. What about you?"

"I like all kinds too. I mostly listen to old school R&B and some rap."

"Old school R&B? Let me find out you like that baby making music from the 80s and 90s."

"Definitely do." He chuckled. "I love a good Charlie Wilson, Isley Brothers, Next, Jagged Edge, 112."

"A man after my own heart." I teased with a wink. "That's that Saturday morning wake up early cleaning music. Add in some Anita Baker, Sade, H-Town… man, my mama used to love H-Town. I remember she was sad as hell when Dino died."

"I went to a concert at the American Airlines center recently and H-Town was one of the performers; they had a robot, Dino. It was the most bizarre shit I have ever seen. Like they could have just used a hologram, anything would have been better than that shit."

"Stop it. I've seen that too." I laughed heartily. "I went to a show they were featured in, in Chicago with my best friend. I couldn't believe what the hell I was seeing, I couldn't stop laughing the entire time."

Our laughter died down just as the waiter returned with our drinks. We ordered food and once he was gone again, I looked over at Josiah. I was trying not to stare; I'd done enough of that already. But I couldn't help it. He was gorgeous and it was becoming increasingly difficult not to hop over this table and give the rest of the restaurant a show.

"Why you staring at me like that?" Josiah asked leaning into the table with a smirk on his face. He knew, he fucking knew what he did to me and probably to every other woman that had to look into those beautiful eyes of his.

"Staring at you like what, Josiah?"

"Like I'm a snack or something."

"Aren't you though?" I asked him. "Be for real, you know you fine and I lowkey hate you for it."

"What?" he laughed heartily, holding his stomach. "What I do to deserve the hate? I was born this way, ain't nothing I can do about it."

GENESIS CARTER

"Your confidence is sexy as hell." I sighed gazing at him longingly.

"You're sexy as hell in general. Man, you don't know how happy I am to be sitting here with you again. I swear to God, I didn't think I ever would again."

"No? Why not?" I sipped the glass of wine I ordered.

"Shit, the way you blocked me on everything. I ain't gon' lie I was this close to catfishing you with another page."

"Stop it." I shook my head and playfully rolled my eyes. "I'm happy to be here with you too though. I told myself that when I moved here, I would give myself six months to get my life together and then I was going to casually send a hey big head DM."

"Not hey big head." We both laughed at that, but I was very fucking serious. I was going to look for him and hope he wasn't with anybody else. God knew my heart, he knew where I needed to be and he did it in his time frame, not what I thought would be mine. "What am I going to do with you?"

"Hopefully." I looked up at him over the rim of my wine glass. Lifting it to my lips, I took a quick sip before continuing; "Everything."

∼

"Baby Boo." Jamie hollered into the phone as soon as I answered for her. I had just gotten home after spending all night and day with Josiah. Tomorrow would be my first day at my new job and I didn't want to stay over with Josiah because there was no way I was walking into that building with him. I was sure before the day ended tomorrow though, everyone who worked at the school would know about Josiah and I considering some of our colleagues saw us kiss and leave together.

"Jamie, I miss you." I sighed putting my bag down on the floor of my bedroom and then flopping down on my bed.

"I miss you too Bookie butt, but it's okay because I plan on coming to visit soon and we can hang out. How's Dallas?"

I had been so wrapped up in Josiah that I had neglected to tell my best friend in the whole world what was going on. Even now, as I sat on the phone with her, I didn't know if I wanted to full on tell her what was happening. Of course, Jamie knew about Josiah, I told her about Mexico; I hadn't told her the full story just like I hadn't told Parris the full story either. But with Jamie, I had good reason not to. I didn't want her to feel any type of way about it considering she was Jonathan's twin sister.

"It's good." I sighed. "Um, you're never going to believe what happened."

"What?"

"Remember the guy from Mexico? Well, turns out he works with Parris; he's a teacher at the school she works at."

"Bitch, stop lying."

"I wish I was." I chuckled rubbing my hand down my face nervously. "We went out Friday to meet some of her colleagues and he was there. To say I was shocked would be an understatement. I mean how fucking random was that?"

"Fuck how random it was; did he dick you down like he did in Mexico?" Jamie asked causing me to laugh. She was a mess, anytime it had to do with sex, she was all for that conversation. Jamie was a free spirit and I loved that about her.

"I've been with him all weekend since Friday." I admitted blushing, my thoughts leading me through the events of this weekend.

"What did he say when you first saw him?"

"He didn't say anything actually, he just… kissed me and I—"

"Kissed you? In the middle of the club? Bitch I would have jumped on that nigga right then and there."

"I almost did." I laughed and she joined in. When my laughter died down, both ends of the line got quiet.

"What's up Babe?"

"There's something I didn't tell you about Mexico." I sighed preparing to get this out the way. It wasn't like me to keep things from my best friend, and this was weighing heavy on me. A part of me was afraid of her reaction, the other part was afraid she'd pull me back down to my senses and make me realize that I was moving too fast and being stupid.

"Spit it out hoe, what happened?"

"In Mexico, for me, it wasn't just about the sex. I mean; I told myself that it was, but it wasn't. I swear to God Jai, I don't know what it was, but he had me feeling some type of way. When I realized how my feelings were developing, I left a day early and blocked him."

"Damn Kali, for real?"

"Yeah." I nodded as if she could see me. "I know it's ridiculous, but I really was feeling him."

"And what were you scared of?"

"That I was dishonoring Jonathan." I replied honestly. "That me catching feelings for some stranger was somehow being disrespectful to my husband."

"Kahlia, stop it." Jamie sighed. "Look, I know how much you loved my brother and I know how much he loved you. But, baby, Jonathan is gone and like I've told you before; just because he's gone doesn't mean you have to stop living your life. We both know he didn't want that for you. You're young, you have so much life to live; why waste it?"

"Jonathan was the love of my life."

"Maybe he was, maybe he wasn't. At the end of the day, he

isn't here anymore. If you fell for that stranger, how do you know that he isn't the love of your life?"

"Love? No, we're nowhere near there yet."

"Are you trying to convince me or yourself?" she chuckled. "From what it sounds like, you're very close. You told me you spent all weekend with him. I'm guessing it wasn't just sex?"

"No."

"Because you want to explore something more with him, something deeper?"

"Yes."

"Kali, go for it." She replied and suddenly I released the deep breath I was holding before tears starting to fall down my face and sobs escaped my lips. "What's wrong? Why are you crying?"

"I didn't think you were going to... I thought you wouldn't approve."

"Why wouldn't I? Because Jonathan was my brother? Like I said, we both know he wouldn't want you to spend the rest of your life alone. I'm glad you're finally opening up to it actually. I was scared for you for a minute there friend. I thought all you'd do was have meaningless sex with randoms. Not that there's anything wrong with that; I'm all for that. But you're not that type of girl Kahlia. You're the type of woman who is supposed to be someone's wife, someone's mom. If this man is making you happy, then I'm happy."

"You don't think it's too fast?"

"Love don't get a time frame babe. Hell, Khloe and Lamar fell in love and then got married within 30 days?"

"Lamar was a crackhead behind closed doors, I don't think I want to be compared to them."

"Bitch, he had issues, but their love was real. Old folks say all the time how they knew within days that they were going to marry each other. If it's true for them, why can't it be true for our generation?"

"I love you, Jai." I smiled. "Thank you for being supportive."

"Don't thank me yet, I still need to meet Mr. Mexico. I need to plan a trip to Dallas anyway."

11

JOSIAH

"How's your first day?" I asked Kali sitting on the edge of her desk in her new classroom. When I walked in, she was hanging decorations; pictures of famous artists, mostly black all around her classroom.

We'd started the first day back in a long meeting before being dispersed to our own classroom and offices to start setting up. It was going to be a long week of learning, team building and dull meetings. The only thing I had to look forward to besides practice, was Kali. I never imagined I'd be this excited to be at William P. Tate High School. I had broken my one rule when it came to this place; never date someone I worked with. Kahlia Mitchell was the exception.

"So far so good." She smiled in my direction. "Everyone has been welcoming; mostly I think, because my sister is their boss. How about you? How's your day so far?"

"Better now." I said wrapping my arms around her waist and bringing her closer to me. "So, I was thinking that I want to cook dinner for you tonight. You down to come by later on?"

"Josiah Mackenzie, you asking me on another date?" she

cooed wrapping her arms around my neck and I nodded my head. "What you tryna cook for me?"

"I make a mean Cajun pasta and I been craving it as much as I crave you."

"Stop it." She playfully rolled her eyes. "You be tryna game me."

"Is it working?" I chuckled and she shook her head laughing too.

"Maybe."

"I'm feeling you so much, I just want to spend as much time with you as possible. We can do dinner and a movie, then I can do you afterwards." I nuzzled my nose in her neck causing a girlish giggle to escape her lips. "I want to wake up to you tomorrow. Can we make that happen?"

"Ugh, I guess. You're so obsessed with me." I knew she said it in jest, but she didn't know the half. So, I responded the only way I could; truthfully.

"I really am." Hearing that seemed to sober her as she smirked sweetly. I placed a quick kiss on her nose then her lips before removing her from our embrace. "I got practice, but I get out at around 5:30. I gotta stop by the grocery store on my way home. You can meet me there later."

"I'll see you then." I got up from my seated position on her desk and walked towards the door. "Josiah—" she stopped me in my tracks. Turning around, I saw her biting her bottom lip as if she was struggling with a thought. "The feeling is mutual." Nodding in acknowledgment of her words, I made my way out of her class and down the hall so I could get back to my own classroom.

My heart seemed to expand, and butterflies rose in my stomach. Kahlia Mitchell had me sprung and on one hand, I enjoyed the feeling. On the other hand, it terrified me that I was putting my all into another woman. The fear of being hurt again always seemed to stay in the back of my mind. I wanted her, was absolutely obsessed with her yet a small part of me kept reminding myself of how I was played before.

As soon as I made it back to my classroom, my cell phone rang. Seeing it was my mom, I immediately answered.

"Good afternoon, Beautiful."

"Hi Sonshine." She replied in return. "How you doing?"

"I'm good Mama; first official day back to work. They gave us a break from the workshops we been doing to start setting up our classrooms. How you doing?"

"I'm good baby." She sighed. "Just was thinking about you; you been heavy on my mind all weekend. I don't know why but I felt like something was going on with you. Everything okay? Texas treating you right?"

"Everything is good this way Ma." I told her and then I contemplated telling her about Kali. "Actually, everything is better than good; it's great."

"Yeah? How so?"

"I met somebody, and I really like her a lot. It's all been happening fast, but Ma; I think this might be the one."

"Sonshine that makes me so happy." She gasped in awe. "You got a minute to tell your mama all about this woman?"

"Yeah, I got a minute." I sat down behind my desk. "Her name is Kali and she's absolutely beautiful. We met in Mexico and reconnected recently; she moved here to Dallas. Ma, I'm feeling this girl so bad it's ridiculous and honestly; it's scary as hell."

"You said you met her in Mexico? That was what a few months ago you told me you were going there?"

"Yeah, it was back in May." I sighed. "We spent three days together, then we kind of lost touch." I was stretching the truth. "But we reconnected a few days ago. She moved here, her sister is my boss, and she works here now. I wasn't expecting that, wasn't expecting to see her and I wasn't expecting for these feelings to be so raw and real."

"Sounds like you're in love Sonshine." I could hear the smile in her voice. "But I want you to take it slow Josiah. It's only been a few days since ya'll reconnected."

"And in those three days I haven't been able to get her off my mind. Even when she's next to me, I'm thinking about her. I think about what our lives will be like a year from now, five years from now and hell; even twenty years from now. But we both have our issues; mine being the obvious."

"And hers?"

"She was married before, lost her husband. She says she's getting over it, but I don't know mama; it sounds like she really loved that man. How the hell am I supposed to compete with that?"

"You don't Josiah." She sighed. "You just be your own self and have your own relationship with her. Don't go comparing the two and wondering about things that aren't relevant to the life you're trying to build with her. I can tell by the way you talk about her that she's something special. So, when does the woman who went through 12 hours of labor to get you here; get to meet this special someone?"

I bit down on my bottom lip. I knew the subject was going to come up. She always had a way of bringing it up without saying the words exactly. But was I ready to go there? Was I ready to see my family again after all of this time? And with Kali on my arm?"

"I don't know Mama." I told her truthfully. "I still need to figure some stuff out."

"Okay Sonshine." She relented with a deep sigh. "Well, you just let me know when you're ready and I'll make sure everything is set up on my end. I'll let you go; I know you're busy. I love you, Josiah."

"Love you Mama, talk to you later." Without another word, her end of the line disconnected.

PRACTICE WAS LONG AND EXHAUSTING, but I still found my spirits to be up knowing I was going to be spending my night with the woman who had been occupying my mind. After ending practice, I made my way back to my office, collected my things and then left the school.

I stopped at Kroger on my way home to grab some things for dinner then I stopped at the liquor store to grab a bottle of tequila and a few bottles of wine so we could celebrate our first day back to work. When I got home, I got comfortable; taking a shower then I turned on my speaker so I could listen to music while I cooked.

Right before I started cleaning my chicken, I pulled out my cell phone and shot a quick text to Kali to see if she was on her way.

> Hey beautiful, I made it home. You on your way?

> Kali: Yeah, I was in my groove with this painting. Give me about thirty minutes and I'll be there. Can't wait to see you.

> In my own groove in this kitchen with the music blasting. Code is 0523 for the door. Come right in.

Making sure my phone was connected to Bluetooth, I turned on my cooking playlist and then got started on dinner. The Cajun pasta I was making was something I didn't get to make that often because I didn't want to make the pot full only to eat it by myself. Tish had Rich on some kind of health kick since she was trying to lose the baby weight, so they weren't going to be able to help me eat it.

As I prepared this meal, I couldn't help but to think about

GENESIS CARTER

the fact that I was cooking it for somebody I planned on being around long term. When I bought my house, I bought it with the thought that my family would live here. But then, everything went down, and I couldn't back out of the deal, so I still packed up and left, just came a lot sooner than originally planned.

I had just finished frying my chicken breasts when I heard the door chime letting me know it was being opened. Looking toward my left, I smiled seeing Kali walking in with a small bag in her hand and a bottle of wine. I stopped what I was doing, going over to help her.

"What's up baby?" I asked giving her a quick peck on the lips.

"I brought wine." She gave me the bottle of wine in her hands.

"I got a couple of bottles as well and tequila. I figured we could celebrate our first day of work. Go get comfortable; I'll pour us a glass of wine; food is almost done."

"Okay." She smiled pulling me back down to her and taking another kiss. "It smells good. Make my glass of wine tall. I have paint everywhere, I'mma take a shower really quick." She walked off and I shook my head, knowing she wasn't kidding.

I went back to the chicken, placing it on a napkin covered plate to let it rest while I made the sauce. Just as I was stirring in the heavy cream to my sauce, Kali was walking out in a light pink pair of silk pajama shorts, and a button up top. Her hair was pinned up into a high bun and she had a pair of glasses on her face, looking at her phone.

"Parris thinks we're spending too much time together." She shook her head catching me off guard. I wasn't expecting the conversation to start this way.

"Whoa, you want some wine first?" I asked pushing her full wine glass towards her. She grabbed it, her long white fingernails wrapped around it. I watched her take a sip of her drink and went back to stirring my sauce, waiting for it to thicken. "Now, what's going on?"

"I think she's just concerned; it's been less than a week and we've spent every single day together since the night of the club." She shrugged. "She's just worried, which makes me believe she thinks I have something to worry about. Should I be concerned Josiah?"

"About what?" I snorted a laugh.

"You. Are you out here just going through the entire staff?"

"Nah." I laughed shaking my head. "Absolutely not. I don't usually date people I work with. You're the exception." I turned around and winked at her and she playfully rolled her eyes. "No seriously, I don't. A lot of them like me, but I ain't never showed no interest. And we've had conversations before about my previous dating life. We both have said we've had a few flings, nothing serious."

"I know; I just wanted to make sure I didn't have to be looking bitches upside they head every staff meeting or every time I passed them in the hallway."

"You ain't got nothing to worry about." I told her grabbing the pan for the sauce to pour it over the noodles which were resting. "Hey, do me a favor, can you check on the garlic bread?" From the corner of my eye, I saw her get up and come towards me, grabbing an oven mitt and I stepped to the side to allow her access to the oven. She placed the cookie sheet on the stove and then peered over to the pasta.

"That looks so good, and it smells good; I'm so excited to eat. You're tryna fatten me up?"

"Maybe." I shrugged moving over to the chicken and cutting it up into strips before placing them inside of the pot with the noodles and sauce. I continued to mix everything together then went to grab plates adding food to both of them then cutting the garlic bread and adding that as well. I placed her plate in front of her then grabbed my wine and my own plate, sitting beside her at the counter.

I bowed my head in a silent prayer before grabbing my fork, placing the first forkful of pasta into my mouth. To my right, an audible moan sounded causing a big smile to spread across my face as I looked over at Kali.

"Oh my gosh Babe, this is so good." She said before doing a little dance in her seat.

"Damn, I get all of that?"

"With any luck you might get a little extra." She winked.

"So, I talked to my Mom today."

"Yeah? How was it?"

"It was good, I told her about you." She didn't respond, but the scraping of her fork against the plate told me she probably had her mouth too full of food to respond. "She asked about meeting you." I glanced over at her, and her eyes were already on me. "I told her I would think about it."

"You think we're there?" she finally spoke, grabbing her wine glass and taking a long sip.

"Nah, we ain't gotta be." I shrugged. "I don't think I'm ready to go to Atlanta any time soon anyway."

"You think she's going to tell your family you met somebody serious?"

"Who said anything about me telling her it was serious?" I snorted. "I told her I met a big booty chick, and I was having some fun."

"Go to hell." She playfully pushed me. "I know ain't no black mama wanting to meet the big booty chick their son is just having fun with. Your mother wouldn't waste her time just like I wouldn't waste mine if I had a son."

"A son? What if you have a daughter?"

"Nah, I'm a boy mom. I helped raise Mason and the relationship I have with him is so important to me. God told me, he had plans for me to raise a couple of sons. Dark brown skin, hazel eyes." She looked up at me again. "They are going to be little heart breakers and I'mma have to keep all the girls away from them."

"How soon you tryna make that a reality? The little chocolate boys with the hazel eyes?"

"Not that soon." She shrugged. "But, neither of us is getting any younger and we agreed to not play games. We're both in this for the long haul, right?"

"Right." I agreed. "So, by the end of the year?"

"Josiah." She laughed shaking her head. "No."

"Oh, I was just checking because if you're ready I'm ready."

"Neither of us is ready. You should have seen your face in Mexico while we were in the jacuzzi."

"Oh, you mean when you let me raw dog you."

"Stop it." She groaned hiding her face with her hand. "We were in the heat of the moment, and I don't just go letting anybody do that. Your face before I told you about my birth control was hilarious; you were so scared."

"Hell yeah. I wasn't tryna make no accidental vacation baby."

"You're terrible." She laughed. "But I get it. That would have not been ideal."

"But one day, though, we gon make some babies. I'm all for practicing until we're ready."

"You're dangerous, do you know that?"

"So are you Kali Mac, so are you."

"Kali Mac?" she asked confused, and I nodded, placing the last of my pasta in my mouth then taking a sip of my wine glass.

"Manifesting it."

"You are so corny."

12

KAHLIA

The first day of school quickly came and went. Before I knew anything, weeks had passed, and I was acclimating perfectly to my new life. If you had asked me years ago if I saw myself teaching high schoolers the fundamentals of art, I would have laughed at you. I had taught a couple of private art classes, but I didn't think I would be this good with teaching as I was. I was enjoying myself so much, I had even asked about starting an after-school photography club. Most of my cameras had been collecting dust in my art room and I missed it.

My life outside of teaching was even better. Josiah and I were all but living together which was frustrating at times because he was such a neat freak and I was nine times out of ten, a hot mess. But he accommodated me and gave me space in his bathroom, drawers and even a small part of his closet.

"Ms. Mitchell, is this right?" Trenell, one of my students asked showing me her drawing. I'd had them drawing the scenery outside of my classroom window, the trees, the perfect view of the football field and the parking lot.

"Looks good, don't forget the shading on the trees." I grabbed her pencil and helped her a little.

"Thank you."

"Of course." I smiled just as the bell rang to end the 4th period class. "Okay everybody, hand in your materials, we'll finish up tomorrow. Everyone is doing such a great job, I'm so proud of ya'll. See ya'll tomorrow."

"Bye Ms. Mitchell." Multiple people said in unison as they handed in their things and then exited the class. I went over to my desk, monitoring as the stragglers left their drawings on my desk and exited. In just a few weeks, the class had come a long way. Some of the students were naturals, but for those who art didn't come natural for them, they seemed to be doing well also with a little bit of guidance.

Just as I was gathering the pencils, my cell phone rang. I quickly grabbed it up, seeing it was a Dallas number I didn't recognize and answered it.

"Hello?"

"Hi, is this Kahlia Mitchell?"

"It is, who am I speaking with?"

"My name is Delilah Robinson; I don't know if you remember me, but we met a few years back in Miami. You were there with a friend of mine, Antwan Ledger displaying some work."

"Yeah, I sort of remember. How can I help you?"

"I wanted to meet with you about something. I have an art gallery here in Dallas and I was hoping to discuss doing an exhibit of your work and some other opportunities I think you might be interested in."

"Wait, is this for real?"

"Yes. Antwan and I have been discussing you and he told me you moved to Dallas not too long ago. I purchased a couple of your pieces for my own personal collection, and I wanted to share your art with the city of Dallas."

Shocked was an understatement. I had spoken to Antwan a few weeks before I left Chicago and mentioned I was moving to Dallas. Antwan and I both went to Hampton and had been good friends for years, sharing our love for art. He never mentioned knowing someone who owned an art gallery in Dallas, not once.

"Listen, let's get something on the books so we can meet. When will you be free?"

"I um—I'm teaching at a high school so I can be available any time after 4 during the week."

"Good, let's meet say, Thursday evening? We can discuss this over dinner."

"Of course. Does 7pm sound okay?"

"It's perfect. I'll send you some details via text. It's a pleasure speaking with you Kahlia, have a good rest of your day."

"You too." I mumbled before disconnecting the call. "Oh my God."

The excitement building up in me was immeasurable. I wasn't even looking for anything here in Dallas; was choosing to focus on teaching until I built up a network here. Little did I know, God was working behind the scenes for me and thank God because in the past four weeks I'd finished 3 paintings and needed somewhere to display them. I had thought about putting them up for sale on my website, but for some reason I hadn't.

Continuing to gather up my supplies, I straightened my desk then grabbed my keys so I could meet Parris for lunch. We'd agreed last night to spend our lunch period together to get some sister time in. The last few days I'd been with Josiah during lunch but mostly because Parris was always so busy. I made my way out of my classroom, locking up and then headed towards the front office.

"Hey, you; you ready to head out for lunch?" I asked Parris walking into her office just after noon. I was hoping to take an extended lunch period, my next class wasn't until 2 and I was starving. Plus, after the phone call I'd just gotten off, I could use a celebratory cocktail with lunch. "I got some exciting news and I want to tell you all about it."

"I'm shocked, I thought for sure you were going to flake on me." She replied pushing back from her desk. "Let me grab my purse."

"What do you mean you thought I was going to flake on you?" I asked her confused.

"Nothing Kali, let's go I'm so hungry." She grabbed her bag then led the way out of her office before we made our way down the hall towards the back of the building where the teacher's parking lot was located. "You driving or you want me to?"

"I can drive." I mumbled still trying to figure out what the hell she meant.

I hadn't flaked on any plans I had with her, so it was a little off putting hearing her say that. After getting in the car and putting our seat belts on, I pulled out of the parking lot and the only sound in the car came from the radio which was on low. I was raking my brain trying to figure out what the hell Parris was talking about and after a while, I couldn't stand it anymore, so I decided to ask.

"What did you mean by you thought I would flake on you?"

"Dear God Kali, I knew it was just brewing." Parris sighed shaking her head. "I didn't mean nothing by it."

"Obviously you did, which is why you said it. And I'm hella confused because I don't flake on our plans."

"You've flaked on me a time or two. When we're supposed to hang out, you're suddenly going to Josiah's house or you're staying longer with him, so you don't come home and hang out with me."

"Really Parris?" I glanced over at my sister. "That's not fair."

"It's also not fair when I get stood up by my sister so she can hang with her little boyfriend. You were the same way with Jonathan. I should be used to it by now." I gripped the steering wheel tightly, so much so that my knuckles were visible. Biting down on my bottom lip, I tried to think about my words before I used them.

"Used to what Parris?"

"Used to you getting in a relationship and diving headfirst into these men. I mean, it's only been just under a month since you've been with him, and I barely see you. You came here to be with me and Mason, not to be all up under a nigga."

"Why are you so fucking pressed? I like spending time with my man, after not having one for years I think I've more than earned it. All that time I spent mourning Jonathan, refusing to get into anything serious and when I do; it's a problem?"

"I didn't say it was a problem, I'm glad you're happy. I just want you to stop rushing into things. You barely know him."

"I know enough." I scoffed. "I know that I have never felt what I feel for him, for anybody else including Jonathan. It's scary, but I'm trying to navigate it and wrap my mind around it. I'm fucking 32 years old Parris and Josiah is 35; we both agreed neither of us is trying to play games so yes, we're a little accelerated but is that a bad thing?"

"It can be, especially if you get hurt. What if it don't work out and now both of ya'll, who work together have issues?"

"I think we're adult enough to not let our personal issues affect our professional lives. And I mean, if it gets to be that big of a deal I will quit. Teaching isn't my first choice in jobs; I enjoy it, but I'm an artist first and foremost."

"Yeah, you say that now, I guess we'll see."

"We'll see? So, you praying on my downfall?"

"That's not what I said Kali, stop being ridiculous. Obviously, I want you to be happy, but like I said find some balance in it. You dived headfirst into Jonathan and when he wanted to go to Hampton, you went to Hampton. I asked you to move to Dallas a long time ago, but Jonathan wanted to stay in Chicago, so you stayed there."

"It's our hometown Parris, you act like it's some foreign country. I was staying with my husband, somewhere that was familiar for the both of us."

"All I ask is that you exercise a bit of caution. This thing with Josiah is still new. It's okay for you to spend time at the house for more than a few hours. Mason and I spent all that time convincing you to move here so we could have you with us, not for you to be off with yo nigga."

"Maybe if you were off with your nigga more often, you wouldn't be worrying about what I'm doing with mine." I mumbled and from the corner of my eye, I could see Parris' head snap in my direction.

"Excuse me?"

"What's up with Fabian? I know you've seen him a couple of times and from what you told me ya'll are really into each other. Maybe if you spent a little more time with him, then you wouldn't be worrying about me. You're done raising me Parris, I'm a big girl, I don't need you to hover."

"Hover? Girl, I tell you I want to spend more time with you, and you think I'm hovering? That's fucked up Kahlia, seriously. And don't fucking worry about what I got going on with Fabian; we are good around here. I just missed my fucking sister is all and the little bit of time I finally get with you; this is the bullshit you're on."

"We gon' act like you didn't start it? You made the comment about me flaking on you, knowing that hasn't happened."

"Okay Kahlia." She sighed shaking her head and picking up her phone from her lap. "I'm not about to argue with you about it. I said my peace."

"And I said mine."

∼

THE REST of my day was stressful. After coming back from lunch, I was in a bad mood, and I was glad when the bell rang for my final class because I needed some me time. I was irritated as hell about the things that Parris had said. I didn't think I was doing any of the things she said I was doing. I certainly had never flaked on her and for her to act like my relationship was a problem was disheartening. Of all people, she knew what my life had been like these past few years since Jonathan's death, she knew how hard it had been for me; and I finally get a little bit of happiness only for her to try to snatch it away.

Finally gathering my things, I left out of my classroom and made my way out of the parking lot; saying goodbye to students as they left. As I was pulling out of the teacher's parking lot, my cell phone rang; it was connected to my dash, so I answered seeing Josiah's name flash across the screen.

"Hey."

His side of the line was quiet for just a second before his voice boomed from the speakers of my car.

"What's wrong?"

"Nothing."

"Kali, tell me what's wrong. Where are you?"

"I'm headed home Josiah."

"I figured as much when you didn't come to my office and meet up like we normally do. You ain't gon' tell me what's wrong?"

"Nothing's wrong." I lied again, knowing the words Parris

said to me were still roaming around in my brain. I hated it, hated that the things she said were getting to me like this.

"Okay, you don't want to talk about it right now; cool."

"There's nothing to talk about honestly." Another lie.

"Kahlia, who you tryna convince me or you?"

"Neither of us. Listen, I'm getting another call. I'll talk to you later."

"Say less." He responded before disconnecting the call. Shaking my head, I felt a flood of tears threatening to release from my eyes. I didn't know why I was being like this with him, it wasn't his fault. But he was the reason for the problems I was having with my sister; problems I didn't even know I had.

True enough we'd spent a lot of time together in the past few weeks; but I thought that was normal for new couples. I craved him, craved his presence so I felt like it was only right for me to be with him so much. Josiah was like a light at the end of a very dark tunnel for me. Any time I got to spend with him was treasured and I didn't think I was wrong for wanting to constantly have that feeling of trust, comfort, and love around me.

Love… It was a word I had been battling with in relation to my feelings for him for quite some time. The more time I spent with him, the more I thought about it; love had been present from the beginning and I just didn't even know it. There was no doubt in my mind that he was the man for me, the man who was sent to me from God. From the outside looking in, people would think we were rushing into things, but for me at least; I didn't think we were moving fast enough.

I wanted to love on him every minute of every hour of every single day; that's how attached I felt to him. His light was very present in my life and if that kind of thing wasn't sent from God, then what other reason was there to explain it? I liked to think I knew he felt the same way, even though neither of us had said those three little words every couple in any relationship longed to hear. I felt it from him. I felt it in the way he handled me, in the affirmations he spoke into me, I felt it in the time we spent away from one another; I was so deeply in love with this man; there could never be any denying it. So, why was that a problem? What was so wrong about that? Love doesn't wait for time to catch up, when you know, you know, and I knew back in Mexico.

So, I called Josiah back not wanting there to be any issues between us. I needed his peace, and I needed that comfort that only he seemed to be able to offer me lately.

"Kali Mac…"

"I'm sorry." I said immediately, sighing hard. "There is something wrong and I just, I didn't know how to wrap my brain around it. I won't get too deep into it; but Parris said—"

"Parris is always saying something Kali."

"I know and I hate that I'm letting her get to me. I think I need to take a break from her for a while. I was thinking, maybe I could stay at your place for a little bit?"

"You can stay forever if you need to." He replied and I knew without a shadow of a doubt that he was being serious. He had hinted a few times about us moving in together, especially since we already spent so much time together; but I didn't think it was the right time for it. All the love in the world couldn't prepare me to move in with another man, especially one as OCD as Josiah.

"I was thinking for like a week or two."

"Whatever you need Kali Mac. Aye, listen I gotta go, practice is about to start. I'll see you at home?"

"Yeah, I'll see you at home." I smiled. "Josiah—" my line got quiet, I wanted to say the words I felt in my soul, but I couldn't bring myself to do it just yet. Fear for whatever reason, consumed me. "Never mind; I'll see you later." Again, we disconnected our call, and I made my way to the home I was sharing with my sister and nephew.

I knew Parris was not going to be happy when she found out I was leaving for a little bit, but I also didn't expect her to be surprised. After we had our disagreement at lunch, we didn't speak to each other the entire time. We'd both hit a nerve with some of the things we said, and when we had disagreements like that, it used to be easier since I lived in a different state. But now, I lived in her home, and I wasn't interested in the awkwardness.

I pulled up to the house not long after and I immediately went upstairs to pack some of my things. I contemplated taking some of my art materials, finally settling on moving the picture I was working on along with one other canvas. It was another hour before I was all packed and had everything in the car. Just as I was putting the last canvas in the trunk of my truck, Parris and Mason were pulling up.

"What's this?" Parris asked getting out of her car and coming to mine. "You moving out?"

"I'm getting some space." I replied. "I'm not in the mood to go back and forth with you. The conversation earlier really irritated me, and it pissed me off quite frankly."

"Okay Kahlia, you know you're such a fucking brat."

"Pot or the Kettle Parris?" I closed my trunk before making my way over to the driver's side of the car. "It's just for a few weeks. We've done this before only difference is I'm not hundreds of miles away anymore. We both know we need time to cool off after earlier."

"Yeah, but we work together Kahlia."

"Yeah, I know. And I need a break anyway. Listen, I gotta go. I love you." I placed a kiss on her cheek before getting into my car and pulling out of the driveway leaving her staring after me.

I cried the entire way to Josiah's house. I cried because I was an emotional wreck. The argument with Parris completely disarmed me in the most uncomfortable way. Her bringing up my relationship with Jonathan was alarming because I wasn't expecting her to compare the two. I felt different with Josiah then I was with Jonathan. I felt more alive and that in of itself was heartbreaking.

I didn't understand Parris' issue. She claimed she wanted me to be happy, but when I finally found happiness after four years, she told me it was wrong. And maybe she hadn't said it in those exact words, but she made me feel like my relationship with Josiah was wrong. I couldn't help the way I felt about him, and I couldn't change it either.

It didn't take me long to get to Josiah's home. When I did arrive, I pulled my car into the driveway on the right side since he usually parked on the left; then I grabbed the bags I'd packed lugging them to the front door and entering the keycode for the lock. By now, my tears had dried up, but the sorrow, the hurt, hadn't changed. I thought I was on the right path; thought I was doing something worthwhile only for Parris' words to keep echoing through my head. That conversation completely overshadowed the call I'd gotten earlier.

I placed my bags in the bedroom before going back out for the art supplies. I hoped Josiah would accommodate me with space to create. I was sure he would, so I placed those things inside of the first guest room on the left then I made my way back into the bedroom so I could put my things away.

Once everything was put away, I undressed getting comfortable in a pair of biker shorts and a cropped tank top. My hair which was in knotless braids was pinned up on top of my head. I went into the kitchen, poured a glass of wine, and then made my way to the back where he had a covered porch with a nice patio set. It was hot as hell in Dallas, hotter than normal but I needed the peace of the outdoors to try to clear my head.

I didn't know how long I'd been sitting out on the back patio, scrolling my social media before I heard the back door being opened. When I looked up, I saw that Josiah was dressed down in a pair basketball shorts and a wife beater.

"Hey." He sat down next to me, reaching for me and absentmindedly I climbed into his lap burying my head in his neck inhaling his scent. The moment he started rubbing my back, the tears started flowing down my face and I wrapped my arms around him.

Neither of us spoke as we sat together, wrapped in each other's arms. I had, had a bad day and this was the comfort I needed. No words needed to be exchanged in order for me to communicate that I needed him, and he understood that.

After a while, my sobs died, and my eyes got heavy. Resting in his arms, while a slight breeze hit us was relaxing, it was peaceful, it was comfortable. Four months ago, when I met him, I didn't know how much being in his arms would come to mean to me. This man… this man that God sent to me, was my everything and regardless of how anybody else felt about it; I knew that we were right.

"Can I say something to you, and you won't think I'm weird? No judgment?" I asked Josiah as I laid on his chest, his arms still wrapped firmly around me.

"We've never had any judgment between us from the beginning Love, it won't start today." He replied rubbing my back. "Tell me."

"I believe in soul ties." I started, nervous about expressing the information I needed to convey. "I believe that God keeps giving us chances to get it right just in different lives."

"Okay, I can see that."

"And I don't know Josiah, I think we may have loved each

other in a couple of those past lives. How else do you explain this intense connection we have and have had since we first met? I don't think that it was a coincidence that we were there together, or that we're here together. What if regardless of what life we have, we're always going to find each other? I know it sounds silly."

"It doesn't. I have been thinking about why this is so comfortable, why it feels so right and what you just said makes more sense than anything else I could come up with."

"I had a dream the other night and I think it was a memory of one of those past lives."

"Tell me about it."

"I just remember us being in Africa, speaking what I came to learn was Swahili and although I didn't speak it, I understood it perfectly. We were standing in the sun, embracing one another. I think you were a King, and I was your Queen. The love, the mutual respect, the comfortability, it was so familiar. We were surrounded by our children; 3 boys and 2 girls, we were so happy; we were in love. I want that again; I want that with you."

"I'm going to give it to you Kali. I'm never going to let you go, you understand." I nodded wrapping my arms tighter around him.

"I think that maybe we had to go through what we did in order to get to each other. I loved Jonathan, like I'm sure you loved your ex. But we lost them and found each other. It sucks that we had to go through it all. Jonathan was a good person. I wouldn't wish death on my worst enemy especially not the way he went, but I can't shake the feeling that even if he hadn't passed, I would have found my way to you."

"You think so?"

"I feel it." I replied feeling my emotions getting the best of me again. I had cried enough today and didn't want to shed any more tears. "I feel it in my bones, I feel it in my soul. I think you were made for me, and I was made for you. This shit is-- scary and beautiful and insane." I looked up at him as a tear pooled over, falling from my eye. Josiah reached down and wiped it. My mouth opened and closed several times, trying to be brave enough to say the words I needed to say to him; words I hoped he would reciprocate.

"Tell me."

"I'm in love with you. I've been in love with you from the beginning. I knew it in Mexico which is why I left you the way I did. I was scared because if I loved you after three days, what did that mean about the love I had for Jonathan? Was that even real?"

"It was real, baby. What you had with him was real and you can't discount it. But what we have is real as well." He sighed shaking his head. "When I found out you left the way you did, I was shattered. That feeling of loss, it hit me differently. I thought losing Angie was bad but losing you was like getting hit by a train running full speed. I knew the moment I left that resort that what I was doing, was mourning the loss of a deep love. That shit was crazy Kali. I knew I wouldn't be myself again until I had you back in my life. And when I saw you again, everything just felt… right. So, I said all of that to say, I love you too."

Overwhelmed with emotions, I leaned up, placing my lips against his. Tears continued to cascade down my face. I straddled him, melting into his body as he wrapped his arms around me.

Hearing him tell me he loved me was everything. I wasn't exaggerating my feelings. I was completely in love with Josiah and while these feelings were confusing and scary, I knew they were real. I knew that I loved him more than anything in this world and I knew that I would love him like this until the end of my days.

13

KAHLIA

"Kahlia? It's so nice to meet you." Delilah smiled as I stepped foot into Evermore Gallery. It was in a good location in north Dallas towards downtown. It had taken me nearly 40 minutes to get here. Parking wasn't ideal, it took me another twenty minutes to figure out the parking situation before I was finally able to walk in here.

"You too." I smiled accepting her handshake. I gazed around the gallery, impressed by the décor; what I loved even more was the talent lining the walls. "This place is amazing."

"Thank you." She smiled walking beside me as I walked around the space. I was excited to even be considered to have my paintings on these walls.

"Impressed?"

"Very." I finally looked at her. "I'm sorry, I'm fangirling a little bit here."

"It's fine girl, we all do it." She waved me off. "Should we head out? We can walk; the place I texted you about is just a block or two away, we can chat on the way there."

"Okay." I agreed and we made our way out of the building, with her locking up behind us. "So, what made you reach out to me?"

"Antwan. He showed me some of your work and he told me you were moving here. My goal with you, is to explore a whole new collection for you. Have you been creating anything new?"

"Yes." I nodded. "Since I've been here, I've just found myself very inspired."

"Good." She smiled. "Can I ask what has inspired you?" I smirked, trying hard not to blush as I thought about Josiah. "A man?" I looked at her shocked. "Yeah, it's definitely a man." That remark caused a chuckle to escape both of our lips. "That will do it every time."

"Do you create as well?"

"No, I'm just a fan and a collector. I opened my gallery about ten years ago and built it into what it is today."

"That's dope. I had a small space in Chicago before I left, for my art and photography; but when I decided to make the move, I gave up the space. I was hoping to do something similar here in Dallas; so, any help you wouldn't mind giving me would be amazing."

"Of course. Mine is the only black owned art gallery in Dallas. Whenever I find talented black artist, I always want to reach out and help. That's why I wanted to meet up with you. Not only to get your work in my gallery, but also for other things which we'll discuss." She looked up at a building and nodding with her head said, "This is us." She opened the door to the restaurant, and we walked in.

"Welcome to Armani's." the hostess smiled. "Did you have a reservation?"

"Yes, for Robinson." Delilah replied and the hostess nodded, pressing a few buttons on her pad.

"Right this way." She waved us on and walked us into the restaurant, towards the back. "Your waiter will be right with you. Enjoy." With a smile she was off. The menus were already at the table, and I grabbed mine mulling over the different options.

We sat in silence for a minutes before the waiter came, introducing himself as Adrian and taking our drink orders.

"So, let's talk about you. You mentioned on the phone that you were teaching, how'd you get into that?"

"My sister is a vice principal at the school I'm teaching at. When I moved here, she convinced me to apply for the job just temporarily until I could get myself together. I actually like it; I've met so many talented kids and I have enjoyed seeing their creativeness grow."

"Young talent is amazing, isn't it? How long do you plan on doing it?"

"Um, I hadn't thought about it." I shrugged. "Not long. I was going to try it out for this school year and figure out the rest later."

"I'm asking because I am planning on moving to New York soon and I was hoping to find someone to help me run things. I've been considering a few people and you're one of the people I was hoping to speak with about it."

"Wow, really? Why me?"

"Because you would appreciate it the most." She chuckled. "And as you mentioned, you did have your own space in Chicago. So, is that something you'd be interested in? I know we still need to iron out some info about your art being in the gallery, but I figured I'd throw that in there for a little extra razzle dazzle." I laughed at that just as the waiter came back with our drinks.

"Yeah, it's definitely something I'd be interested in."

"Well, let's toast to it." She said grabbing her drink. "To new opportunities and new beginnings."

"New beginnings."

"So how was it?" Josiah asked the moment I entered his home. He was sitting on the couch, playing his PlayStation. With a smile on my face, I stepped out of my shoes before putting my keys in the small bowl on the table beside the door.

"It was good. She's looking for a few pieces to put into the gallery. I might start something new just for that." I sat down next to him, placing a quick peck on his lips.

"I like the ones you did already baby, what about those?"

"Those are special." I replied. "And they are for me, personally. When I get a place, I'm going to hang them up."

"You got this place." He chuckled and I glanced over at him. "And don't look at me like that, we both know you not getting your own place. When you're ready to move out of Parris' that means you're going to be ready to finally move in with me."

"This test trial for the next week or so will tell me if I want to consider moving in here."

"Okay Kali Mac, whatever you say baby."

I shook my head. Josiah was dead set on us moving in together. In a month we'd already been spending a lot of time together, more than I'd spent with any man since Jonathan passed. But when you love somebody, you wanted to spend as much time with them as humanly possible.

"Let's say we do move in together; can I make a few changes?"

"Changes like what?" he glanced over at me for a few seconds before turning back to his game.

"Décor changes Josiah. Your place is nice, but it's giving bachelor vibes. I want to add a little color to it. And that bedroom I've been using to paint, I'd want to fully convert that into my art room; would you be okay with that?"

"Yeah, I'm cool with that. I planned on moving that bed out of there anyway to give you more space. I'm pretty handy so if you need me to build you something, we can design it however you want."

"And what about changing the décor?"

"I guess I'd be cool with that. I been in here by myself for so long, I might pout about it, but I'll be okay. I want you to be comfortable here."

"Well, we won't have to consider making changes just yet. We're still on a test run."

He mumbled something under his breath, and I chuckled. I didn't know what he said, but I was sure it had something to do with this not being a test run. I knew him well enough to know he was probably concocting some scheme to keep me here in his head.

"I'm going to wind down and shower. Don't stay out here too long playing 2K."

"Got you." I stood up and kissed him again. I could never get enough of his full lips.

Making my way to the bedroom, I quickly undressed, placing my dirty clothes in the laundry basket, and then starting a shower. Finding my phone, I turned the Bluetooth speaker on so I could listen to music while I did my nighttime routine.

I was so excited about my new opportunity with the gallery, and I was appreciative of Delilah for giving it to me. I had to remind myself to reach out to Austen as well to thank him.

After my shower, I grabbed my phone and climbed into bed so I could scroll Tik Tok until Josiah got in bed. As I was scrolling, a text came through on my phone.

> Mason: Can we have a Tee-Tee/Nephew date this weekend?"

WHEN IT COMES TO YOU

Smiling I clicked into the text thread and started my reply.

> Of course, my love. Anything you want to do in particular?

I saw the three dots letting me know he was typing, and I waited for the reply.

Mason: We can go to Cinepolis and see a movie. They got food there so we can eat dinner too.

> I got you, which movie you want to see I'll order the tickets now.

Mason: Saw X

> Okay, I'll get the tickets now. Get some sleep. I love you.

Mason: Love you too.

Smiling, I went on to the Cinepolis website and ordered two tickets for us. Just as I went back to Tik Tok, Josiah came into the room, sliding into bed.

"What you smiling about?"

"Got a hot date this weekend." I teased.

"With who?" he scoffed causing a chuckle to escape my lips.

"Mason. He requested some alone time with his favorite aunt so of course I'm making it happen."

"Oh, that's dope, what ya'll gon get into?"

"Dinner and a movie at Cinepolis. He wants to see the new Saw movie."

"Cinepolis is dope. It's a little ice cream spot called The Cauldron nearby. If it's cool, I can meet ya'll."

155

"Yeah, that will be nice." I said plugging my phone on the charger then placing it on the nightstand. I snuggled under the covers as Josiah wrapped his arm around me.

"I've had Mason in a couple of my classes. He's a good kid."

"He's the best kid. I was only 16 when he was born, and Parris was taking care of both of us. I helped out where I could; mostly watching Mason and stuff after school. He's the sweetest person I know."

"You're the sweetest person I know." He tipped my head so I could look at him before placing his lips on mine. "I love you."

"I love you too."

14

JOSIAH

"Coach Mackenzie? What's up? How can I help you?" Parris asked after I slightly knocked on her office door. I was carrying a bag from Jamaica Mi Happy, a restaurant I'd heard from Kali that she enjoyed a lot.

It wasn't something I asked about, Kali had been talking about Parris since she'd temporarily moved into my place to get her space. She missed her sister; I knew it and I understood it. I would be lying if I said I didn't miss Joshua sometimes, despite the bullshit he helped put me through. Before everything happened, Joshua was my best friend, my literal A1 since day 1. I missed him like crazy but forgiving him was harder than I could have ever imagined.

With Kali and Parris, their issues were easily solvable; and since they involved me, I was going to do what I could to fix it. I'd never had a bad relationship with Parris before; we'd had a good and cordial work relationship. The problem is she didn't know me outside the walls of this school which is mostly my fault because I didn't let a lot of people into my world, not after the betrayal I experienced. Somehow, for some reason, Kali had been the exception.

"Good afternoon Ms. Nettles, I was hoping we could have lunch together and talk about some stuff. Kahlia told me you liked this place, so I wanted to extend and olive branch." She sighed and for a second, I thought she'd tell me to go to hell; but I knew the food was smelling good, it had my stomach rumbling with hunger the longer I held it in my hands.

"What's in the container?"

"Kahlia said you liked the fillet snapper with rice & peas and cabbage; so that's what I got." She licked her lips before biting down on the bottom one. I could tell from the inquisitorial look on her face that she was contemplating if she wanted to have this conversation with me. I could admit, having it here, at work, was not ideal; but I didn't think a pop up at her home would be a better option.

"Is there hot sauce?"

"Yeah. And she said you liked Dr. Pepper; so, I got you one of those as well." I smirked with a slight nod.

"Fine, come in and close the door." I turned to close the door behind me and then proceeded over to her desk, sitting down in one of the chairs on the opposite side of her. I placed the bag on the desk and handed her, her container. "Kali know you're here?"

"She knows I offered to buy you lunch; I took her some food already. She's letting some of the kids finish their work in her class so, I took it upon myself to come up here and see if we could talk." She grabbed her container and opened it before immediately digging in.

"So, what do you want to talk about?"

"Your sister." I told her plainly. "There seems to be some discord because of my relationship with her. I know things are happening fast for us and you're looking out for her but I'm having a hard time seeing why it almost feels like you're trying to dissuade her from getting close to me. I just honestly want to resolve whatever ill feelings you have or at least come to an understanding so we can move on. I fully intend to be in her life for the long haul."

"The long haul huh?" she scoffed. "Ya'll just met and already it's the long haul?"

"We just met and already I know I love her more than anybody else in this world." There was a pause filled with nothing but silence as we stared at one another. Shaking her head, she placed her fork in her container and scooped some of the rice and peas in her mouth. "I know it sounds ridiculous; hell, if it wasn't happening to me, I wouldn't believe it myself."

"How do you know it's love and not lust? My sister is a good person Josiah, and her last relationship left her weakened. I'm not trying to see that happen to her a second time."

"That's different, her last relationship only ended because her husband died. I would expect any person male or female to be left weakened after an experience like that."

"You don't understand, Kahlia loved that man so much that her life was completely different without him. She stopped doing a lot of things she loved including producing her art because of the love she had for him."

"And now I'm the muse who is pushing her to achieve her dreams." I shrugged. "You don't know me and that's fine; I can tell you that I'm a good person too. I was raised right, my parents are still married, still together so I know what healthy relationships look like. I can assure you that your sister is in good hands with me."

"Just like that, you expect me to be okay with all of this? She's my baby sister, I helped raise her. In some ways, she is my child."

"But we both know she's not a child. Your sister is not even capable of being taken advantage of. She's one of the strongest, most beautiful, and amazing black women I know. I can see that she was raised well, and I thank you for your part in that. I don't want there to be no bad blood between ya'll because you don't want us to be together."

"I never said I didn't want ya'll to be together. I told her, things were moving fast and to slow down. But now I see somebody should be telling you the same thing. Ya'll all in bliss now, but what happens in ya'll first disagreement? Kahlia is mean Josiah, and I don't know you from John; how I know you ain't the ill-tempered kind of man."

"I'm not. I'm a good dude and I hope my actions from the time that you've known me while we've worked together can speak a little bit to my character. And I hope that you will be willing to get to know me better as well. Like I said, I'm in this for the long haul with Kali. I'm not going anywhere unless she wants me to."

"I see." She sighed placing her fork down and crossing her hands in front of her. "You said you loved her, have you told her that?"

"I have."

"And she said it back?"

"She said it first. There is no way for me to explain what this is between us. Hell, I've been just as confused about it since the first day I saw her in Mexico. That woman is special to me, she makes me feel like I can be and do anything in this world as long as she's by my side. This ain't a game for me; hell, I'm too old for games. I'm looking for a wife, somebody to have kids with and in such a short amount of time I know that person is going to be your sister."

"How do you know?"

"Because I feel like we've done this before. She said something to me a week ago; she said she believed we knew each other in past lives and without a doubt I felt it too. She is mine and I am hers. There has to be a reason why our lives are playing out like this. That woman is my wife both mentally and spiritually. It's not going to be much longer before I make her my wife in this lifetime as well."

"Sheesh. Kali is a lucky girl. I don't understand it and I probably never will; but I respect it. I love my sister and I just want the best for her. All I ask from you, since you plan on being around for a while; is don't hurt my sister."

"Listen, I'mma tell you something about myself that's personal. I don't talk to many people here, but since we're practically family—" I smirked playfully in her direction, and she shook her head with a snort of a laugh. "I'mma tell you how I ended up here in Dallas from Atlanta."

"I'm listening." She picked her fork back up and continued eating.

"I was engaged before—"

"Engaged?"

"Yeah. She was my college sweetheart. I met her and thought we were building our lives together. My best friend Rich and his wife moved here to Dallas about a year or two before I did, and Rich convinced me to move here as well. I came down for a trip to look at a few houses and left my ex at home, during that trip. When I got home, I found out she'd been with my brother, in our home, in our bed. So, I left Atlanta and haven't been back since."

"Damn, that's—I'm sorry that happened to you."

"It's all good." I shrugged. "I've moved on. But I say all of that to say, I've been hurt like that before. I have no intention of ever having Kali feeling that level of pain; not from me, not ever."

"You talk a good game Josiah Mackenzie, make sure you can back it up. I don't fuck around when it comes to my baby sister."

"Good because neither do I."

GENESIS CARTER

∼

"You got her living with you and shit?" Rich asked as we sat in my living room playing Call of Duty. Kali was in her art space, painting, with her music blasting.

She was trying to give me my space, but I didn't want any space from her. All I craved all day every day was to be near her. Rich showed up needing a break from the baby and she moseyed off into the room to paint.

"She's staying here for a minute. She had got into it with her sister, but I lowkey ain't tryna let her go home. Ya boi in deep Rich."

"I see." He laughed, pushing me. "I like this look for you. You seem really happy brodie."

"I ain't been this happy in a while." I admitted. "I think I'mma take her home to meet Ma Dukes."

"Damn for real? You taking yo ass home finally and with Shorty on your arms? Shit is gon get real. What you think Ang gon' think?"

"I honestly don't give a fuck." I shrugged. "I ain't thinking about that damn girl. She got her life and her new baby, and I got my life here. I'm going to see my mama and pops."

"When you gon go?"

"Probably try to ring in the new year there. Kali been heavy on this Lucky Daye shit, and he got a small show in Atlanta a few days before New Years Eve. I figured I'd take her to the show, then we ring in the new year with Ma Dukes and Pops; a little getaway before we come back here for work."

"That sounds like a bet. I know Tish was talking about going home soon too. Shoot me the details and we probably go with ya'll."

"Will do."

"I meant to tell you, they coming here with the baby in a

few weeks. I figured I'd tell you now, so you have a heads up. I think it's at the end of the month, some shit Tish and Ang set up."

"Oh yeah? Thanks for letting me know so I can steer clear of yo crib. Guess Imma miss my visits with Riley during that time."

"Or you can come through with ya girl and we can chill. Shit, you happy in yo relationship now, why not show them that?"

"I don't need to show them shit and they don't get to know shit about my life."

"Yeah a'ight." He sighed shaking his head. "But aye, let me get my ass home before Tish starts calling me. The baby been kicking both our asses and I need to go give her a little break."

"Bet." I stood up and dapped him up before giving him a quick hug. "Hit me tomorrow and be safe driving home Rich." He nodded and started heading to the door just as the door to the guest room where Kali had been holed up, opened. She was wearing a pair of biker shorts and one of my t-shirts. Her braids were pinned up on her head and she had a scarf tide around them. There were a few paint smudges on her face, almost as if she'd absentmindedly swiped her face.

"You leaving?" she asked Rich and he nodded.

"Yeah, I gotta go relieve Tish." Rich told her. "But I was telling Mac that we wanted to have ya'll over for dinner sometime soon. Tish been asking about you. She still can't believe Mac got a girlfriend."

"I'd love to have dinner with ya'll, just let us know when." Kali replied coming to my side and wrapping her arm around my waist. "It was good to see you, be safe."

"Good to see you too Kali, ya'll be good." Rich waved one last time before exiting the house. Turning to look up at me,

Kali smiled, and I bent down swiping my finger over the paint smudge.

"You made a mess." I said before placing a kiss on her lips.

"I always do." She playfully rolled her eyes.

"How's it going in there?"

"It's going." She shrugged. "I missed you, so I had to come out. I didn't run Rich off with my loud music, did I?"

"Nah, he be having his shit so loud I swear he gon' go deaf soon." I chuckled. "You hungry? I can whip us up something really quick."

"I am hungry, but not for food." Her eyebrow bounced up and down in a playful manner causing me to laugh. "I'mma go run a shower. You save your little game and meet me in the bathroom?"

"Abso-fuckin-lutely." I bent down placing another kiss on her lips, swiping my tongue against hers before pulling back.

"Don't be long." She said removing herself from our embrace as she turned around, I slapped her ass causing a girlish giggle to escape her lips. I watched her as she walked down the hall, her hips swaying as she walked off. I bit down on my bottom lip, loving the view of her ass poking out in the shorts. Her body was beautiful, both with and without clothes on.

I walked over to the front door and locked it before coming back and finding a place for me to save my game. Once that was done, I made sure the house was locked up and lights were off before making my way to the bedroom where I heard the shower running. I undressed from the bedroom door to the bathroom door. When I entered the bathroom, Kali was already in the shower waiting on me.

The moment I entered the shower, Kali dropped down to her knees looking up at me expectantly. I stroked my dick, turning so my back was to the steady stream of hot water. I rubbed my mushroom head along her thick lips and groaned at the prospect of my dick being in her mouth.

"Open." I ordered and she obliged without hesitation. When her tongue snaked out and licked my pre-cum, I couldn't help the groan that escaped my lips. With her eyes trained on me, I slowly fed her my dick until she gagged. "Fuck Kali." I held onto the wall as she bobbed up and down my shaft, her lips swollen, and her eyes filled with lust. "I fucking love you."

15

KAHLIA

After spending a little over two weeks with Josiah at his home, I figured it was time for me to have a conversation with my sister. We still hadn't spoken much outside of work and when I went to pick up Mason for our date, she was in her room and hadn't come out despite her knowing I was there.

I wasn't even 100 percent sure if I wanted to come back, but I also didn't want to overstay my welcome at Josiah's. So, after I finished up at work, I made my way to her house so we could have a conversation.

I tried to practice in my head along the drive of what I could say, what I would say. I knew that she and Josiah had, had a conversation but now it was time for our conversation. I hated these make up conversations Parris and I had after we fought, they were always so awkward, just as awkward as the original fight. Still, when I pulled up in front of her house twenty minutes later, I got out of the car and made my way inside using my key to open the door.

When I walked into the house, I could hear music blasting and the smell of fried chicken filled my nostrils. As I turned the corner from the door, I saw Parris in the kitchen dancing to Teena Marie's *Square Biz*. I walked over to the countertop and rested my chin on the palm of my hand watching as she flipped the chicken and twirled around, twirling until her eyes landed on me.

"What the fuck Kali?" she held her hand against her chest. "Alexa, pause music." I couldn't help the laugh that escaped my mouth. It was so genuine, so loud, so boisterous and it was so real. "It's not funny you fucking asshole, what the hell are you doing here?"

"I live here, or did you forget?" I asked walking over to the plate of chicken that she had cooling off. I snagged a piece, breaking some of it off before placing it in my mouth savoring the crispy skin.

"I didn't forget, but you obviously did. What, did you come to get more clothes?"

"I came to talk Parris." I sighed leaning against the counter and looking over at her as she continued to cook. "Where's Mase?"

"Upstairs doing homework."

"You cooking a lot of food, you got company coming over?"

"I done got used to cooking for three." She shrugged. "I always keep extra for you. I don't know why, I'm wasting food."

"Parris, we gotta stop doing this." I told her. "I know I probably shouldn't have left the way I did but I just felt like I needed to get away."

"You've been running away like that since you were little Kahlia. Anytime you didn't agree with something somebody said to you, you seem to think you can't face your problems."

"Except this wasn't my problem Parris, this was yours. I know you had a conversation with Josiah, and I appreciate you for having it. This thing with us, is real. I'm in love with him."

"He told me." She mumbled glancing over at me. "Is it real?"

"I feel it in my soul; I feel him in my soul. That man is for me Parris, I'm telling you. It's so hard to explain and it may seem ridiculous to somebody looking from the outside in but, I'm so in love with him."

"I just don't want you to get hurt Kali."

"I don't want to be hurt either. But, if I am, that's life. You can't protect me from everything Parris. I'm a big girl, I can handle things. I appreciate you though, so much for all that you have done and continue to do for me." She didn't respond but I could tell she was just letting my words sink in.

"So, you coming back home?"

"I was thinking about it." I said finishing off the piece of chicken I was eating.

"He doesn't want you to leave though, I know it."

"He doesn't. But I don't want us to be consumed with one another. Not fully, not just yet."

"He's going to marry you, Kahlia." Parris whispered before looking over at me. "And I think you're going to say yes. Imagine that you having two great loves in your lifetime and I'm still struggling to have just one."

"Fabian seemed like a nice candidate. What's up with that?" I saw the smile appear on her face, before she tried to quickly remove it.

"I like him, a lot; but I'm taking things slow. I don't want Mason to feel some type of way."

"Girl, Mason doesn't care." I chuckled. "When we went on our little date he told me as much. He said he be hearing you on the phone giggling like a little girl and know you talking to some man. He just wants you to be happy Parris, and so do I. I get taking it slow, but also, we're too old to be pussyfooting around. Make your intentions clear, make your expectations clear and if he can't handle either then move on and find somebody who can. But I hope he can; he's cute and if you had another baby with him that kid would be so cute."

"Girl, I am not thinking about no more damn kids." She laughed, waving me off. "But, speaking of kids… the way Josiah talks about you; I'd swear he's ready to pop a few in you and soon. How do you feel about that?"

"I mean." I tried hard to contain the smile that threatened to spread across my face. Truth is, having kids had been heavy on my mind especially now that I was in my thirties and my biological clock was ticking. "I think about it sometimes, but I want to enjoy him for a little while longer. And I also need to be married. Having kids out of wedlock is not for me."

"Trust me, having them in wedlock ain't no better. Lamar was a piece of shit husband and father. At this point I could have had a baby with anybody married or not and it would have been better than him. But I'm grateful to have Mason and I wouldn't trade him for the world."

"He's the best person I know." I let her know. "My life wouldn't be the same without him so thank you for that. I'm not his mom, but he's taught me so much about raising a kid. You did such a good job with him Parris, seriously."

"Appreciate that." She smiled before placing the last batch of chicken to rest on the plate. "You staying for dinner?"

"Yeah, I'll stay. Let me just text Josiah to let him know." Pulling out my phone I saw that it was just now 5pm which meant he should have been getting out of practice.

"Invite him, there's more than enough." Nodding, I went into our text thread and sent a message.

> Hey, I'm at Parris' was going to stay for dinner. She wanted me to invite you.

I waited before seeing the three dots moving to let me know he was responding.

> Josiah: Bet. Practice just ended, I'll hit you up when I get close. I miss you.

> I miss you too. See you soon.

"You ain't even gotta be smiling that hard." Parris snorted with laughter. "Girl, that nigga dick must be immaculate because ain't no way you sprung already."

"Alexa, play *I'm Sprung* by T-Pain." I called out and after a few seconds the song started playing and I started dancing to it, while singing the lyrics causing Parris to roll her eyes.

∼

I LOOKED over at Josiah as I packed the last of my things into my bags. He wasn't happy, but we'd talked about this several times. I'd been here long enough, yet he was trying to hold me here forever.

"Stop looking at me like that." I sighed. "You've known all week this was my plan."

"I don't like this, Kali. I want you here with me, waking up next to me every morning and in my bed every night like we've been doing."

"Josiah—"

"You can just move in. I mean we already on the fast track, there is no need for you to be holding up space at Parris'."

"I'm not holding up space, I live there."

"You could live here instead."

"Baby, I love you, but I don't think we're ready to live together yet."

"What you mean? We been doing that the past few weeks.

I wanted you to move in before, but now it shouldn't even be a topic of discussion. We got a system and us not being together disrupts that system."

"It doesn't Josiah, don't do that. We were together before I stayed here these last few weeks. It's time for me to go back home."

"Kahlia, you about to piss me off."

"Why does this make you so angry?"

"Not angry, just... frustrated." He walked over to me and wrapped his arms around my waist. "Look, we love each other, right?"

"Yes."

"And we both agreed that this is the track we want to be on as far as our relationship goes, right?"

"Yes, but—"

"But what?"

"I don't want to crowd your space. I am a lot Josiah, what you've witnessed so far is tame. I have a lot going on and with me trying to create for this art exhibit, I don't want to ruin what we have. I am telling you; I can get mean and—"

"And that's just something I'm going to have to figure out how to deal with huh?"

I paused, not expecting that response. I don't know what response I actually was expecting, but it certainly wasn't that. He was prepared to deal with my bullshit, almost willing to take it on even, that surprised me, it threw me for a loop for sure.

"Why?"

"Why what Kahlia?"

"Why are you just willing to deal with my bullshit now?"

"Because I plan on dealing with it for the rest of my life, so I might as well get used to it now. You think dealing with a woman with a strong personality scares me? It doesn't, not if that woman is you. It's like you've said before, this pull, this connection we have is so fucking deep. This ain't about you or me individually anymore Kali, this is about us as a whole. We are partners, we have already established that we have been partners before you and I even knew it. I read up on that soul ties shit and it's real. You been mine, you gon' stay mine for whatever lives we find ourselves in. So, no you're not moving back with Parris, in fact I'm insisting that we go over there now and get the rest of your shit because it's coming here to our home."

He stood up tall, with confidence while staring me down and my mouth moved to object, but no words came out. What the fuck was happening? I had no clue on how to react to a man bossing up on me like Josiah seemed to be doing. It wasn't about control, I didn't feel like it was but, in his words, in his stance, he was standing on business with me, and I folded.

"Let's go then." I started out of the room, but he pulled me back to him, placing a kiss on my lips then lifting me up and carrying me out of the room, a trail of girlish giggles in our wake. He grabbed his keys from the bowl near the door and then we made our way to the garage where his truck was parked.

It was ridiculous the way I folded, the way I just gave in to his whim but there was absolutely nothing I could or was even willing to do to change it. He had me, just like I had him, wrapped around each other's little fingers. This man... my man... he consumed me and resisting him would have been impossible even under normal circumstances especially once those beautiful hazel eyes trapped me in their gaze.

16

JOSIAH

"What up Rich?" I answered the phone as I was getting dressed, placing the phone on speaker.

"Aye... we got a problem." Rich sighed and I paused, hearing the slight distress in his voice. We were supposed to be on our way to his home for dinner. Kali was in the bathroom putting on makeup as we spoke.

"Hold up." I replied before putting my shirt over my head and then picking the phone off the bed, taking it off speaker. "What's up?"

"I didn't fucking know let me start by saying that shit."

"Didn't know what?"

"Angie and Josh here with the baby." Again, I paused, my mouth getting a salty taste and my stomach churning. "Apparently Tish got the weekends mixed up and forgot."

I didn't fault Tish for still communicating with Angie, even after everything that happened. She'd grown friendly with her when we were together. They had built a friendship so I wasn't surprised when shit hit the fan and she maintained her relationship with Angie. I didn't respect it, but I understood it.

"Okay?"

"I get it, if you don't want to come; but Angie still thinks—"

"Let me run it by Kali and I'll call you back." I sighed. "This is some bullshit, Rich."

"I know Mac, I fucking know. When they showed up, I was confused as fuck. But what can I do?"

"Let me hit you back." I replied as Kali walked out of the bathroom, fully dressed in a two piece skirt, and fitted camisole. Her braids was pulled up into a high ponytail with curls on the ends. Her makeup was flawless, she didn't use much of it and I loved her that way.

"You look cute." She smiled walking over to me and smoothing down my shirt before placing a kiss on my lips. When she stepped back from the kiss, she looked up at me. "What's wrong?" I sat down on the bed and sighed, holding my head in my hand.

"Rich just called."

"Uh oh, did they cancel last minute? It's okay, we look too good to be staying in the house let's go find—"

"Angela and Joshua are here." I stopped her and looked at me confused but the moment she realized who I was talking about, her plump red nude lips formed an o.

"Why?"

"Angie and Tish are friends." I explained. "They became cool during college after we started dating. I guess she mixed up the dates they were going to be here. Rich called and told me, so I'd know before we went over there. But, if you don't feel comfortable Baby, we don't gotta go."

"Josiah, I'm good, but what do you want to do?" she asked sliding into my lap and wrapping her arms around my neck. "If you want to go, we can, if not, like I said we can go find a nice little lounge and listen to some live music. I think Parris said she was going to the place Fabian works again."

"If you don't mind, we can go." I told her.

"Are you ready to face them? How long has it even been?"

"Years." I shrugged. "I ain't seen either of them in years. They've been here a few times, but each time I always avoid them."

"How about this, we can go over there since that was our plan. But, if at any time neither of us wants to be there we can leave and go hang out with Parris. I don't want you to be uncomfortable, I know I won't be uncomfortable, so you don't need to worry about me."

"Okay, let's go and then if we ain't feeling it we'll leave." I sighed. "Call Parris and tell her to be on standby to send us a fake emergency text."

"Got you." She chuckled, getting up from my lap and grabbing her phone. I grabbed mine and called Rich back.

"Yeah." He answered.

"We on our way. But, if we not feeling it, we gon leave just giving you a heads up."

"I understand. I'll let Tish know. See ya'll soon." I started to disconnect the call, but he stopped me. "Aye Mac... this is our bad for sure; I'mma make it up to you."

"No need Rich. We good, I'm already knowing. See you when you get here." This time I did disconnect the call and I finished getting ready before meeting Kali in the living room so we could go.

"This food better be fucking delicious." Kali said causing me to chuckle. We walked out of the house going into the garage and she handed me the keys to her Lexus. I opened the passenger side door for her before going over to the driver's side.

Her car was parked right next to mine, in her designated spot. Since we'd moved her in, a week ago, we'd been finding places to put all of her things. I made room in the master closet for her clothes, and we'd made moves to officially set up her art room; removing the furniture that was inside and setting her things up in there instead.

As we drove the short distance to Rich's I felt my palms getting sweaty and my stomach continued to churn. I wasn't ready, I didn't want to face them, which is why I knew I wasn't going to be able to go to Atlanta, despite what I'd told Rich about wanting to take Kali there to meet my mom.

I felt Kali's hand slid into mine and I glanced over at her. She pulled my hand up to her lips, placing a gentle kiss on it.

"I love you, you got this." She affirmed to me. "I'm going to be right there with you. If you don't want to stay, we will not stay. I think you need this though Josiah; because this confrontation is preventing you from going home to see your mom and I can tell you miss her. Once you get this out of the way, you can go to Atlanta."

"You gon' come with me?" I asked looking over at her as we approached a red light. "Ma Dukes said she wanted to meet you anyway."

"That's something I'd be willing to do." She agreed. "Let me know when and we going. Your mom looks like she gives good hugs."

"She do, the best. I miss her and you're right, getting this over with will be a step towards getting back to Atlanta. I love you baby, thank you for being here."

"I wouldn't be anywhere else." She smiled leaning over and capturing my lips before the light turned back green.

We made it to Rich's place ten minutes later and after parking I looked up at the house taking a deep breath.

"Parris on standby?" I asked Kali and she laughed.

"Yes, she said let her know and she got you."

"Bet, let's get this over with." I got out of the car and went around opening the door for her, then helping her out of the car. I pocketed the keys but held on tight to her hand as I escorted us to the front door. Ringing the doorbell, I waited for it to be answered and it was, not long after, by Rich and Tish both.

"Mac, I'm so sorry I completely forgot." Were the first words out of Tish's mouth the moment she saw it was me. "I thought it was next week instead of this week."

"It's all good." I said pulling her into a quick hug. "Tish, this is Kali. Kali, this is Tish."

"OMG, you're beautiful." Tish smiled pulling Kali in for a hug. "It's so nice to finally meet you. Mac has been keeping you from me."

"For good reason." I heard Rich mumble, and I knew exactly what he meant. The moment Rich told Tish about Kali; I was sure Angela knew. They were thick as thieves and there was no way Angie didn't know there was a Kali.

"Thank you, it's so nice to meet you too. I can't wait to get my hands on that baby. Josiah has been showing me pictures, she's precious."

"Well come on in. We had some unexpected guests, but I'm sure Mac filled you in already. Dinner is just about done, just got a few things to finish up in the kitchen." She wrapped her arm around Kali's and pulled her into the house.

"I can help you, if you need help."

"Perfect. We can let the men go chat and you can help me in the kitchen." As soon as we walked into the house, Angela, and Joshua both came into view. My eyes first went to my twin brother whose face matched mine to the tee. The only difference between us now was that I'd decided to cut my hair and his hair was still fairly long. For a second, we stood there staring at each other, an awkward silence resonating between all of us.

"Mac." Rich nudged me and my eyes flicked in his direction before I pulled Kali close to me.

"What's up Josh?" I asked my brother.

"Josiah…" he responded. "It's good to see you." I didn't

return the sentiment. It wasn't good to see them, wasn't good to see either of them; but they'd put me in a predicament where I almost felt forced to be doing so. "You remember Ang—" I cocked my head to the side, confused on if he was as dumb as I thought he was. "Of course you do, my bad... I just—"

I sighed and took a step back taking Kahlia with me. She held her arm around me tight, looking up at me. My eyes connected with hers and the small smile playing at the corners of her lips calmed me. I knew she could feel how bad I was shaking, yet with every moment she looked into my eyes, I calmed.

"It's all good." I told him. "What's up Ang?"

"Hi Josiah." She smiled. "Like Josh said, it's good to see you. It's been too long."

"Not long enough." I commented.

"Mac." I heard Rich say from my side.

"I'm Kahlia." Kali said holding her hand out to Josh. One look in his direction and he quickly put his approaching hand down.

"Joshua. It's good to meet you."

"You too." Kali replied placing her hand back at her side.

"This is Angie." Josh nodded towards the woman I once loved. Finally, my eyes fully took her in. She was beautiful, of course she was. Her almond colored skin glistened in the light. The blonde hair she now wore looked great against her skin. Her eyes, as pretty and as brown as they were the day I met her.

"Hi, I'm Kahlia." Kahlia turned to Angie and Angie's eyes roamed up and down Kahlia's entire frame, sizing her up.

"Hi." She replied dryly and my neck snapped in Kali's direction feeling her slightly tense up around me. Before anybody could say anything, the loud wail of a child flowed into the room.

"I think that's mine." Angie said. "Excuse me."

"Kahlia, you still okay with helping me in the kitchen? I just need to finish up a few things before we sit down to eat."

"You good?" I asked Kahlia and she blinked up at me with a smile.

"Of course. Go hang with the guys." Her eyebrows bounced playfully up and down causing me to laugh. She ran her cupped fingers up and down my chin before winking then following Tish to the kitchen. When they left, Josh, Rich and I stood around awkwardly.

"That Mavs game is on." Rich finally broke the silence, nodding his head in the direction of their living room so we could settle in before dinner. I sat in an armchair while Rich and Josh took the sofa, Rich strategically place in between us.

"Ya'll been to a Mavs game yet?" Joshua's voice boomed over the white noise from the tv; it was white noise because I couldn't pay attention to the game, too busy trying to calm myself down.

To think that after all this time, I was still hurt, only spoke to the affection I once held for my ex-fiancé and my brother. I never in a million years thought I would be sitting here, in this situation now; having not spoken to either of them in years. They were two of the most important people in my life and now I couldn't stand to be in the same room as them.

"Mac…Mac." My head snapped towards Rich then over to Josh. "You good?"

"Yeah, I'm just; my bad what were you saying?"

"I was telling Josh about those tickets we copped to see the Mavs. Remember we had those cheap ass 400 level seats and when we walked up to the AAC those young dudes approached us. We thought we were getting robbed, but they was selling those fucking too good to be true seats in the 200 levels, damn near to the floor?"

"Yeah, I remember." I laughed. "You told me not to trust it

because all they wanted was $300 for the pair; but I got them anyway. We had one of each ticket in our hand as we walked up to that door scared to get rejected with the lower level seats. But when we got up to that door what happened?"

"They scanned the tickets, and they were legit." He chuckled shaking his head. "I thought for sure they were going to call the cops on us. We sat down in our seats, fucking amazing seats by the way; and for the first thirty minutes, I was sitting up straight, eyes on a swivel thinking the cops was going to show up any minute now or somebody was coming to claim their seats and then I'd have my ass in jail, and Tish would be cussing me out. This nigga Mac was reckless, not giving a fuck back then, he ain't have nobody at home but I bet if you try to get his ass to do some shit like that now; it would be out of the question."

"Yeah, well, a beautiful woman keeping your bed warm will do that to you." Josh added his two cents. From the corner of my eyes, I could see Rich mouth the word 'fuck' before his eyes too went over to Josh.

"You're right; I'mma go check on my beautiful woman." I stood up from my seat before making my way towards the kitchen.

"You couldn't spend five minutes alone in there?" Tish asked as soon as I walked in. She, Kali, and Angie were all standing around in the kitchen, placing the food on serving dishes and sipping wine. "Food is almost done Mac, and we're having girl talk. Whatever this is, couldn't wait?"

"Love don't wait." I replied grabbing hold of Kali and placing kisses all over her face. She didn't push me away, didn't shy away from my affection; in fact, she embraced it tilting her face in more angles playfully so that the entirety of her face was covered in kisses. I bent down so I was close to her ear and whispered; "You sure you good?"

"Uh huh." She nodded. "I'm fine. You good?"

"I am now. Tell Parris to be ready with that phone call." That caused her to laugh loudly.

"I got you." She chuckled. I removed myself from our embrace before winking at her and making my way down the hall towards the bathroom.

I quickly emptied my bladder then washed my hands before splashing water in my face. I was worried. Worried that Kali was peeping my uneasiness. I was worried she would know I wasn't as over this shit as I had told her I was. Grief hits different, even if there is no physical death involved. I was definitely still grieving though, grieving the loss of my first true love, and grieving the loss of one of my best friends. I wasn't even sure I'd ever truly get over it and I was worried she would leave me one day because of it.

Drying my face off with a paper towel, I made my way out of the bathroom, walking down the hall and on my way down, I heard the faintest cry coming from one of the rooms on the left. The door was slightly ajar, and I went inside.

My God daughter's nursey always blew my breath away especially seeing the mural of black ballerinas on the wall behind her crib. I loved the idea of having a daughter, I knew deep down I was a girl dad for sure.

Walking over to it, I expected to see her round face staring up at me; instead, I was staring at a small little boy, with the same hazel eyes as mine. When I imagined what my children with Angela would look like, he was it. He was caramel like her with short curly black hair. His eyes were big and inquisitive and as I neared him, he cooed; I supposed thinking I was his father.

I wrapped my hands on the edge of the crib looking down at him, his crying stopped the longer he stared at me. My God daughter Riley still sound asleep next to him; her daddy was also a heavy sleeper. I bent down and looked at the little boy. He was beautiful and I hated that I would never get to know him on the level he would need; every nephew needed a strong, fun uncle but I knew I couldn't give that to him, not right now at least.

"He's beautiful, isn't he?" The sudden echo of her voice gave me chills. I stood straight before turning around to face her, alone, for the first time in years. "I don't know if your mom told you, but his name is Joel Henry Mackenzie." I closed my eyes biting back the ping of anger that ran through my chest. "Henry was Josh's idea. He said he wanted to honor you even if—"

I walked towards the exit where she stood, partially blocking the way.

"Move Angie." I glanced over at her. "I ain't looking for no conversation."

"Josiah, I just wanted to say how sorry I am for what happened." She said rubbing her arms. "I know that it's a long shot, but I'm hoping that one day you and I can be friends at the very least. My son needs as much family as he can get, and I was hoping—"

"Nah." I swiped my finger against my nose. "You and me ain't friends and can't never be friends. This was what you wanted Angela."

"This is not what I wanted. Of course I was in love with you, but—"

"But what? You thought you could have your cake and eat it too? Fucking me and my brother and you was just gon keep doing that shit until I found out?"

"That's not fair I—"

"And to think, you did all of that bullshit just to become somebody's baby mama, when I was tryna make you, my wife." I scoffed shaking my head. "I wish you well Angie, I do. But if I never had to see yo' fucking face again in my lifetime, I would have been cool with that too. Excuse me." I slightly nudged her out of the way, walking out of the room, not fazed by the tears sliding down her face. She had done this to herself.

"Kali." I called throughout the house making my way back down the hall. Her head popped out of the opening to the dining room, eyebrows arched high to the heavens as I made my way to her. "We're leaving."

She didn't object, she just took my hand, and we made our way out of the house and to her car. I opened her door for her, making sure she was in before making my way to the driver's side. I could hear Rich calling after me, but I ignored the fuck out of him. This was a bad idea, it was a mistake and for as long as I lived, I hoped I would never have to see either of their fucking faces again.

17

KAHLIA

It had been two weeks since that incident at Rich and Tish's home when Josiah stormed us out without a word to anyone. I trusted him enough to know that whatever it was, he wasn't feeling that shit and even if I wanted to stay; nothing would keep me from being by his side when he needed me, for whatever reason.

As we drove away from the house that night, I remember looking over at Josiah, hoping he would be willing to talk to me and tell me what was going on. I would have never questioned him in public, but privately, in each other's company I felt the need to ask questions. What I wasn't expecting, was to be immediately shut down allowing a weird vibe to linger in between us and out of nowhere, the first brick of my wall went up.

The bricks had been slowly rebuilding themselves to form the wall I let up with other people. I loved him, but I was questioning the reason why he was so adamant on leaving and not talking about it. I hated the doubt I had experienced since then, hated this nagging feeling in the pit of my stomach. I almost felt like I was being unreasonable.

But as I lay in bed next to him, waiting on my alarm to go off, I wondered what he had been thinking. He was sleep when I got in last night; I'd been working with Jeremy who I'd convinced to spend some time in Dallas, to curate my pieces for the exhibit at the gallery. When I got in bed, wine drunk after a nice dinner I treated Jeremy to, I was completely naked. I missed Josiah all day and I was done feeling disconnected to him; so, I came in and pounced on him, wanting to feel him inside of me.

As I kissed his lips, enticing him to wake up and notice me; I felt rejection from him, for the first time with just two little words; "Not tonight". Sex was so pleasurable between us and our connection so deep, so beautiful that we usually couldn't keep our hands off one another. I didn't respond to him, just slid out of the bed making my way to the bathroom, slamming the door behind me.

I ran a quick shower to help me cool down and I felt so fucking odd. Still, after the shower I wrapped my body in a towel then made my way out of the bathroom. I glanced over at the bed and noticed Josiah was awake, sitting on his side of the bed shoulders bent.

"Kali, what's the problem?"

"I don't have a problem." I snipped grabbing pajamas from my drawer and quickly throwing them on.

"You mad because I ain't tryna have sex right now?"

"No, I'm mad because you've been acting very fucking weird the past two weeks. We've been feeling off Josiah, you can't act like you don't feel it. I've been trying to figure out what it is, I know it has something to do with Angela. I was wondering where she'd gone. So, what happened at that dinner? Ya'll were back in each other's presence for five minutes and you're already questioning what we have?"

"What?"

"Look, I get that seeing her made some feelings flood

back and maybe you're questioning everything we've been through these past few months; but if you're going to leave then give me a heads—" my words were stopped when he suddenly snapped off the bed and in two steps was in my space, cupping my face with his big hands and smashing his lips against mine.

"Don't ever question my devotion to you. Seeing Angie don't have shit on what we are to each other. Don't do that shit Kahlia; neither of us is going anywhere." His forehead touched mine before he whispered; "Wewe ni wangu wa milele."

"Na wewe ni wangu."

We'd learned those words in Swahili. After the first time I dreamt about our past life as King and Queen, I remembered a phrase that we'd constantly said to one another. With the help of Google translate I understood what the words meant.

When I figured it out, I repeated the words to Josiah, insisting that whenever we needed each other, we'd utter those words; but it became an everyday thing since the day we agreed to it. Hearing those words relaxed me, my breathing slowed, heartbeat slowly decreased from its previous fast pace.

"I love you, let's go to bed." Josiah whispered, placing one last kiss on my lips before grabbing my hand and helping me into bed. I laid on my side and felt his arms wrap around me. It wasn't long after, that I heard the sound of his snores; yet I couldn't sleep if I wanted to.

It's why I was waiting slightly impatiently for the alarm to go off and I could get out of bed. There was so much going through my head, too much in fact that I just wanted to focus on one thing which was getting my day started and figuring out my next moves. I loved Josiah, but I couldn't lose myself in him as I'd done with Jonathan and this feeling, I was feeling was so very close to it that it scared me.

At 6:00AM my alarm went off and I immediately hopped out of bed, scurrying past Josiah just as he stretched properly shutting the bathroom door to get my hygiene in order for the day. While brushing my teeth and washing my face, I grappled with whether or not I was going to continue to ignore the daunting feeling I had emanating inside of me, or if I was going to get the answers I was looking for.

I decided on the latter, hoping to get it out of the way now instead of trying to deal with it later. We needed to be dressed and out the door in a little over an hour which wasn't nearly enough time, but it would have to do for now. After placing my face towel out to dry, I took a deep breath then opened the door bumping into Josiah's bare chest. Taking a step back, I looked up into those bright eyes staring back at me seductively, a fire burning in them that I'd felt before, sometimes craved.

"Good morning." His hoarse whisper broke the silence between us.

"Morning." My eyes roamed his chest up to his face. "I was just leaving so you can have the bathroom."

"Okay." His tongue swiping across his lips, but he didn't move, continued to stare at me.

"Baby, you gotta move so I can get out."

From the corner of my eyes, I could see his hand moving up towards me before his fingers gently outlined my hardened nipples causing a gasp to be caught in my throat. His lips slowly lowered to mine. I wrapped my arms around his neck as he lifted me, placing me on top of the vanity countertop. He still thought I was mad about the sex, which was frustrating, yet no matter how frustrated I got, I wasn't about to stop it either.

His hands cupped the meaty flesh of my thighs, spreading them wider as he stood between my legs. I locked myself in his embrace, my head flying back as a loud moan escaped my lips while his lips placed soft, deliberate kisses along my neck. Feeling his hands on the seed of my shorts, my heart seemed to race anticipating his touch between my folds. He pushed my shorts to the side, and his finger glided down from top to bottom.

My arms wrapped around him, ready for him to enter me and when he did, I groaned; his own groan throatily escaping his lips. Reclaiming my lips as he delivered deep and sensual strokes, his tongue swiping against mine, sending shivers throughout my body. Snatching his lips away, his strokes got deeper, faster, driving me insane. Together we found the tempo that bounded our bodies together, our breathing and heartbeat in perfect harmony.

"Fuck Kali." Escaped Josiah's lips as he continued to fuck me deep. "I want to start a family with you baby. Can I give you, my babies?"

I barely knew what he was saying, so agreeing to it was nothing as long as he was doing what he was doing to me; I would agree to just about anything.

"Yes." Poured from my lips. It was like hearing my agreeance caused Josiah to increase his speed even more. Feeling my walls constrict around him, we exploded in a downpour of fiery pleasure. My body seemed to melt against his, our arms still wrapped around one another, the room slightly spinning.

"You, okay?" his voice cracked a little before he cleared his throat.

Smiling up at him, all I could do was nod my head as words yet again escaped my mind. He unwrapped my legs from his waist before chuckling and removing himself from our embrace. I watched lazily as he walked over to the shower and turned it on before taking his shorts and boxer briefs which were at his ankles all the way off. He walked back over to me, then helped me out of my clothes before carrying me to the shower.

We washed ourselves in silence and my mind went back to just a few minutes ago replaying the interaction in my head, the pleasure, the tingles, the ecstasy and the very few words spoken between us.

"You weren't serious right?" I asked after we'd stepped out of the shower. Josiah was halfway out of the bathroom entering the bedroom when he turned and looked back at me.

"About what?"

"The baby. I mean, obviously that's the plan for us to start a family one day; but I'm thinking more distant future."

"Why not now?" he asked, and my mouth opened trying to explain my position, but I kept falling short of a response. "Kahlia?"

"I just... I don't think right now is a good time for it." I shrugged folding my arms across my chest. "We aren't even close to marriage, but you want to think about having a kid right now?"

"Not even close to marriage?" He stood staring at me obviously baffled. "Kahlia, are we not in the same relationship? Because I thought we were on the same path."

"I didn't say we weren't on the same path—"

"What else would you call it if I'm ready to shop for rings and you don't think we're anywhere close to marriage? What the fuck is happening right now?"

"Nothing, I just—" I sighed, taking a deep breath, closing my eyes trying to find the right words to use. "I don't know Josiah; I feel a little disconnected from you ever since we left Rich and Tish's house a few weeks ago."

"You been feeling disconnected from me for two weeks and ain't said shit?"

"Ain't said shit? What you mean? I been trying to talk to you, but you keep shutting me out."

"Because ain't shit to talk about." He mumbled turning and going towards the closet. I followed him, figuring I'd already started it, I might as well see it through.

"Okay then why did we leave like that? I knew we had an exit plan, but you executed it before I thought you would. What was said between you and Angela that made you so mad? I'm not even going to ask why you were alone with her."

"Oh, is that what the real problem is? I was alone with her for five minutes."

"And obviously enough happened in that five minutes to the point where you stormed us out of that house the way you did. So, what happened?"

"Ain't shit happen Kahlia." He sighed grabbing a pair of boxer briefs and sliding into them. He then grabbed a Polo with the school logo on it placing it over his head then sliding a pair of dark khakis on.

"You're lying." I shook my head disappointed. "Something happened because like I said, ever since then I've felt a disconnection between us."

"Let's just drop this." Josiah walked around me going back into the bedroom.

"Tell me or don't plan on speaking to me until you can gather enough balls to tell me what's up."

"Nothing fucking happened." He sighed sitting down on the bed and placing his head in his hands. "On my way back from the bathroom, I heard a baby crying; I thought it was Riley, so I went in to check on her. I wasn't expecting to see my nephew there staring up at me. He was… he was beautiful Kali, and he was exactly what I thought my son would look like."

"Your son with who Josiah? Her or me?" his eyes flipped

to mine and the silence between us spoke volumes on its own. A raw sense of grief seemed to overwhelm my body as tears immediately pooled in my eyes. I felt lost, confused, shocked but before he could see a tear drop, I rushed towards the bathroom locking myself inside.

"Kahlia, baby..." his voice boomed from the other end of the door. I sat down on the edge of the closed toilet, silent sobs escaping my lips. Which each sob, my body shuddered, and my heart ached. "Kali, I'm sorry open the door so we can—"

"Get away from the fucking door." I managed to croak out. "Please, just leave me alone Josiah."

"I'm not fucking leaving until you open the door." And hearing that broke my heart even more. His voice sounded pained, like he was in anguish as if I had just told him that I fantasized about what my babies with Jonathan would have looked like. I felt humiliated and disrespected. Five fucking minutes, that's all it took for him to lose sight on what we had been planning with one another. Five fucking minutes in her presence was enough to make him fold.

"I don't want to see you."

"We gotta go to work Kahlia, you can't stay in there all fucking day. Come out and we can talk."

"I'm done talking." My tears subsided and I just felt drained.

"Baby, tell me what I gotta do to fix it. I didn't fucking mean—I mean, it's not like that and I promise you I don't want Angela."

"Just her fucking kids." I chuckled, shaking my head. "You lied to me."

"Lied about what?"

"Everything, it feels like." I said feeling another twinge of ache in my chest. "Just go Josiah, I need a minute and if I come out of this bathroom right now, I'm going to hit you."

"I don't want to. I need to stay here with you."

"You're going to be late, and I don't have a class first period." I reminded him. "Just go. We'll talk later."

"Kali…I love you." My silent sobs were deafening to my own ears. I hated this, hated this feeling. This crushed me; there was no other way to put it.

The pain I was feeling, the hopelessness; you'd have thought Josiah and I had been together longer than we did. Like I'd lived a million lives and loved him a million times. And if something like this could hurt so bad, what the fuck was I going to do if anything worse happened?

I listened carefully as he walked around the bedroom a little more, probably gathering his stuff for work before he travelled down the hall and finally the sound of the garage raising and the roar of his F150 surrounded me. As soon as I heard the garage closing, I let my sobs rain out of my mouth.

Was I being unreasonable? Were my feelings not valid? We were supposed to be end game, my mind, body, and soul told me so. I thought that I was his forever, and he was mine. Ridiculous as it may sound, it was how I had imagined us, up until two weeks ago when Angela came back into his life unexpectantly. He still loved her and in knowing that I felt betrayed.

∼

I MADE it to work just after 8:30. Once I was clocked in, I tried to zip past Parris' office, but the box of supplies I'd carried in was holding me back. Just as I walked past, the door to her office opened and she walked out followed closely by Autumn.

"Kahlia, come back here." Parris called and I rolled my eyes playfully so Ms. Sanchez the secretary chuckled and shook her head.

"Hey Sissy, I was just heading to my classroom." I pointed towards the door, hoping my urgency to not talk here in front of other people; especially not in front of Autumn who seemed to be hating on my relationship with Josiah from the beginning. I was starting not to believe him when he said he never fucked her because she was coming on way too strong.

"We need to talk Kahlia."

"Can it wait until later? I really need to get to my classroom and set up some stuff. We can go to lunch, on me; I promise."

My fingers were crossed behind my back like a child because I had every intention of locking my classroom doors and sitting in the dark for my lunch period; or sitting in my car and calling Jamie on my lunch break so we could talk trash and plot. I could hear her now saying fuck these niggas and to be the boss bitch that I was and fuck somebody else; Jamie wasn't the most level headed of the two of us. I of course would hype her up like I was going to do it; but deep down, we both knew I wasn't about that life, and I'd never do that to anybody I cared for.

"I will meet you in your classroom at twelve thirty." She advised before going back into her office. Relieved, I turned to make my way out of the office again, little did I know I had unwanted company.

"Hey girl." Autumn smiled; her two front teeth slightly bigger than the rest. "How have you been? Parris told me you moved out; did you move in with your man?" My eyebrow arched up to my forehead as I glared at her. "I ain't mean no harm; just checking on you. Josiah is a player from what I heard, and I don't want to see you hurt. I told Parris I was going to tell you; I just heard so many things."

"I'm not concerned." I replied. "But thank you for yours."

"Of course, girl, you know we gotta stick together."

"Autumn, we're not friends." I reminded her. "Please don't

discuss my business with my sister; she'd never tell you anything; which I'm assuming she didn't because you came to me fishing for information. I know you called yourself having a thing for Josiah, but I'm here now so stop wasting your time." Without another word I turned and headed in the direction of my classroom.

My time until lunch went by in what felt like a blur. I don't remember going through my lesson plans, barely even remember speaking to any of my students. As the time for 4th period came to an end, and the bell rang I jumped up at the same time as my students hoping to avoid not only Parris but Josiah too. All of the texts he'd sent me throughout the day went unanswered.

Just as I had placed my purse over my shoulder, I was stopped by Parris standing in my classroom doorway. Cocking her head to the side, she stared at me with her arms folded across her chest.

"Where were you going? I told you I was going to meet you here?"

"I um… I was just going to go take a nap in my car. I didn't sleep well last night and I'm tired."

"You can't bullshit a bullshitter, Kali." She shook her head. "What's going on?"

"I don't want to say." I told her and I didn't; mainly because I didn't want to hear her say she told me so. I believed wholeheartedly that my relationship was legit, our feelings were legit, but Parris probably couldn't wait to say it. "But I um, I need a favor."

"What Kali?"

"I need to leave early."

"You got here late." I pleaded with my eyes while keeping my head on a swivel. "Bitch why the fuck you look like you on the run? Did he hurt you?"

"No Parris, I just need some space. I was thinking about

WHEN IT COMES TO YOU

going to Baltimore for the weekend. There's a flight at 4 and if I go home now and pack, I can make it to the airport in time."

"Kahlia don't just leave like that. Regardless of whatever issue ya'll got going on right now, leaving this way without him knowing is not right. Obviously, you don't want to tell me what happened and I ain't about to pressure you to do so, but I know if ya'll love each other the way ya'll claim to, it can be fixed."

I nodded but didn't respond because I was starting to even question the love. Was it real? Hell, it certainly is on my end. I knew how I felt about him; his feelings for me were in question which sucked because before two weeks ago, I felt so sure, that we were sure about each other.

"I hear you and I receive it." I sighed. "So, you're going to cover for me?"

"Fine." She rolled her eyes and sighed. "But don't try to pull no shit come Monday. You better have your ass in this building."

"Pinky swear." I promised holding out my pinky and she cupped it in hers. She pulled me into a hug and rubbed my back. "I love you, sissy."

"Love you too. Now get out of here before I change my mind." I placed a quick kiss on her cheek then exited the classroom. I started to turn right to go towards the exit, but instead I turned left to make my way towards Josiah's office which I knew he would be in as he usually did football duties during his lunch break.

It took me a little over five minutes to get to the office and when I did, I knocked gently before his deep voice invited me in. When I walked in and he looked up seeing it was me, he stood up and met me at the door. When he tried to embrace me, I found myself stepping out of the way which garnered a confused look on his face.

"I just came to tell you I'm leaving."

"Leaving to go where?"

"I'm going to take the weekend and go visit Jamie." I rubbed my forehead. "Parris is covering for me so I can leave now and be at the airport by 4. I'll come back Sunday and then I'll decide if I will come back to your home."

"Our home."

"That's... that's not my home Josiah. It hasn't been, not really. —" he started to interrupt me, but I put my hand up to stop him. "I just need some space and I need you to respect it and understand it." He sighed walking back to his seat then rubbed the top of his head multiple times. "Josiah—" he looked back up to me and I walked towards him. "You gotta make sure this is what you want, that I am what you want. I told myself before that heartbreak wasn't in the cards for me because I wasn't going to get close enough to someone to like them; a lot let alone love them. I wasn't prepared for you and then I quickly realized I needed to be. I fell in love with you. I want you; I just need you to make sure you want me too."

"I do, I just—" I placed my finger on his lips silencing him.

"Please. Try anyway, for me. You owe me this at the very least." We stared at each other, so many words being conveyed in our eyes.

"Okay." He relented.

"Thank you." I held on to his hand. "Now stand up and kiss me." Slowly, Josiah stood up, towering over me, and wrapping me up in his arms. I stood on the tips of my toes and placed my lips on his.

I knew what I was doing was the right thing to do. I was taking care of us by giving us room to breathe. From the beginning we went into this headfirst, we fell fast and hard and this was not an ordinary thing for people. These weren't ordinary feelings, and we weren't ordinary people. Josiah Mackenzie in some form, in some life, with some name was the love of my life, I just needed him to deal with his shit first.

"I love you." He whispered against my lips, and I pulled back to look at him.

"And I love you."

18

JOSIAH

Coming home to an empty house nowadays just didn't sit right with me in my spirit. It's like nothing was right until that beautiful woman of mine walked into the house. She made it peaceful; she made it safe; she made it a home.

She said she would be back, but I couldn't help but to think that maybe she wouldn't be. She was right about the disconnect between us; I'd felt it too. I didn't feel it right away though, it took me a few days to realize what was happening. I still desired her, still craved her, but mentally seeing Angie and Josh fucked me up so bad that I started to question everything I'd been building with Kahlia. It wasn't fair to her, I knew that; but I couldn't let her go.

I made my way into our bedroom seeing traces of her all over it. Her perfume bottles were scattered on top of the dresser. There was a book on her nightstand that probably contained more smut than a Playboy; shit she admitted was her guilty pleasure. One of her scarves was next to it. Articles of her clothes were scattered on the floor; she knew I hated that shit, but Kali was always gon' be Kali. I fucking missed her already.

"Fuck." I mumbled to myself. Leave it to me to fuck some shit up; but that shit with Angie fucked my head up. Who knew that a conversation less than 5 minutes long could have such an impact on me.

Getting undressed, I went into the bathroom and ran a shower. It was going to be an early night for me which was unusual for me on a Friday night. After my shower, I grabbed my cell phone and ordered some food before sitting on the couch in front of my tv. I'd turned the tv on, but I wasn't even sure what was on it. I'd just used it as white noise while I scrolled social media, trying to distract myself from thinking too hard.

As I scrolled, a post from Kali's business page flashed across my screen promoting her exhibit at the art gallery. It was fast approaching. She'd been working so hard on getting it organized and I was excited to be in her element with her. I was already proud of her for making the moves she was making; I could only imagine what it was like to experience things as she did.

I shared the post to my story and again on my page on IG; the IG post syncing up on my Facebook page as well. Since I was on her page, my fingers seemed to have a mind of their own when I clicked on her name and began to scroll her page.

I knew she was right; I knew I needed to really deal with my feelings about my situation with Angie and Josh. I remember Rich telling me this was going to be a problem in my life with Kali; I didn't want to hear that shit then, but I understood now. I thought I was over it, thought it didn't matter anymore since she had come into my life; but that wasn't true. Now, I knew, that for her, I had to get it together.

Without thinking, my hand went to my contacts and clicked on her name so I could call her. I knew she was in the air and her phone was on airplane mode by her phone going straight to voicemail. Of course she didn't have a greeting with her voicemail, she opted to let the automated system do it for her. When I heard the tone, I hesitated tempted to just hang up. Suddenly I found my voice.

"I respect it and I understand it; why you thought you had to leave. Space will probably do the both of us some good, it's only for a few days right? Shit, who am I kidding; you ain't even been gone that long though and I'm missing you like crazy baby. Be safe, call me when you can and most importantly; make sure you come home to me. I love you, Kahlia."

Yeah, my spirit wouldn't be right until I had her home.

～

I DIDN'T EVEN REMEMBER FALLING asleep. I stayed up, late, playing Call of Duty, solo drinking and checking my phone every ten minutes hoping Kali would call me; all I got a little past midnight was that she'd made it to her friend safely. When, I tried to call her, she didn't answer so I drank some more until I passed out.

With a pounding head, I eased up from my uncomfortable position on the couch. The sun was out and shining bright as hell. Slowly getting up, I grabbed my phone and staggered down the hall towards my bedroom so I could relieve my bladder then get back in bed until my headache wore off.

After flushing the toilet, I hobbled out of the bathroom and into my bedroom before falling on the bed and placing the covers over my head. Had it not been for my buzzing phone, I would have been able to fall asleep. Grabbing it off the nightstand, I squinted trying to focus my eyes on the screen as I read the text that had just come through.

> Rich: U good bro?

Confused, I started to send my reply.

> Yeah. Why?

> Rich: U told me Kali left yesterday. You don't remember calling me at 2AM?

> Hell no. Wtf I say?

> Rich: Get dressed, let's hit the gym. I'll be there in 30.

There was no point in telling him I was hung over; it seems he probably already knew that. The gym was the last place I wanted to be right now, but something told me it was exactly where I needed to be. Groaning, I got out of bed again then went into my closet to grab work out gear. I brushed my teeth, washed my face then made my way to the kitchen so I could fill my water jug.

Once it was filled, I went into my junk drawer, grabbed the bottle of Excedrin, and popped two pills before taking a long swig of my water. I knew I needed to eat something, so I grabbed a fruit bowl and began to pop pieces of pineapples and watermelon in my mouth. It wasn't nearly enough to help cure my headache, but it was something and I figured I would burn the rest of it off in the gym.

It wasn't long after that Rich texted me letting me know he was outside. I grabbed my gym bag then locked up my house. Slowly walking up to his car, I saw him laughing and shaking his head. Hell yeah, he knew I was hungover.

Knowing I was about to get an ear full; I threw my gym bag in the back seat before getting in the passenger seat.

"What's good bro?" Rich held his hand to dap me up and I accepted it. "On a scale from one to ten how much of that bottle you finish last night?"

"I got a couple shots left." I shrugged. "So, tell me what I called and said."

"Plenty." He shook his head. "You really think Kali is done with you over that?"

"Could you blame her? Imagine Tish telling you she wants to have your baby, then you find out she wants your baby because she's been imaging what her and her ex's kids would look like. You'd want to leave her too. I can't lose this girl Rich; after everything, after all we've given to each other, I cannot lose her. But I can't have her and have these problems too, these thoughts of regret."

"Regret about what bro?"

"What you mean regret what? Everything that happened four years ago."

He chuckled, gripping his hand tighter around the steering wheel.

"Mac, I know you loved Angie but shit, you different with this one. I ain't seen you this happy, this alive since before that shit happened four years ago. I see why it took you so long to move on, you were looking for you something special; same as I did with Tish. Angie was a lesson and what the fuck happened to you was a blessing because it exposed ain't shit ass people and got them the fuck out of your life. Why you think you my only friend and only nigga I love enough to call my brother? Because nobody else made the cut besides you and Tish. It ain't no question where you need to be and stop regretting shit."

"Damn nigga." I scoffed.

"You asked." He shrugged. "But seriously, stop self-sabotaging yourself. When, not if, but when, she comes home you better make sure you fix that shit if that girl is what you really want. Lock that shit down and don't fuck it up again."

"I hear you."

I tried to keep my mind off the shit going on in my life while I was at the gym, but I couldn't help checking my phone constantly, hoping I'd hear from Kali. Each time I looked at my phone I grew more and more disappointed.

What the fuck was this? She hadn't even planned on speaking to me at all? This feeling became eerily familiar; the loss, the ache, it was how I felt the moment I found out she'd left my ass hanging in Mexico. Was this going to be a regular occurrence with her; leaving when shit got a little tough? I hated this shit, hated feeling hopeless like this. All I wanted was my baby, needed her, craved her.

We spent a few hours in the gym before Rich let me know that Tish wanted to throw some food on the grill. I had him drop me off at the house so I could clean myself up and let him know I'd be there as soon as I got fresh; promising to stop and grab something to throw on the grill.

After showering and getting dressed, I made my way out of the house. I stopped and grabbed a bottle of Hennessy and some meat to put on the grill. I made it to Rich and Tish's an hour after leaving the house. When I got there, I handed Rich the bottle and handed Tish the food I'd brought knowing she was particular about the way her food was seasoned.

"Where Riley?" I asked grabbing a glass from Rich as he poured some of the Hennessy inside of it.

"She should be getting up." Tish said. "Go grab her for me, please." I nodded sitting the glass on the counter and then walking towards her nursery. As I approached her crib, a sense of déjà vu overwhelmed me. I went back to the day I saw my nephew; Joel Henry Mackenzie and I resented him, an innocent child, for something he had no control over.

GENESIS CARTER

She said giving him my middle name was Josh's idea and, in that moment, I realized that Joshua was who I was madder at. Angie should have been loyal to me, but she didn't have the same loyalty to me that Josh did. My brother, my twin, we came into this world together and I just... I expected so much more from him. It could have been anybody else, I just wished to God it hadn't been Josh. Angie took so much from me, too much to keep track of and I had let her; was continuing to let her. I had to end that shit here and now.

Hearing Riley's coos broke me out of my trance as I smile down at my God daughter. Lifting her up out of her crib, she stretched in my arms, and I adjusted the pink bow on her head. I snuggled her close to me, placing kisses on her big cheeks. She was Tish's spitting imagine; it was like Rich didn't help making her at all.

I carried her out of her room and made my way back into the kitchen when I entered, I saw that one of Tish's friend Natalie was there. I knew Natalie well, had fucked her a time or two back during my more reckless days. But that had ended long ago, had to cut her off because she was trying to take up a position that at that time, I was determined to keep permanently empty.

"Josiah, hey." Nat smiled when I entered the kitchen. I handed the baby to Tish.

"What's up?" I asked grabbing my drink and then making my way out of the house through the back door so I could sit outside with Rich. "Tish tryna kill me bruh." I said to my friend the moment I was in his presence.

"Nigga, nobody told you to fuck her friend." Rich laughed flipping some meat on the grill. I sat in one of the patio chairs watching the Cowboys game that was on the tv. I loved their outdoor space; it was completely covered and decked out with nice furniture, built for entertainment. I was trying to get my own space together at my house; I was hoping to figure it out with Kahlia since she'd moved in.

I wanted to make my house, our home. Hearing her say she didn't feel like it was her home crushed me. I didn't want her to feel like that; I wanted her to love being there. I wanted to raise our family there, to grow with the space.

"That shit happened on accident; we was drunk."

"All five or six times?" he laughed again. "Fuck outta here."

"It's more people coming right? I'm already in the doghouse, I ain't tryna be deeper inside it."

"Yeah nigga, it's more people coming." He shook his head. "Speaking of that doghouse, you ain't heard from Kali?"

"Nope." I replied taking a sip out of my glass. "I'm tryna give her, her space; but this shit is hard as hell. We ain't gone this long without talking since—well, since Mexico."

"What you gon' do about it Mac?"

"Whatever it takes." I replied. "I love that girl man. I love her real fucking bad."

"Well, you already know what I said earlier. I don't think I gotta repeat that shit. Get your girl man."

"I'm trying."

As more guests arrived, I found myself distracted from my problems. It was nice to be around other people, it was nice to enjoy friends. I was on my third glass of Henny when I saw from the corner of my eye, Natalie making her way towards me.

"You been talking to everybody but me stranger." She smiled using her hand to shield her eyes from the sun. "How have you been?"

"I'm good Nat. How you been?"

"Same." She shrugged. "What's new in life with you?"

"A lot."

"Yeah, Tish was telling me you got a little girlfriend."

GENESIS CARTER

Natalie smirked, hand on her hip, titties on display in front of my face.

"Oh, she did huh?" I asked taking a sip of my drink and glancing over at Tish who was sitting with Riley not too far away.

"I didn't believe her because last I checked you told me you were going to be single for the rest of your life. What happened?"

"Found somebody that made me change my mind." I pulled my phone out of my pocket feeling it vibrate. My heart swelled seeing the Facetime request from Kali. "Excuse me." I brushed past Natalie making my way into the house. As soon as I was through the threshold, I answered the call with a bright smile.

"Why you smiling already?" Kali asked smiling wide as hell. I'd missed seeing that smile. Her teeth perfectly aligned which she told me was from years of wearing braces and to this day, wore a retainer. I remember finding it once, she'd left it out wrapped in tissue on the bathroom counter; it scared the fuck out of me.

"I miss you and I'm excited to see you." I told her. She looked like she was outside sitting down, but she was on a high level since I could also glimpse high rises behind her as the wind blew her hair in her face; the sound of traffic surrounding her. Her braids, the ones that weren't flying around, were framing her face and from what I could see, she had on a yellow top. I wasn't sure if it was a dress or a shirt but regardless; the bright yellow material looked beautiful against her deep brown skin.

"What you been up to?" she asked before taking a sip of the red liquid from a wine glass.

"Missing you, Kahlia."

"Besides that, Josiah." She playfully rolled her eyes, the

corner of her lips twitching very obviously trying to keep from smiling.

"Shit, I went to the gym with Rich this morning. Now I'm at his crib, him and Tish threw a little kickback, and they got food on the grill. What you up to?"

"Missing you." She smirked and I couldn't help the smile that appeared on my face.

"Besides that, Kahlia." I mocked her causing a chuckle to escape her lips.

"Just hanging out." She shrugged. "Jamie had to run out for work so I'm sitting on her patio watching traffic. I was trying not to call you, trying to give you space, but I couldn't help it my fingers just clicked on your name."

"Oh, is that what happened? You can call me whenever for whatever baby." She stared at me, biting her lips; she had something to say but didn't know how to say it. I knew it because I knew her. "Spit it out Kali."

"Spit what out?"

"Whatever you thinking about." I sighed finding a seat in the living room which was quiet and much cooler than the outside. The Dallas heat was not letting up on us, despite the fact that it was already Fall.

"Are we going to be, okay?" her eyes seemed to pool with tears the same way they did yesterday morning. I had broken her heart, and it was still hurting. I regretted that conversation so bad, wished I had kept my mouth shut.

"I want us to be Kali. This shit don't feel good for me. I'm sorry baby, I'm so fucking sorry about yesterday." I paused, my throat aching with the sense of foreboding. I wanted to be honest with her, but the last time I was honest, I overshared and now we're sitting here miles apart talking over Facetime instead of being next to each other. "I know you're mad, but I need you to give me grace the same way I give you grace Kahlia. We're both still trying to figure shit out, neither of us is perfect."

"Josiah, you told me you were thinking about babies with another woman right after asking me to have one for you. How was I supposed to react?"

"I don't know." I replied honestly. "I don't know why you thought traveling hundreds of miles away was going to help anything. You could have stayed and talked about it so we could work things out. Whenever shit gets hard with us, are you going to keep running?"

"Running? I'm not running Josiah." She said defensively, a frown line forming on her forehead.

"You ran from me in Mexico. You ran from Parris when she pissed you off and you ran from me again going to Baltimore. You're a runner and that shit ain't cool."

"This was a bad idea, I gotta go."

"See, you tryna run again." I told her. "Kahlia, stop this shit. You can't run from every conflict you have baby. I get why you want to run, after what you've been through, but this isn't the solution." She didn't respond, her lips pursed in defiance, but she didn't hang up. "Did I fuck up? Absolutely. I can't apologize enough for it. I got some shit I need to deal with, I know that. The problem is that you don't seem to know that you got shit you still need to deal with too."

"Like what? I don't have any baggage, I dumped it into the ocean before I met you. The one thing that could have held me back was long gone."

"Is it?" I asked watching her fidget with the heart shaped pendant on her necklace. "You cling to him whenever you need comfort. I didn't realize how much it bothered me until just now, seeing you fidgeting with that damn thing while I'm tryna figure our shit out."

"Don't."

"Don't what?" I sighed. "You can bring up my shit, but I can't call you out on your shit?"

"It's not the same."

"It's not the same? We're both clinging on to the past shit. How the fuck are we supposed to move on together when we can't get past these issues?"

"No, I'm mourning my dead husband, and you're still mad your brother fucked your bitch, it's different." She snapped sharply and for the first time, I questioned her. Questioned her feelings for me because to be that fucking petty when all I was tryna do was be truthful; it was foreign to me. It made me question whether I really knew her at all.

"Wow."

"You saw that bitch for five fucking minutes, and she had you in your feelings."

"And you ran off to your dead husband's sister to do what? Feel closer to him? You cling to that fucking necklace like it's some comfort to you whenever you're distressed. You never fucking take it off; it's a slap in the fucking face to be honest. You said you moved on; you went to spread those ashes so you could move the fuck on; but I guess that never happened which makes you a liar. I'm not about to compete with a dead man Kahlia."

"Fuck you, I didn't lie about shit. You, who hasn't seen his parents in years because you're so butt hurt that your brother and yo' bitch couldn't keep they fucking hands to themselves. That bitch obviously didn't love you, which is why she's where she's at now. But here you are, clinging to the memory of a life you'll never get with her. I thought you meant it when you said you wanted it with me. But I guess you didn't; which makes you the fucking liar Josiah; not me. And let's be clear, I'm not about to compete with a hoe who couldn't tell the difference between you and your brother."

I could hear my heart beating through my chest with the

way the silence surrounded us. We stared at one another, both obviously angry, both questioning everything between us. I could see the questions, the regret going through her mind, in her eyes and I knew my face was doing a shit job at hiding my feelings.

"I shouldn't have called you. I should have—"

"Should have what?"

"It doesn't matter. Goodnight Josiah."

"Kahlia, I'm not done talking to you."

"Well, that's too fucking bad." She replied before hanging up on me. When I tried to call her back, I got a message saying I couldn't reach her right now; and I knew she'd blocked me.

"Fuck." I squeezed my cell phone in my hands, stopping just short of crushing it.

19

KAHLIA

"He's not wrong Kali." Jamie said after I'd told her about the conversation Josiah and I had, had. We were eating at a really good Thai restaurant she said she frequented. It was near her apartment, close to the water so we were sitting outside taking in the slight breeze.

"What?"

"You heard what I said." She sighed. "You said you went to Mexico and spread Jonathan's ashes so that you could move on. You still wearing that necklace, walking around with it on every single day as a reminder of him and I love that, but I also see how Josiah could be feeling a way about it. You are forever holding my brother up on this pedestal that it's going to be difficult for any man besides him to reach."

"That's not fair."

"Life ain't fair boo. Like I've told you so many times before; I know you miss him but if this is going to work with Josiah you need to let go fully. I'm not saying to forget him and what he meant to you; but you can't cling to him Kahlia; it's not healthy for any relationship you find yourself in outside of him. I am not saying this is all on you, he obviously has his own shit to figure out. Nevertheless, ya'll both need to figure it out and maybe consider doing it together. I like him for you, I haven't met him in person yet, but from what I know about him; he's the one Kali. He made a mistake. It was a stupid mistake; one ya'll should be able to move past."

"It's not that easy Jamie."

"Kahlia, stop. So, what the conversation got heated; but emotions were flaring, and shit was said. Oh well, get over. You have been lucky in this lifetime to find love twice, boo. I haven't found it once and I may never find it. Fix this, please. This pride you have, it ain't worth it. I ain't saying you gotta fix him, but you do have to let go of Jonathan and find out what your life is without him."

I didn't respond, just grabbed the wine glass I'd been drinking out of and took a sip before looking out over the water. Conflict with Josiah was not something I wanted to experience. But I was a fool for thinking we could get through life without having these kinds of tough conversations.

"You ready to go?" Jamie asked snatching me out of my thoughts. I nodded and she waved her hand to the waiter to ask for the check. It wasn't long after that she was signing the slip, and we were making our way towards the door.

We'd walked to the restaurant as it was a short distance away from her apartment. Along the way we enjoyed hearing the music from bars and street vendors. Other than the music, the walk was quiet and when we made it back to her place, I went straight to the guest room I'd been sleeping in to make sure my things were packed. I had an early flight tomorrow.

I grabbed some pajamas then went into the connecting ensuite so I could shower. After my shower, I went back into the bedroom and sat down on the bed, grabbing my cell phone going to unblock Josiah's contact; it was petty of me to have done it in the first place. It was nearly 11pm here which meant it was 10 in Dallas. Pressing the Facetime app, I clicked his name as it was the last, I'd called then waited for him to answer; hoping that he did actually answer.

"Kali Mac, I see you unblocked me." He chuckled sarcastically. It looked like he was at home, in our bed. His chest was bare, his durag was on and I could hear the TV in the background.

"I've dreamed about them." I whispered and he stared at me; confusion written all over his perfect face. Those beautiful eyes pulling me in without him even trying.

"About who?"

"Our kids. I know what they look like, I can see their faces every time I close my eyes. And hearing you say…" I sighed, trying to keep myself together. "You said you imagined your babies with her and all I could do was see our babies faces. If a family with me, a future with me, is not what you want—"

"You know damn well it's what I want Kahlia; don't do that." He shook his head. "I want you; I only want you. You are my world, and nothing feels right because you're not here. It's been a day and I'm going crazy without you."

"I need this to work Josiah, I need us to work. We need to figure this out, together."

"Promise me, you'll stop running." I licked my lips before looking away from the screen. "Kahlia."

"I promise." My hand went towards my necklace, but I stopped myself.

For so long Jonathan had been my comfort and then this necklace that held his ashes became my comfort. He was all around me, I'd found ways to keep him nearby. But I knew he couldn't be that for me anymore, he couldn't be my comfort because that was now Josiah's role in my life.

So, I did something I never thought I'd ever do; I reached behind me and unclasped my necklace; sliding it off and placing it in one of the compartments in my purse.

> Josiah: What time does your flight get here?

I WAS SITTING in the airport waiting to go home. I'd said my tearful goodbyes to Jamie with her promising she'd visit me in Dallas soon so she could be at my art exhibit. I was tired, exhausted, from being up all night talking to Josiah knowing I needed to be sleep. We were on the phone so long, I fell asleep with the phone propped up on my pillow as if he was asleep next to me.

> Should get to Dallas around 1pm so I should make it home by 2-3pm.

> Josiah: Can't wait to see you, have a safe flight.

I sent back a bunch of kissing emojis just as they called for boarding on my plane. I got on with the second group, finding my seat in the 4th row, thankful I had purchased a seat with extra leg room, and had purchased a window seat. I didn't want anybody to bother me, and I didn't want to bother anybody. So, as soon as I was seated, I pulled out my Air Pods, put on my music, then propped the travel pillow around my neck. I'd be home in a few hours so I could see my man.

I spent the entire plane ride sleep and when the flight attendants made the announcement that we were landing, I excitedly woke up, placing my things up and bracing myself for landing. After the conversation Josiah and I had last night, I felt a lot better about us. We both had taken accountability for the hidden issues we were having despite neither of us ever bringing them up. The baby conversation was off the table for now, we agreed we weren't ready for that move just yet; plus, I was adamant that I would not be popping out any children until I had a ring on my finger.

After landing we deplaned and I hurried down the walkway, into the airport and then made my stop to the Garrett's Popcorn storefront in DFW airport. If there was anything I missed about Chicago; it was this popcorn being so readily available for me. When Jonathan was alive, he would bring me a Garrett's mix every week because he knew how much I loved it.

After grabbing my popcorn, I made my way towards the exit; I'd only brought a carry-on bag so there was no need for me to stop at baggage claim. As I walked through the revolving doors, I stopped in my place when Josiah appeared in front of me holding a bouquet of flowers. I couldn't help the smile that spread across my face as I walked over to him.

"What are you doing here?" I asked wrapping my arms around his neck as he pulled me into a hug. He placed his lips on top of mine.

"I couldn't wait to see you. I took an Uber here so we could drive back together."

"You're cute." I said as he took my bag from me and handed me the flowers.

"Where'd you park?"

"Not far." I walked out of the door, and he followed me.

We made our way to the parking garage, and I was thankful that the flight flew in the same terminal that it left from. When we made it to the car, he opened the passenger door for me, put my bag in the backseat and then got in the

GENESIS CARTER

driver's seat. Once he was settled in his seat, he grabbed my hand placing a kiss on the back of it.

"I know you're tired, but I need to stop at the grocery store right quick and grab something for dinner."

"That's fine." I yawned. "I needed to grab a few things for the week anyway. I can't wait to get home; I need to wash this flight off me and take a quick nap."

"Nah, sex, shower, then you can nap."

"Josiah." I laughed.

"What? He missed her." He placed the hand he held in his lap, and I felt how hard he was. My hand went towards his belt buckled and he glanced over at me as he approached the toll booth to get out. "Don't make me pull this car over Kahlia."

"Then stop starting shit you can't finish." I playfully snatched my hand away and he laughed.

We stopped at the grocery store first, going aisle to aisle, hand in hand picking out items for dinner tonight and that we would need for the week. As we were standing at the checkout line, I chuckled seeing the cashier couldn't keep her eyes off Josiah. When she glanced over at me, she looked shocked and embarrassed to see I'd caught her ogling him, but I let her know it was okay. I knew it was his eyes, those beautiful hazel eyes that always seemed to pull you in, even if he wasn't trying to do so.

After leaving the grocery store, we made our way home. I was glad see the house as we approached, and he pulled into the garage next to his truck. I got out and went to grab bags, but Josiah stopped me letting me know he had it before sending me inside.

As soon as I was through the threshold of the house, I felt home. Despite what I'd told Josiah, this was in fact my home. I knew it was because this is where he was, this is where we would raise our family. Making my way through the house, I noticed how spotless it was; Josiah, of course was a neat freak. Even the bedroom which I'd purposely left a mess was cleaned up, everything in its place.

I slid off my shoes, placing them in the closet and then went into the bathroom so I could run my shower. While I was walking back to the closet to grab underwear and clothes to put on after my shower, Josiah walked in carrying my bag.

"Why the shower running?" he asked, and I laughed, shaking my head. I knew exactly what he was getting at, and I was not about to do this with him.

"I need to shower so I can take a quick nap."

"I said sex, shower then nap." He grabbed me gently by the waist pulling me into his body.

"Or, how about, shower, nap, dinner, then lots of sex before bed." I wrapped my arms around his waist looking up at him. "I'm really tired and I always shower after I travel. You gonna break my routine?"

"Fine. I'mma prep for dinner, and I'll come check on you." I smiled placing a kiss on his lips before bouncing to the bathroom, shutting the door, and getting undressed for my shower.

By the time I was showered and dressed down in leggings, a Hampton University t-shirt and had my hair tied up, I climbed into bed and scrolled my social media. It wasn't long after that my phone had slipped out of my hand falling to the bed just as my eyes closed.

∽

I WOKE up from my nap smelling food and my stomach instantly rumbled with hunger. Besides, the popcorn I'd managed to scarf down on the drive from the airport, I hadn't eaten anything. Slowly getting out of bed, I wiped the sleep from my eyes, grabbed my phone and made my way out of the room.

"I was just about to come get you." Josiah smiled. "Food's done."

"It smells so good baby." I said walking over to the island countertop which is where we normally ate dinner. Josiah sat a plate down in front of me; steak, loaded mashed potatoes and broccoli with cheese. I groaned and my mouth watered. "You know the key to my heart."

"Yeah, I do." He chuckled sitting his plate down next to me. "You want a glass of wine?"

"Yes please." I grabbed my knife and fork before absent-mindedly doing a happy dance.

"There's that happy dance."

"Don't laugh at me, I'm hungry." I replied. He placed a glass of wine down in front of each of us then sat next to me.

"Fork down Kahlia, we still gotta bless the food."

"God knows my heart; I just want one bite." I groaned but one look in his direction and I reluctantly placed my knife and fork back down before accepting his outstretched hand.

Josiah said a quick word of grace before I was finally able to dive in. I loved his cooking; he wasn't lying in Mexico when he said he was a good cook and he cooked for me often. The steak was delicious, the potatoes were flavorful, and the broccoli was perfectly steamed, the cheese sauce creamy. We ate mostly in silence, the only conversation coming from Josiah who kept pointing out that I was fucking the food up and my only response being the middle finger. When I was done eating, I pushed my plate away from me and gulped the rest of my wine.

"I need to shower, then we can watch the new episode of Walking Dead." Josiah said standing up and I nodded still stuck in my food coma. "Can you load the dishwasher?"

"Yeah."

He bent down and placed a quick kiss on my lips before heading down the hall to our room. Slowly, I got up and grabbed both plates, emptying the excess food into the trash then rinsing them off and placing them in the dishwasher along with all the other dishes in the sink except for the pots which I always hand washed.

By the time he was out of the shower and back in the living room I was finishing up with cleaning the stove and counters. I washed my hands then made my way over to the couch so we could cuddle and watch one of our favorite shows. Just as we had gotten comfortable and were about to play the episode, his phone rang.

"Shit." He said looking at it and seeing it was his mom. "I can call her back." His hand hovered over the decline button, but I stopped him.

"It's okay, answer." I replied and he shrugged before accepting the call and placing it on speaker.

"What's up Beautiful?"

"Sonshine." Ms. Claudette's voice boomed from the phone. "Did I catch you at a bad time?"

"No, me and Kali just sitting here watching tv."

"Oh, tell her I said hello."

"She can hear you Mama, you on speaker."

"Hi Ms. Claudette." I smiled greeting the woman who was responsible for birthing this beautiful man whose arms I was wrapped in.

"Hello to you Ms. Kali." She replied. "How you doing?"

"I'm doing well, you doing, okay?"

"Yeah, just missing my sonshine as usual." She replied and Josiah playfully rolled his eyes.

"You laying it on thick Ma."

"What? I am. I heard your brother got to see you, but I can't get a visit."

"That shit was on accident." Josiah replied a little too

forcefully and I nudged him giving him the evil eye. "My bad Ma, I ain't mean to curse."

"It's okay Josiah, I understand." She sighed. "He said you looked good; he said you looked happy."

"Did he?"

"He said you left abruptly though, and I was just calling to see what happened."

"I don't want to talk about it Ma." He sighed and I rubbed the back of his head soothingly. "And honestly, I ain't tryna sit here and talk about Josh."

"You never are Josiah." Ms. Claudette said before coughing almost uncontrollably. I looked at Josiah alarmed.

"Ma, you good?"

"Yeah, it's fine." She sighed. "I just got a little cough. So, Kahlia can I get your help in convincing my son to come see me?"

"How about we send for you and Pops to come visit us?" Josiah suggested before I could respond. "You know me, and Kali don't get that much time off during the school year."

"Thanksgiving break is coming up and so is Christmas. I've already invited you for Thanksgiving, but you make up excuses every single time Josiah. So, I'm going to ask the lady of the house to help me instead."

"Ma—"

"Kahlia?" Ms. Claudette ignored him. I looked at Josiah and licked my lips before speaking. "Do you think you two can make it for Thanksgiving? I don't know if you had plans with your family."

"No, I don't." I told her. "Not really."

"Work on him for me then will you Sweetpea?" I could feel Josiah staring a hole in the side of my face as I tried to find the words to say to his mother.

"I'll try." I told her.

"Alright, that's all I ask." She coughed again and I felt it, there was something not right.

"You sure you're okay Ms. Claudette?"

"Everything's fine. I'll let ya'll go."

"Love you Ma."

"I love you more Sonshine." She replied before the call was disconnected. I grabbed the remote to try to play the episode before he could say anything.

"I'm not going to Atlanta for Thanksgiving Kahlia."

"Well, I am." I shrugged. "I'm buying my ticket tomorrow and if I buy yours too, I bet you get on that damn plane."

20

JOSIAH

"I can't believe I let you convince me to do this shit." I shook my head as we went through TSA. We were just in time for our flight to Atlanta. I was so adamant on not coming that I had refused to pack my bags, refused to do anything and I knew I was on Kahlia's shit list because she ended up doing it for me.

"Stop being a brat." She snipped placing her things on the conveyor belt and shaking her head. I placed my things in her bin then followed behind her into the line waiting to go through the metal detectors.

I had originally planned on spending Thanksgiving break with Rich and his family, but Kahlia had made good on her promise the day after we'd spoken to my mom and purchased two tickets to Atlanta with plans for us to spend the entire four-five days there. I wasn't happy about it, tried to argue my case, but she wasn't hearing it. Even after my experience with seeing Angie and Josh before, even after the damage it caused to our relationship, she refused to see reason.

"This ain't a good idea Kahlia, I'm trying to tell you." She didn't respond as it was her turn to go through the detectors. I watched as she raised her hands above her head and was asked to step out before she moved on to collect her things. I followed the same process then joined her in grabbing our things.

"Honestly Josiah, you should have been made this trip to see your parents. I get that you were upset with them for accepting your brother and I think your feelings are valid; but--"

"But?"

"But, if you're ever going to get over what happened and move on with me, you need this. It's just a place, it's just for a few days. Besides, each time we've spoken to your mom since her asking us to come, that cough has not gotten better. What if there is something wrong and she just doesn't want to tell you over the phone?"

I didn't say anything, mostly because I had been thinking the same thing. Claudette Mackenzie was one of the strongest people I knew. She didn't complain when she was sick, she just took it in strides. But Kali was right, there was something about her cough that didn't sit well with me. She'd had it too long.

After grabbing our things, we made our way towards our gate. We were flying with Delta and since Kali was a frequent flyer with them, she'd put us on the upgrade list when we checked our bags in. I had travelled first class before, knew how comfortable the seats were and I needed the extra space, so I was hoping to get lucky.

I was so tired. We'd been up all night arguing about whether or not I was getting on the plane and then we had to be up early today for work. It was the last day before the break, so we only had a half day, but we came straight here after work. I had planned on sleeping on the flight since I knew that we'd be busy as soon as we stepped foot into

Hartsfield Jackson; we had to get our rental, check into our hotel, and then go see my parents for dinner.

"I don't want no problems between us no more." I told Kali once we found seats near the gate just in case they called us for the upgrade. She looked over at me and sighed.

"Me either, but you also can't keep avoiding these issues either." She placed her hand on the side of my face. "Just don't shut down on me. If you want to talk, I am here to talk. If you just need to vent, vent to me, okay?" I nodded then sat back in my seat. There was nothing I could do to stop it; this trip was happening. I just had to wrap my mind around all of it on this three hour flight.

Six hours later and three hours after arriving at the airport, grabbing the rental, and checking into the hotel; I found myself standing outside my parent's door. Looking up at the house I grew up in, it seemed smaller than it used to be.

My Pops was retired military, having dedicated the majority of his life in service. My mom was retired as well, she was a social worker up until about six years ago. I remember she used to tell us stories about some of the cases she was over; involving kids and women who suffered through domestic violence and child abuse. It was sick hearing it. I could never imagine hitting my woman or abusing my kids.

"You gonna ring the doorbell?" Kahlia asked and I nodded but my hand didn't move to reach it. I was nervous as hell. Although I talked to my mom often; I had barely spoken to my Pops, and it was because he was mostly on Josh's side; spewing bullshit about my need to get over it. He favored Josh, I'd always known it growing up, but the love I got from my mom always overshadowed anything I wasn't getting from him. "Baby…"

"Huh?"

"Ring the doorbell." Kahlia nodded towards the white doorbell, and I sighed before pressing it. She grabbed onto my hand and rubbed my arm. "I'm nervous, I hope they like me."

"Doesn't matter if they do or don't; I love you and you're not going anywhere." She looked up at me with a wide smile, I bent down and kissed her lips just as the door was opening.

"My Sonshine." My mom's beautiful face appeared at the door, her smile just as wide and bright as Kahlia's had been moments ago. She opened the screen door and immediately pulled me into a hug which I reciprocated. Claudette Mackenzie was just as beautiful as the last time I'd laid eyes on her. She had skin that matched mine and Josh's, thick curly hair, a button nose, and full lips which she kept covered in nude lipstick. She was short all my life, standing just barely above 5'0.

"Hey Mama." I slightly lifted her in my arms and chuckled as she squirmed to be let go and put down. She always hated when we lifted her, it was a running joke between all of us since she was so short. By the time Josh and I were finishing elementary school she was officially the shortest person in our family and hadn't grown an inch since then.

"Oh, I missed you so much." Her voice cracked and I just knew when I let her go, she was going to be crying. "Josiah Henry Mackenzie you are a sight for sore eyes."

"So are you, Mama." I smiled finally setting her on her feet. She rubbed my face before turning to look at Kahlia. "Ma, this is Kali."

"You are beautiful." She crooned before pulling Kali into a hug. "Welcome my dear. It's a pleasure to have you and thank you for getting my baby home."

"It's nice to finally meet you in person." Kali said holding on to my mom tightly. I knew she was probably missing her own mom which was why it was so important for her to see me reconnect with mine.

"Well come on in, Daddy went out to pick up the Chinese food. I hope you two don't mind, I been a little under the weather, so I didn't cook anything."

"You're good Mama." I told her, shutting the front door behind us and walking into the house. Everything was exactly how I remembered it; my mama wasn't big on change. All of our pictures still lined the walls, paintings they'd collected, flowers in vases all over giving the house a florally smell.

"Kahlia, this Chinese place is one of our favorites. We've been ordering from them since the boys were young. The food is excellent. I do apologize, I guess I should have asked if there were any dietary restrictions; I know Josiah eats everything."

"I'm the same way, I am not picky, and I have no dietary restrictions."

"Good." Mama smiled then she looked at the gift bag Kali had in her hand. "Is that for me?"

"Oh yeah." Kali said handing her the bag. I had no idea what was in it, and when I asked her about it; she told me to stop being nosey since it wasn't for me. "I thought you might like to have this." Mama accepted the bag and after taking out the tissue paper, she pulled out a 5x7 picture frame.

"Oh Lord, look at this." She laughed.

"Josiah and I met in Mexico; I'm sure he's told you. We went out to tour the city and I snapped this picture of him. It's one of my favorites." Curious I nodded for my mom to show me. It was a black and white photo of me standing on a boat gazing up at a real pirate ship. I went back to that moment and felt like a kid all over again; I had never in my life thought I'd see a pirate ship and there I was standing in front of one. I could see why it was her favorite, I looked so happy, I was so happy in that moment pointing out to the ship in amazement. Seriously, the inner child in me was excited.

"I haven't seen that smile in so long." My mama said caressing the framed picture. "Thank you for this, I'll add it to my Josiah wall."

"Josiah wall?" Kali asked, her eyebrow lifting up.

"Mama, don't." I warned, knowing where this was leading. I wasn't interested in having my girlfriend see my embarrassing kid photos.

"Yes, Josiah and Joshua each have their own wall of photos starting from pre-k through college. You wanna see?" She stood up and held her hand out for Kali which she accepted. Reluctantly, I got up as well and followed them to the hallway where the left side of the wall was dedicated to me.

"Oh my God." Kali squealed before looking back at me. I could see the amusement in her eyes as she viewed my toothless photos, bad hair day photos, and photos of me when I thought I was cooler than I actually was.

We went down the hall, looking at all my pictures. When we got to college years, there were several pictures displayed of me, Rich, Angie, and Tish with our Howard University gear on; pictures of Rich and I after we pledged Alpha dawned in jackets with our line names.

"Howard." Kali scoffed, shaking her head.

"The real HU." I playfully pushed her, and she rolled her eyes.

"Yeah right."

"What's this about?" My Mama asked taking in our playful banter. We'd been doing this since we met, she knew damn well Hampton was not it.

"Kali went to Hampton University; the perpetrators who think they are the real HU."

"If your mom wasn't standing right here—" Before she could finish her sentence, the sound of the door opening pulled our attention in another direction.

"Claudette, I'm back. I see a nice car outside, Josiah here?" My mom led the way back up front and I grabbed Kali's hand escorting her in the same direction. When we neared the front door, my mom was giving my dad a kiss and he handed her one of the bags which I quickly took.

"Josiah, it's nice to see you son." My dad said staring at me with identical hazel eyes; it was the only thing Josh and I had gotten from him. His salt and pepper hair looked good on him. He was taller than me, but not by much and he'd put on a little weight. Still, he was the same man who had raised me, taught me lessons, molded me into the person I am today.

"You too Pops." I held out my hand and he looked at it for a second before accepting it then pulling me into a tight hug.

"You have been missed; phone calls are not enough."

"I know and I apologize. Things just got a little heavy for me and I needed—"

"I understand." He replied. "Glad you're here." He pulled back from our embrace then looked over my shoulder. "Well, well, who is this?"

"This is Kahlia." I told him.

"She is a beauty." He chuckled walking over to her and holding out his hand. "It's nice to meet you Kahlia, I'm Jeremiah."

"Sheesh, these eyes." Kahlia said causing us all to laugh. "I'm so sorry, that was—"

"Real." My mama said wrapping her arm into hers. "Don't worry, I got stuck by them too. That's how I ended up with two kids. Let's go eat, I'm starving." Kahlia looked back at me, and I couldn't help the chuckle that escaped my lips as we all moved to the dining room.

We sat around for dinner, and I felt good about the fact

that Kahlia was experiencing my parents. They seemed to love her, and she seemed to loved them as well. We laughed and Kali listened to stories about how I was growing up. Seeing her here, with them, only made me believe even more that she was the perfect fit for me and this family.

∼

KALI and I spent the day before Thanksgiving sightseeing. She said this hadn't been her first trip to Atlanta, but this was the first time here with a native, so I got to show her around all my favorite spots. I took her to Atlantic Station so we could ice skate and she did some shopping of course. She'd brought her camera along, so she snapped pictures of us throughout the entire day.

For dinner we grabbed pizza from Nancy's and watched outside of our hotel window as the city below us moved around; traffic, the people, the view it felt good to be home. That night I made love to my woman under the light of the Atlanta skyline; fucking her so deep, so passionately, so fucking nastily that she was snoring before long.

Waking up the next day, we were refreshed, showered and out the door for an early start. Kali had promised my mom that she would be there to help her cook and of course I had gotten recruited to help as well. As we drove towards their home, I couldn't help but feel the nerves building in my stomach from knowing I'd be in the room with Angie and Josh again.

"You okay over there?" Kali asked sliding her hand into mine. I glanced over at her and smiled with a nod before focusing back on the road. "You know what I've been thinking?"

"Huh?"

"Promise not to be mad if I say?"

"Spit it out Kahlia." I smirked over at her playfully.

"I don't think your problem is with her." She muttered uneasily. Again, I looked over at her, confusion blatant on my face. "Well, I know it is, but not really. I think your real issue is with your brother. At the end of the day, he owed you more loyalty than she did. She was just a girl; granted a girl you fell in love with, but she was nothing compared to him. You and he came into this world together Josiah. He's been your closest confidant since you were kids and he betrayed you in a way you never imagined. When we saw them at Rich and Tish's house, you could care less about her, all you could focus on was him. So, maybe you need to have a conversation with your brother. I'm not saying it has to be today, in fact, I think it absolutely shouldn't be today, because today is for your mom; but soon."

"I ain't even gon hold you baby, that shit is real as fuck." I told her. "I been thinking about that, for a while. It's just real to hear it out loud. I don't know if I can avoid the conversation today. When else would I have it?"

"If you're going to have it Josiah, you need to speak to your parents first. And when you have it, it needs to just be you and your brother."

"I know. I'll think of something."

"If you need me, at any time, you just come get me; understand?"

"I got you baby." I raised her hand up placing a kiss on it. I felt safe with her, so thankful that she was in my life. I didn't know what I would do without her being here. She just didn't know how much she'd saved me, had changed me for the better.

We made it to my parent's house not long after. When we pulled up, I saw a blue Jeep Wrangler in the driveway, and I knew immediately it was Josh's. He loved that fucking car, this one looked like a newer model. Shaking my head and sighing, I rang the doorbell, and it was immediately opened by my mom who smiled pulling me into a hug before going for Kahlia.

"Did you have some fun yesterday?" she asked her walking into the house holding her hand. Mom had taken over Kahlia's attention.

"Yes, I got so many pictures. I'll make sure to print some off for you and send them so you can add them to his wall."

"I'd love that."

As we made our way into the house, Joshua was the first person I spotted. When he saw me, he stood up and approached. I glanced over at Kali, and she stood as a buffer between us, escaping my mother's grasp to be by my side instead.

"Joshua, it's good to see you again." She waved. "How's the baby?"

"He's good." Josh glanced over at her with a smile, one I didn't like seeing while his eyes roamed her frame. Protectively, I pulled her close to me. I trusted her, of course I did, but I didn't trust his ass worth shit. "Jo, what's up?"

"What's up." I replied with a head nod.

"Can we talk?" he looked over at Kali who was glued to my side. "Alone."

"Nah, I—"

"Kahlia, Sweetpea, let's get started." My mama said pulling Kali away from me. "I prepped some things last night but there's still so much to do. And I want to hear more about this art exhibit you got coming up; maybe Jeremiah and I will be able to come and support."

"Yeah, of course." Kali replied before looking at me. I nodded for her to go ahead and then I turned to Josh.

"Can we talk?" he asked again.

"Nope." I replied taking my coat off and hanging it up then following behind Mama and Kali. Before I could get too

GENESIS CARTER

far, he grabbed my arm, and it took everything in me not to swing on him. "Aye, don't fucking touch me nigga."

"Josiah." Our Pops stood quickly from his spot. "Don't."

"Leave me the fuck alone Josh, dead ass." I snatched away from him making my way into the kitchen. When I entered, my mama and Kali were both staring at me. "Don't..." I told them.

"I wasn't going to say anything." My mom smiled. "Wash your hands and help me sonshine, just like the old days." I nodded before going to the sink to wash my hands.

Despite the conversation I'd just had with Kali, I wasn't fucking ready to talking to Joshua. He didn't want to hear the shit I had to say and I for damn sure didn't want to hear shit he had to say either. What could he possibly say to me? If he thought I needed an explanation on why he fucked my fiancé, he was very much mistaken. Still, I couldn't help glancing over at Kali as I chopped veggies. I knew she was going to feel some type of way, I could see it in her eyes when she did look at me.

"I finally got Joel fed and sleep." Angie's voice suddenly boomed from the entrance to the kitchen. "How can I—" I looked over at her, but her eyes were trained on Kahlia who was conversing with my mom, laughing. "Oh, I didn't know they'd arrived. Hi Josiah." I didn't respond, just continued doing what I was doing.

"I believe you met Josiah's girlfriend Kahlia." My mama interrupted the awkward silence.

"Yeah, Hi again."

"Hi." Kali replied.

"How can I help?" Angie asked my mama and she immediately put her to work. I was glad when someone turned on music and the sounds of Frankie Beverly and Maze echoed through the kitchen. I needed the distraction, needed to focus on something other than using the knife in my hand to ram it through the side of my brother's neck.

I almost felt like this was a mistake, being here. But every time I glanced up and saw how happy Kahlia was, saw her smiling and laughing with my mom. Somehow, I just knew this was where we needed to be for this holiday.

After a while, I took a break and made my way into the living room. My Pops and Josh were watching football. I sat down on the couch opposite them and focused my attention on the tv screen. As if on cue, I turned my head slightly seeing them exchange a look.

"What?" I asked looking at my Pops.

"I just... I thought maybe now is a good time to have this conversation between you and your brother, before dinner. There's a lot we all need to talk about."

"I'm not interested." I dismissed them both. "Now ain't the time."

"Now is the time, Josiah." My Pops replied. "There's... there's some stuff you need to know."

"Like what?"

"You need to talk to your brother first, ya'll need to make this right."

"Make what right?"

"This bullshit between ya'll. It's been years and there are more important things to worry about."

"Pops, this the same thing you tried to pull last time." I chuckled. "You always on his side."

"I'm not on his fucking side. I know what he did was foul, I fucking know that." He pounded his chest. "You think I didn't fucking tell his ass that? I haven't seen you in years because of it, because of the shit he did. But he is sorry for that shit Josiah, you gotta know that."

"I am Jo." Josh mumbled and I looked over at him. "I fucked up, I know that. I can't explain why I did the shit; I just did and there's nothing I can do to take it back. After my son, there's nothing I would do to take it back. I don't regret him, but I do regret hurting you in the process."

"Fuck outta here."

"Josiah." My Pops warned but I didn't give a fuck.

"Nah, that's bullshit Josh and you know it."

"Maybe we should take this downstairs to the basement. We don't need the women in the conversation."

"I think that's a good idea." Joshua stood up; I glanced up at him then over to my Pops.

"Josiah, please son."

Shaking my head, I stood up and followed behind them as our Pops led us down to the basement which he also kept as a mancave. With the door closed behind us, I stood as far away from Josh as I possibly could, afraid that if I stood closer, I would strangle his ass for sure.

"Now listen here, this shit needs to be squashed and I mean it. It's gone on too long Josiah, too damn long. It's not right that we ain't seen you in years, none of it is right."

"Look, at the end of the day, I know I fucked up." Josh told me. "I ain't mean for this shit to go down like this, but it just happened. I wasn't expecting it to happen. And like I said upstairs, I regret hurting you, but I don't regret being with Angie and having my son."

"I was just collateral damage, right? Just fuck Josiah. Ya'll both meant the world to me. I loved the fuck out of that girl, and we was about to get married. Why did you have to go after her Josh?"

"That shit just happened the first time."

"And after that? Ya'll could have told me; you could have said something before I proposed to her. I ain't even gon' ask you how long that shit was going on, because it had to be since before I had proposed. You sat there fucking my girl while she wore a ring on her finger that I gave her. I was planning our future and ya'll both was just saying fuck mine."

"I didn't want to fucking tell you because I knew it was going to end up here, Jo. I knew how much you loved her, but I loved her more."

"Yeah, a'ight." I scoffed. "Ya'll were some shitty people who did a shitty thing to the one person who would have done anything for either one of ya'll. And at the end of the day, Angie was supposed to be loyal but nigga, you, yo' ass was supposed to be my A1. We blood, twins, shared a fucking womb and you didn't give a fuck about me."

"That ain't true."

"Oh, it ain't? If you did, this shit wouldn't have gone down like this. Ya'll wouldn't have been sneaking around in my shit fucking every chance ya'll got if you gave a fuck about me. I lost everything behind ya'll, had to start the fuck over and I didn't trust nobody. Ya'll did that shit to me, but I'm supposed to just sit here and act like everything is all good now?"

"I ain't saying you gotta act like we good. I just—" he paused, a pained look in his eyes. "I miss you, Josiah. I miss my brother; I miss my friend. I need you to believe me when I tell you how sorry I am. You're right, I owed you more loyalty than I gave you. But I'm telling you, when it came to that woman, my heart been in this shit for the longest and there ain't shit I can do about that. I got a son now, we got a son, I want you in his life. I want you to teach him shit that I can't. He innocent in this bro."

I didn't respond, just paced back and forth across the basement. My feet didn't lead me near him because my fists were balled and ready to fuck his ass up. His apology was ringing in my ear, Kahlia's words from earlier were in my ear. Josh was the source of my pain, Angela had culpability as well, but mainly it was Josh.

"All these years I been mad at Angie but man Josh, I have been mad as fuck at you. I might be able to forgive you one day; not saying it's today or any time soon, but I won't ever forget this shit. We won't ever be close again and as far as me having a relationship with your son; that's something I'm going to have to think about as well. I just want to move on with my life."

"I get it." He walked closer to me, and my eyes roamed his frame, wondering what the fuck he was doing until he held his hand out to me. I accepted it and without hesitation he pulled me into a hug. "I'm sorry Josiah, seriously."

"Good because you should be."

"Thank the lord." Pops said from behind us, as we backed out of our embrace. He sighed, sitting down in his recliner. "Now, Josiah; there's something you ought to know. I think you should sit down for this."

I looked over at Josh who was already taking a seat cross from him. I slowly followed suit, making my way to a chair opposite him. My eyes flashed between Joshua and my Pops, both with worried looks on their faces.

"What's up?" I finally asked, breaking up the silence.

"Mom thought I should be the one to tell you. The reason she's been trying to get you here so bad, it's because she's sick Josiah."

"Wait... what?" I felt like he was speaking a foreign language; like I was in a live action episode of Peanuts and an adult had walked into the room to speak.

"Stage 3 breast cancer." The air seemed to be knocked from my lungs at hearing that news. My eyes watered, lips trembled as I stared at my father who looked to be on the verge of tears himself. She is the love of his life, which meant he wasn't dealing with this new that well either. But I knew the only thing preventing his tears from falling were his two grown adult sons sitting before him. He had always been the macho type, a man's man, but I saw his resolve weakening as the seconds ticked by.

"How long has she known?" I swiped away a few tears that had pooled over my eyes.

"That doesn't matter."

"Why didn't she… why didn't she tell me sooner?"

"She's been trying to get you home Son." He sighed and I felt Josh reach over and pat my shoulder a few times, his way of telling me he'd been through these same emotions. His head was hanging low, trying to hide his own tears; I knew.

"Okay, so what's the plan? What are we doing about it; chemo, surgery?"

"Chemo first, she wants to start in the new year and get to enjoy the holidays. If chemo works to shrink the tumor, she'll have surgery. But we don't want ya'll to worry. Mom is strong, we all know that. That lady is going to outlive us all if she has any say so about it."

"She's the healthiest person I know." I shook my head in disbelief. "I don't get it."

"Healthy people fall sick all the time Josiah, you know that. We can't worry about how it happened; we just need to focus on getting her well. We can all do our parts in that. That's why I wanted you and your brother to get on the same page about things because, it's more important shit in life Son, do you understand? We can't take care of her if we're divided and as much as she takes care of us, we owe her that at the very least."

I nodded in agreement. I knew he was right and now I knew I had to try hard as hell to forgive my brother. We absolutely had to be there for Ma Dukes like she'd be there for us. I needed to be able to contact Josh if for whatever reason I couldn't get ahold of our parents.

"We gon' get through this." My Pops said getting up from his seat and walking over to me. He grabbed my hand, pulling me up out of my seat then wrapping his arms around me. "We're stronger together than apart; you hear?"

"Yes Sir."

We talked for a little while longer before going upstairs and watching football until the food was done. Before we gathered for dinner, I took my mom to the side, embracing her for several minutes making sure she knew I would be here and do whatever for her. I was a mama's boy after all. Not wanting Kali to be out of the loop, I asked my mom's permission to tell her; but she said she'd already filled her in while we were downstairs talking. She knew I was going to need Kali's support to get through this; she was always thinking about us even when she was the one that was going through it.

When we gathered around the table to eat, Josh entered the dining room holding my nephew and as soon as I looked at him again, my heart raced. I looked over at Kahlia and she smiled up at me, slightly. It was as if she could feel the nerves in my body.

"Give him here." My Mama squealed reaching for him. Once he was in her arms, she placed kisses all over his face. "Joel, this is your uncle Josiah and your auntie Kali." She held him up so we could see him.

"He's beautiful." Kali smiled looking at Angie and Josh.

"Thank you." Josh smiled. "He accepts compliments from all women, he's going to be a lady's man for sure."

"Just like his daddy and uncle." My Mama chuckled.

"May I?" Kahlia asked and I followed her gaze to Angela who looked like she was caught off guard. But I had seen the twinkle in Kahlia's eyes the moment Joel appeared. She was a baby person, any time we'd spent with Riley, she couldn't put her down. Even the kids at the school, teenagers and she always held a tenderness for them regardless of how bad they are.

"Um…" Angela's eyes bounced from me to Josh and back to me again. "Ye-yeah, it's okay if you want."

Excitedly Kahlia held her hands out towards the baby and my mom slowly placed him in her hands. I looked at him and realized how much he looked like Josh, like me. Yeah, he was exactly who I imagined my child with Angela would look; but I knew the child I had with Kahlia was going to be more of her than me, at least I hoped so.

"He's beautiful." Kahlia looked up smiling towards Josh and Angela. "He has those eyes." She looked up at me and smirked. "But he looks like you Angela."

"Thank you." Angie blushed. "And those eyes are deadly aren't they."

"Are you kidding? This one can get me to do anything with one look."

"Anything?"

"Aht, none of that nasty talk in front of your mother. My old ears don't need to be hearing that." My mama shook her head causing us all to laugh. "Let's dig in before the food gets cold."

"You want me to take him?" Angie asked Kali and Kali shook her head.

"No, you go ahead and eat. I can't imagine either of you gets to enjoy a full meal together without holding him. I don't mind; I helped take care of my nephew and I got used to eating with one hand."

"Thank you, you're a lifesaver."

"I'll make your plate just let me know what you want." I told Kahlia and she nodded, adjusting Joel as he fussed a little.

The food was passed around the table and Kali continued to hold and feed Joel. He seemed to like her as much as she seemed to like him. He nestled himself in her arms after he was done eating and burping and she continued to soothe him into sleep as we ate and talked amongst ourselves. It was strange to be here, laughing with all of these people at this table especially considering what happened between us. But every time I looked over at Kali, she was already looking at me, easing me through it, letting me know she was here for me, through glances.

Before Kali and I were due to leave for the night, she gathered us all into the living room so she could get a picture of us for our first Thanksgiving together as a family in four years. Moments like these were always important to her. It was something that I had learned that about her; she wanted to mark important events with a photo. As she stood in front of us prepared to take the picture, my mom stopped her.

"Wait, aren't you getting in?"

"No, I take the photo; I'm hardly in them." She replied.

"Come on now, you're a part of this family now. Set it up somewhere and get in this picture." My Pops said waving her over. Kali looked at me and I chuckled with a shrug. "Come on now." Accepting defeat, Kali checked the focus on her camera and set the camera on top of the mantel. She ran over to me, sitting down in my lap.

"It's going to beep twice before it will flash, five seconds. Five...four..." I placed a kiss on her cheek and squeezed her against my body, wrapping my arms around her hearing a giggle escape her lips. "Three...two...one."

"Cheese." Everyone said in union before the camera flashed not once, but three times.

After making promises to get copies to everyone, Kali and I put on our coats and made our way out of the house. We had to pack for our flight tomorrow and my mama asked us to come over early so we could have breakfast with her and Pops before we left.

When we were on the road, I glanced over at Kali whose eyes were closed and her head was resting against the window. She looked at peace and I reflected on the calmness I felt with her all day, all weekend, hell for the entire time I knew her.

"Kali." I said rubbing her leg and she peeked one eye open. "Thank you for getting me here."

"Of course. I'm here for you always because I love you so much."

21

KAHLIA

"You nervous?" Josiah asked rubbing my shoulders as I stood in front of the mirror gazing at the white cocktail dress I'd opted to wear for my event tonight. I'd purposely picked the second week of December to hold the event since it would be cheaper for those coming out of town to come to Dallas.

"Of course, I am." I sighed running my hand down my dress. "I'm an artist and I'm sensitive about my shit." That made him laugh out loud. "Don't laugh, it's not funny." I whined.

"Okay, okay, I'm sorry." He wrapped his arms around me. "I've seen some of it and I've loved what I've seen. I don't know much about art, but I know enough to know that you are dope as fuck at what you do. You got this. You got so many people coming out to support you, including ya man." He smiled before kissing my nose and lips. "Come on, Mama and Pops waiting on us."

I nodded before accepting his hand and then grabbing my clutch off the bed. Josiah escorted us out of the bedroom down the small hall and into the living room where his parents were dressed and waiting on us. They'd made good on their promise to come see my exhibit especially since they wanted to spend as much time with the family before Claudette's chemo started in the new year. We'd agreed to spend Christmas here in Dallas, but we were going to fly back out to Atlanta for the new year. I was grateful for their support and looked forward to spending my new year with them.

"You look beautiful." Ms. Claudette smiled pulling me into a hug.

"Thank you." I replied before hugging Jeremiah as well.

"Come on, we don't want to be late." Josiah led us out of the house before turning to lock up. We all got into my Lexus, then Josiah pulled out of the garage so we could head to the gallery. On the drive, my leg shook, and I remained quiet listening partially to the conversation happening around me. Every single time my phone vibrated in my clutch I looked at it, answering texts from everyone and calls from Jamie as well as Parris, asking if I was on the way.

"Relax." Josiah said from my left, placing his hand on my thigh. I looked up at him and the moment those hazel orbs focused on me; a calmness went through me. His hand went to my inner thigh, before resting there for the entirety of the car drive.

When we pulled up to the event, I saw that it was already in full swing. Delilah had opted to getting valet for the event, so Josiah stopped in front of the valet podium, and we all got out. I waited for Josiah to get the ticket before he came to my side, and we were back off towards the entrance. My eyes roamed his body, dressed in a black Polo, black slacks, and black Steve Madden loafers. His hair was freshly cut, and he smelled so fucking good.

"Before we go in." I stopped him just short of the door, nodding at his parents for them to go on in. I stared up at him. "Thank you for being so supportive this entire time. I know these last few weeks I haven't been easy to deal with, I'm glad you didn't give up on me."

"Almost did." He replied with a wide smile, his arms wrapped around my waist looking down at me. I tried to wiggle out of his grasp, playfully rolling my eyes. He laughed loudly,"I'm joking. You know I ain't going nowhere baby, it's me and Kali Mac until the death of me. I'm learning and I'm adapting. But if you really want to apologize you can make it extra nasty tonight."

"When do I not?" I smirked placing a kiss on his lips. "I love you."

"I love you." His lips touching mine with every word he spoke. "Let's go so I can show off my fine ass girlfriend and her artwork."

Cheesing, we held hands before walking into the gallery. The moment I entered applauses rang around me. I greeted people I knew and some I didn't know before Delilah waved me over to a small platform in front of my signature piece. It was an acrylic painting of the colorful Tanzanian grassland surrounding an African village, the sun on the horizon in the distance.

I'd seen the view in one of my dreams about a past life I seemed to remember Josiah and I having. It was the soul tie that was always most prominent in my memories. I was his queen, and he was my king. Where we uttered the words; "Wewe ni wa milele wangu."

"Before we begin, I just wanted our featured artist to say a few words about what you're going to see here tonight." Delilah said her voice echoing around the room. I peered out to the crowd. I recognized so many faces, my family, friends, some co-workers, people I knew from the art community. I had even invited some of my art students who showed interest in art. Most of them attending with their families.

I accepted the microphone from Delilah before continuing to look out over the crowd. My nerves kicked in, they always did, any time I had art on display, any time I was highlighted for my work. My eyes roamed around before they landed on the beautiful hazel orbs, I had spent months gazing in to and had dreamed about.

"I won't be long." I finally spoke. "I just wanted to say thank you to everyone for coming out. It's been a little while since I've done one of these; a special thank you to Delilah for giving me this opportunity." I waved in her direction, waiting for her applause. "You know, when she asked me to do this, I admit I was a little nervous. For so long I had stopped painting, and instead focused on my photography. I was uninspired so, I couldn't create. But then, earlier this year, I found my muse." My eyes focused in on Josiah, smiling. "Anyway, I've been very inspired since and I haven't been able to stay out of my art space. This art that you will see, these photographs, have been inspired by grief, strength, power, forgiveness, joy, happiness, and love. So, I hope ya'll enjoy and thank you so much for coming out."

I handed the mic back to Delilah and immediately went to Josiah's side so we could walk around the gallery together. He stayed by my side throughout the entire night while I visited with everyone who came. He relaxed the most around our friends and family; each stop we made we went to a different piece so he would get a chance to look at everything. Every person I saw, Parris, Jamie, his parents, my friend Antwan, Mason, Rich, and Tish, all congratulated me, and it felt good to have so much support.

My favorite visits were my students who were more infatuated with the fact that they could confirm the rumor that me and Josiah were dating. All year long students had been speculating but no one had been able to confirm it. I'm sure when we got back to school after break, news would spread like wildfire; knowing the power of social media it had already started.

All in all, the evening went off without a hitch, I had even had a few purchases which was exciting since I planned on adding it to my travel fund; the more we saved, the longer we could stay in Europe for the summer like we talked about. Right now, we'd worked up to a month's worth of travel, but after these purchases, we could afford to stay another few days in Europe or travel locally to Florida so we could visit Disney, Universal and then go to Miami to lounge on the beach and turn up a little.

When almost everyone was gone, I excused myself to go to the bathroom. It was the first time I'd been able to escape, wanting to spend as much time with my people as much as possible. Once I was done relieving myself, I washed my hands then freshened up my makeup and puffed out the head full of curls I sported for the tonight. I walked back into the room seeing that only family seemed to linger in the space, everyone crowding around my signature piece talking.

"Hey." I approached them immediately taking Josiah's hand. "Are we going to eat? I'm starving."

"Yeah baby, we just need a minute." Josiah whispered into my ear. "Stay with me, okay?" He pulled back from our embrace and I stared at him my eyes swimming with confusion. "Can I have everybody's attention?" he called out to our friends and family who all quieted down, focusing on him. I stood back, gazing at him, my weight shifting from my left foot to my right. All eyes were on us, but my eyes only saw his. "I want to congratulate Kahlia on an amazing event, the work you have displayed here for us tonight has been amazing baby, seriously congratulations." A round of applause seemed to ring through the crowd.

"Kahlia, I have loved you from the moment I laid eyes on you. It feels like it's been forever since we met even though it's been less than a year. For a long time, I was lost, trying to find my way, but not fighting hard enough to find it. I want to say thank you baby, for wanting me to be better and for showing me better. I love you, so fucking much and I just…" he lowered to his knee causing my hands to go up to my mouth in surprise. My eyes were wide in shock, I couldn't believe my eyes. He pulled a small black box out of his back pocket and opened it, displaying one of the most beautiful diamond rings I had ever seen. "I refuse to spend the rest of my life without you. Wewe ni wa milele wangu." The number of tears that started to fall down my eyes was startling. "Will you marry me?"

My head nodded before I could get the word *Yes* out of my mouth. Josiah placed the ring on my hand then stood up pulling me into his body, hugging me and kissing me. I sobbed into his chest, knowing my makeup was going to be ruined. I wasn't expecting this, not at all. I'd wanted it, craved it most days lately, but I wasn't expecting him to do it.

"I love you, so much." He whispered into my lips, tears spilling down both of our faces at this point.

"I love you." I replied attempting to wipe his tears away. "Always."

EPILOGUE

(TWO YEARS LATER)

Kahlia

"Jojo, come to Mommy." I coached my son as he stood to his feet. His facial expression displaying his determination to take his first steps. From across the room his younger twin brother Jahlil stared at him; he'd walked already just days before, and this was old news to him. He was so much like his father it was amazing; he grew bored quickly.

"Come on Jojo, come here to Daddy." Josiah said to my right also coaxing him forward. I rolled my eyes. We'd been in competition since Jahlil started walking and had immediately gone to his father. But Josiah knew that his namesake was a mama's boy and would be by my side in no time. Not to say he didn't mess with his daddy, he absolutely did, it was the cutest sight to see. But Jojo loved me more and we all knew it.

Josiah looked from me to his daddy, unsure of whose

WHEN IT COMES TO YOU

arms to go to. Both of us trying to coax him to come to us. His eyes finally landed solidly on mine, and he took a step. My excitement almost got the best of me, yet I stopped myself from screaming. I nodded my head encouraging him to take more steps and he did. With each step he took, my eyes got wider, my smile was wider. When he was in my arms, I lifted him in the air and ran around the room with him in my arms, his laughs echoing the room.

"Good job my sweet boy." I kissed the side of his neck, digging into his rolls of fat while he continued to laugh.

"Alright, alright." Josiah said coming over to us when I took a quick break to rest. He held his hands out for our son, and I reluctantly gave him up but immediately scooped Jahlil into cuddles. Josiah Jr and Jahlil were their father, uncle, and older cousin's spitting image; besides the fact their skin was darker like mine. They'd gotten those big, beautiful hazel eyes that all Mackenzie men seemed to inherit. With one look into those eyes, they, just like with their father, had me wrapped around their fingers.

"Okay, let's get them together so we can take them to Parris." I sighed solemnly. It was a year into their lives, and it just so happened to coincide with the first vacation Josiah, and I would be spending without them. For so long, I wasn't ready, wasn't ready to be without my two precious babies. If Josiah hadn't persuaded me to take this trip, backed up by Parris insisting she would keep them safe, I wouldn't even thinking about going.

We moved down the hall to their nursery, where their bags were packed, and their jackets were laid out for us. I slipped Jahlil into his jacket then grabbed his bag into my free hand while Josiah did the same with his namesake.

It didn't take us long to have their bags as well as ours stacked into the trunk of Josiah's new Escalade. They sat quietly in the backseat with their pacifiers in their mouths, staring at the tv monitors in the back of the two front seats, expecting Gracie to come on the screens like she did any other time we rode in the car with them. Most times, we had the radio playing softly for our enjoyment but if we had it too loud, they grew fussy.

I bit down on my nails, the longer we drove my anxiety slowly getting the best of me. My leg was shaking, and my focus was jarred, glancing out the window pretending to be interested in everything on our path. I was scared to be without them, but I knew we needed this trip, needed to be together just the two of us.

Since the twins had been born, we'd poured our all into them, and for whatever reason we seemed to argue more. I hated it for us, our relationship was being tested. But I refused to give up on him or us. So, I did what I needed to do to stay connected to my husband; including taking this trip we both knew I didn't want to take since I'd be without my babies.

"It's all good Kali." Josiah held my hand before lifting it to his lips. "We need this. Parris has them." I nodded before looking back at them, preoccupied with the black girl magic they were watching to notice that their mother was distressed. "Besides, it will be nice to be back in Mexico."

"I know." I agreed. "But aren't you a little nervous about leaving them?"

"I'm nervous as fuck." He chuckled. "But I know I need my time with you and I'm choosing to be a little selfish. Parris has help, Mason is there and Fabian. They can all handle them. This isn't their first time staying overnight with their aunt."

"You're right." I told him. "But still…"

"We bought travel insurance and refundable and changeable tickets. If anything goes down, we'll leave ASAP. I promise." He lifted my hand to his lips again and I felt a little relaxed but not much.

It took thirty minutes for me to say my last goodbye and get my last hug from them. I cried the entire time we drove to the airport and during the entire thing, Josiah soothed me through it, letting me know he was right here with me.

I didn't feel better until we got on the plane; our first-class seats another treat thanks to my airline points. It wasn't that long of a trip to Mexico from Dallas, but after a few glasses of wine I was relaxing more, the worry just slightly buried in my head.

By the time we landed, went through customs, stopped by the currency exchange, and made our way to our preplanned transportation; I'd had another two shots of tequila. I pulled out my phone to text Parris so I could check on the boys.

> On our way to the hotel, what my babies doing?

Looking over at my phone, Josiah chuckled; "She about to cuss yo ass out."

"I don't fucking care." Just as I'd uttered those words, Parris replied to my text.

> Parris: Minding their business and leaving yours alone. Don't piss me off Kahlia, leave us alone. We'll call you before bed.

"Funky heffa." I mumbled, rolling my eyes, and sighing as I put my phone away.

"Chill baby, we need to enjoy our time here. I need my Queen to give me a Princess." He'd whispered that in my ear before licking my lobe and pulling me closer into him. I felt my face go hot, he'd been talking about it for months, and I'd been considering it. The boys were only a year, by the time their sibling got here they'd be two, enough time in between them. "Or two."

I moaned as his hand went between my thighs, almost forgetting we were in a smaller SUV that was being driven by a nice young man who probably didn't need to be hearing what was happening in the back seat. Josiah had been telling me since we'd taken flight that he planned on making me scream the moment we got to our hotel room. The sweet nothings he whispered in my ears the entire time made me believe him, made me anticipate our arrival even more.

The trip from the airport to the resort took 45 minutes. That's how long I had to endure Josiah's constant flirting, teasing and I knew it would be another 30 minutes before we were checked in and in our room. Regardless of what time we got in there though, I fully intended to allow him to take advantage of me.

It was a quicker check in process than I remembered before we were being shown to our room. Once we were inside and the butler we'd been assigned had left out of the room, Josiah's lips were on mine, lifting me up in his arms as he carried me to the bed.

He knew I had to shower after a flight, but he could care less about any objections I tried to make to him. I felt his desire for me with every swipe of his tongue against mine. I felt it in the way he rubbed his hand along my body, I felt it in the way his fingers slipped down my shorts, bypassing my underwear, and rubbing between my folds.

I moaned, immediately expelling my essence along his fingers. I knew what was coming so I was ready, and she had been leaking since we stood at the check in desk, him standing closely behind me as the attendant went over our reservation and the amenities. I felt him bricked up against my ass and I knew what was coming to me, yearned for it even.

Slowly, Josiah lowered my shorts and underwear, taking them all the way off and throwing them to the side. He lowered between my thighs and with the first swipe of his tongue, my legs shook. The way his tongue swiped between my folds, the way his tongue curled around my bud, I couldn't control the intense, euphoric orgasm that cascaded over me. My body convulsed as I attempted to ride it out.

While I was gathering my breath, I felt Josiah enter me and my eyes rolled to the back of my head. He held my legs on his shoulders, sliding in and out of me, each time eliciting a loud moan and nonstop shaking. It had been too long since I could be loud, could express my absolute joy and happiness with him being between my legs. When his hand snaked around my neck, I lost it; lost myself in him like only he could make me do.

After, we took a short nap before we both woke and showered together so we could go have dinner. We'd made reservations while we stood at the check in desk with the Italian place we'd visited the first time we shared dinner together. This time, flirting openly, talking about everything between growing our family, to my career running the art gallery while still creating myself.

My signature piece from my last big show two years ago was now sitting in our living room opposite the painting I'd made for Josiah depicting us in the setting sun of our African village,. My hand was on his chest, thick gold jewelry adorning our bodies; his hand resting on the swell of my belly while our foreheads touched. Giving him that painting on his birthday was how I'd informed him I was pregnant.

"Happy Anniversary my eternal." Josiah raised his glass of wine to me, and I raised mine as well. "I love you more and more every single day. I look forward to spending the rest of my life with you. I'll love you always and forever."

ALSO BY GENESIS CARTER

SERIES

After the Storm 1-2 (Completed Series)

Happily Never After 1-3 (Completed Series)

Sweet Remedy 1-4 (Completed Series)

Kano and Montana: An Urban Love Story 1-2 (Completed Series)

Triggered: His Love Way My Sanctuary 1-3 (Completed Series)

Fallin For A Legendary Thug 1-2 (Completed Series)

Rapture 1-2 (Completed Series)

STANDALONES

This Love Gon Be The Death of Me

Oh, So He Cheated, Cheated

Born to Love U

Edgewood: Intercepting Love

When It Comes To You

☆*Follow me on Social Media*☆

Instagram: AuthoressGenesisCarter

Twitter: @A_New_Genesis

Facebook: Authoress Genesis

Facebook Discussion Group: Genesis Carter's Lituationship

Made in the USA
Las Vegas, NV
04 February 2025

10effca3-1085-4ed5-8bff-445ed38f59efR01